CW00867420

The Things the River Hides

Some characters and events in this book are fictitious. Any similarity to real persons, living or dead, is coincidental and not intended by the author.

ISBN 978-1-989868-25-6 (Paperback Edition)

ISBN 978-1-989868-26-3 (Electronic Edition)

ISBN 978-1-989868-27-0 (Hardcover Edition)

Published by Cauldron Press

https://www.cauldronpress.ca/

To those wondering in the darkness.
One day, a lamp will shine.

THE THINGS THE RIVER HIDES

A.N. SAGE

CAULDRON PRESS

CONTENTS

The palace shines bright; so bright, it stings the eyes.

Darkness creeps in.

Every crevice stuffed and heavy.

Every corner filled with death.

She slept for too long and when she awakes, she is a shadow of who she must become.

Weak.

Liquid.

Starving.

Rivers red as blood welcome her home.

She is restless, eager, and ready for what lies ahead.

All around, there is only darkness and death.

But in the distance, too far to see clearly,

Is the one she chose.

Settled.

Stable.

Determined.

The rivers too will part

And she will lead them forth into salvation.

1

Whoever said the dead don't talk, lied. All you have to do is learn how to listen.

Some bodies are deafeningly loud, yelling demands and pushing their life stories down your throat. Others are quiet, barely a whisper of song floating through the air and vanishing into nothingness. But they all talk; at least, that's what it feels like.

I stare down at the bloated corpse before me and bite down on my tongue. The skin is silky smooth, unnatural from all the chemicals pumped into it. Perfect. My hand almost never shakes anymore, and when I pick up the airbrush gun to apply the first layer of makeup to the poor bastard lying on the slab before me, I don't even waver. The paint glides on in waves, a glimpse of life returning to an otherwise empty shell.

I shift my weight.

"Don't go so heavy with the blush this time," my mother says. She looks up from the stack of paperwork on her desk, studying my every move like a predator. "The family requested a natural appearance."

It's hard not to laugh, impossible even. The family must have been confused because as far as I can tell, there is nothing natural about what I have to do to their loved one. But Mother says we didn't pick our work, it picked us. A lie. No matter how hard I dwell on it, I cannot recall when I agreed to this dreadful life of helping her run the Cherry Cove Funeral Home.

We lived in the small town of Cherry Cove for as long as I can remember. A typical coastal town with typical coastal folk. Despite the low population, you still need a car to get around and most people own large pieces of property making neighbors a rare thing to come by. Cherry Cove survives on three things. Fishing, tourism, and a whole lot of judgement. You can't take one step without stepping in gossip and it's gotten even worse since the river became polluted, the water turning an eery shade of red and dragging in people from all over the country to come see it. With tourists keeping our sad little town afloat, everyone is on their best behavior. At least in public. In the privacy of their own homes, all bets are off. Behind unlocked doors, the townspeople whisper behind each other's backs and dissect everyone that sets foot on their territory. I should know, I've been a topic of much conversation for most of my life.

Living in Cherry Cove's only funeral home does not help.

There was a time, long ago, when my life was not so intricately entwined in death. A time when Mom smiled every day instead of burying herself in work and putting an ever-growing wedge between us. A time when I wasn't afraid to leave home.

That was before the surgery, of course.

My fingers clamp down on the nozzle and a spray of over-saturated yellow covers my wrinkled apron.

"Careful, Nastya," Mother scolds from her seat.

I close my eyes and count to ten. "I know," I say.

When I can keep myself from lashing out at her, I focus on the body again, eyes running over the ridges of the man's face as I study his features. A sharp chin butting out, an even sharper nose, and cheekbones most people would kill for. The way his hair is greying frames his face in a surreal shade of white, almost like he's facing the sunlight. He looks kind, like someone who cared for others without wanting anything in return. *Tell me your story,* I think. And he does.

The man speaks of his children, painting them in my mind with warm words and loving descriptions. He tells me of his grandchildren and the way they laughed when he pretended to stumble down the stairs only to jump back up with a grin. I don't interrupt him as he recalls the life he'll surely miss, keeping the fact that it was the same fall down the stairs that landed him in front of me. There is no need to argue with the dead, they usually win. They're stubborn that way.

A whoosh of cold air nips at my skin and I tug at buttons of my cardigan to keep from shivering. Somewhere behind me, Mother stirs in her spot, her eyes burning into the rear of my skull. "You want another sweater?" she asks.

I shake my head.

Ever since the thyroid surgery, I am nothing but a walking corpse myself. Always cold and always trembling. It is infuriating and Mother constantly pressing me to keep warm doesn't help. At this point, I'm used to her fussing, yet it still makes the hairs rise on my arms when she does it. Though it could be the frigid cold. It is so damn cold in Cherry Cove. Or the land of constant winter, as I call it.

"I need to go into town to pick up the flowers for the service tomorrow," Mother says. "You'll be all right on your own?"

"Obviously," I answer. "I can go if you want."

She eyes me carefully, gaze drifting over my face as she considers her diplomatic response. "I got it," she finally says. "You need to finish him up before the paint dries."

I'm not sure why I expected her to cave this time and let me leave the prison she has built for me. Mother has been adamant about my staying away from the townspeople ever since I was a kid. Each time I asked, she came up with a handful of excuses. *Finish your homework. I need you to start dinner. It'll be easier if I do it myself.* After a while, she stopped faking it all together and answered my pleas to go outside with a simple 'no'.

Any other teenager would have kicked and screamed, ran away from home and slammed the door behind them. But not me. I knew if my mother could let me be free, she would.

Freedom is not a thing I can afford anymore.

My mouth twists into a sour expression and I stiffen, refusing to look at her. My elbows press into my sides as I force myself to concentrate on the task at hand. The paint gun sputters and comes to life in my hands, my artwork spreading over dead skin to make it new again.

A soft hand rests on my shoulder and I gulp down spit as mother squeezes lightly. "I'm sorry," she says. Her eyes lock on the scar on my neck and I blush, remembering I forgot to cover it up this morning.

"I know."

It isn't her fault. None of this is her fault. After my surgery, our lives disintegrated, and we both had shadows deep inside us as a reminder. I hated the darkness.

Mother's teeth shine through a thin-lipped gesture that does nothing to put me at ease and turns away from me. As she walks away, she favors her left leg and I try not to giggle at the sight of her. She looks like a dazed penguin, all curves and unbalance. I guess that's the price you pay for living with a lame foot.

Mother never told me how she got hurt, not for my lack of trying. Each time I pressed, she deflected, and I chalked it up to her innate ability to put things behind her. To swallow trauma whole, like she was gulping air. She had the bad leg since I woke up after the surgery. I still remember opening my eyes to see her hobble into the hospital room with a tray of Jell-O cups in her hands. That day changed us. Made us anew. I had a scar and Mother had a limp. It was who we were now.

I don't mind the scar, not really. A scar isn't the worst thing you can get after getting your thyroid removed at the age of five. No, the worst thing is what happens after.

One day, you're a regular kid with friends and toys and little care, and then next, you're a freak. Someone people watch when you pass them. Someone they fear. If it wasn't for Christine Sollar, I wouldn't be here in this stupid funeral home plastering layers of makeup on a corpse. Well, if it wasn't for Christine and my gift.

My posture stoops.

Gift is the wrong word for the ability I manifested a few days after the surgery. Curse was a better alternative. I am a cursed creature. A dark chariot of bad news. What else can you call a girl who can predict a person's death?

Psycho.

Loser.

Killer.

I've heard it all. Don't get me wrong, the words still sting even though it's been years since Mother pulled me out of school because the other kids made my life miserable. I tried to tell her they were only afraid because of what happened to Christine, but she wouldn't listen. She had me out of there in a flash, screaming profanities in Russian at every teacher in our wake.

It's one thing I truly admire about her; the way she's able to tell people exactly what she's thinking without holding back. I did not inherit the same gene. Not by a long shot.

Where mother is strong and confident, I am nothing of the sort. I'm what you'd call an acquired taste. Meaning if you get close enough, you might acquire your own demise if I get my hands on you.

Mother and I are the stark opposite of each other and I often wonder if she didn't find me on the street somewhere as a baby and bring me home. Every feature that belongs to me stands in opposition to hers. Instead of the dark, careful eyes Mother was blessed with, mine are so pale, they are almost transparent. As if to make them stand out even more, I was born with silver hair that never seemed to learn how to darken. When I stand next to Mother, I often have to fight the need to tear the auburn locks off her had and glue them to mine. Then there is the matter of our personalities, which is where our differences become more apparent. I am not outspoken. I am not proud. And of course, I have a gift I'm certain Mother is relieved not to have inherited. The ability to see death before it happens.

I never know when the visions will kick into gear, it could be right away or it could be after weeks of talking to someone. But it comes nonetheless. Clockwork. There are many tales of people with my ability, myths told and passed on through generations. Every culture has a story for death and those who touch it. Some call them banshees, predictors of the darkness to come, women who shriek and cry to warn others of their nearing misfortune. People read too many fairy tales, I think. Not that I can't see the resemblance between my gift and the infinite connection to death a banshee has, but I am nothing of the sort. There are two distinct differences between them and me, and it is blatantly obvious to anyone who cares enough to check. I do not mourn those I see in my visions, and I do not cry for them. I learned not to cry a long time ago. To add, unlike banshees, I am not a creature of legends.

Tucking the cardigan into my jeans, I glance down. "You're ready to roll, Gary," I say, winking. "And looking quite sharp, if I may say so myself."

Gary doesn't respond, but in the corner of my eye, I swear I can see his lips curl up. He's happy, pleased. I am too.

Carefully, I clean out the gun's nozzle and put the paint tubes back on the shelf, making sure to stack them in the exact way Mother likes. She is particular about all things to do with the business and I try to respect her wishes as much as I can. No point arguing with your only friend.

When I finish cleaning up, I toss the apron back on the only chair in the room and scan the desk. Piles of paper are scattered all over the mahogany top. Names and dates and photos penetrate my vision as I try to organize the crazy mess Mother left behind into some semblance of a filing system. She is not one for administrative work, which is quite shocking for a control freak. Luckily for both of us, I am a master of filing. Every night when she leaves the office in a state of disarray, I creep downstairs to clean it up. Sometimes, a body still rests on the slab, keeping me company as I toss papers into their proper files. Sometimes, it is only me in the basement of the large Victorian we occupy. Those nights are the best.

So quiet I can hear myself think for a change.

A door slams upstairs and I hear a string of curse words waft down the staircase. My head jerks to the landing, watching feet scuffle through the small crack under the door. Something else slams, a cupboard I think.

I still for a moment, then drop the file folder in my hands and rush up the stairs. My heart races as I reach the door and twist the handle. The light from the hallway pierces my eyes and I squint, blinking away the dryness and pray for tears. They don't come and I am stuck, fumbling through the hallway with needles scratching the back of my lids. When I round the corner to the dining room, I am breathless and heaving over my thighs. The perks of home-schooling and no gym class is how out of shape you get without even noticing it.

Before me, Mother is hunched over the dining table, her eyes are saucers as she waits for me to catch my breath. "Nastya," she starts.

I lift a finger and take a few more deep breaths. "What happened?"

"I left the pickup slip at home," she says. "That dura won't let me get the order without it. Can you believe it? How many people are ordering funeral wreaths in this damn town?"

She is so angry, it rolls off her. I smack my lips as if wishing to feel some of her fire on my tongue. All I taste is stale air. "Can't you go back for them?" I ask.

Mother's face drops. "Of course, I can," she says. "Don't be ridiculous. But I have a meeting in ten minutes and by the time it's done, the shop will have closed. We need those flowers for the morning."

My heart leaps into my throat. "I'll go."

I don't even ask this time, I state it. It's an odd feeling to speak to her this way, with so much assurance. By the expression on Mother's face, she's as surprised with my courage as I am.

She starts to rebut but I wave her off. "It's fine, Mom," I say. "I'll be in and out and I'll steer clear of people. Like you said, we need the flowers for tomorrow."

Shoulders slumping, I am met with a version of my mother I haven't seen before. She seems to be considering my words, and for the first time, I let a glimmer of hope flutter in my stomach. Her lips smash together and I sag in my spot, waiting for another excuse to pour out of her.

"Fine," she says.

My ears perk up. "Wait, are you serious?"

"Don't make any stops, understand?" she asks. "You go to the flower shop and you come right back."

I nod.

"And for the love of God, Nastya, don't touch anyone." She says it as if I actually would. Then adds, "We can't have another incident on our hands. The town is finally starting to simmer down, and I'd like to keep it that way."

Smiling, I break to hug her then stop myself mid leap. We are not a hugging family. Instead, I let my smile widen and pick her car keys up from the table, tossing them into my back pocket as I turn on my heels.

My breath comes short as I walk toward the front door. Every step is a mixture of anticipation and nerves, and when I finally reach it, I am but a puddle of a person. My long legs take the porch steps two at a time, and I hoist myself into the old pickup truck fast enough to bang my head on the roof. The car starts with a groan and I pat the wheel, slamming my teeth against each other as I reverse out of the driveway. The setting sun casts shadows over the house as I pull away, dark lines splitting the brick and drawing my attention to the two snakes carved into the funeral home sign hanging over the porch. The metal is rusted from many years enduring the wetness in the air and it's hard to make out the words from all the ivy crawling up the side of the house, but I can still see the slithering monsters despite it. They watch over the funeral home and the two women trapped inside like slimy knights. No swords, no armor, only four beady eyes and two forked tongues reaching toward each other.

My eyes narrow on the sign as I peel out, dust rising behind me.

I speed away before mother has a chance to change her mind. She might not know it, but she just handed me the keys to the kingdom. Well, the keys to a Dodge Dakota, but to me, they are one and the same.

The country road spreads wide before me and I roll down the window, inhaling the icy air of Cherry Cove into my lungs. On the radio, an unfamiliar pop song blasts and I turn the volume up as I race toward town. To anyone else, I look like a regular teenager speeding to meet her friends.

Yet, I am no such thing.

I am a warrior emerging from battle, full of scars and wisdom and regret. I am a mare jumping over a fence to race into the wilderness.

My hand reaches for mother's scarf crumpled on the passenger seat and I tie it over my neck to hide my scar. Turning the volume up a few more notches, I tighten my fingers on the steering wheel until my palms are slick with sweat.

This is the best day of my life.

2

It's extra chilly in Cherry Cove this afternoon and as I stalk down the narrow sidewalk of Center Street, I can all but see my breath hovering in the air. All around, the street bustles with life and I tighten my scarf over my neck, keeping my eyes low. If I count the steps as I walk, the panic of being seen is almost non existent. Almost.

A door swings open and I jump back, avoiding getting slammed in the forehead by mere inches. As I stumble backward, I am faced with the scowl of a local girl not much older than me with three coffee cups balancing in her arms. Her nails are painted a bright red, matching her obnoxious lipstick to perfection. The girl starts to smile, then her eyes meet mine and the scowl returns. She runs her gaze over me with a huff and swings her long, auburn hair over her shoulder. "Watch it!" she yelps.

My blood freezes. I choke out a pathetic, "I'm sorry," and move around her, giving her a wide berth to pass. I hear her mumble at my back and grit my teeth. *Don't turn around. Don't turn around. DON'T turn around.*

As I rush to put some distance between us, a series of laughs echoes toward me and I stop dead in my tracks. The tendons stand out on my neck and my tongue slaps to the top of my mouth, jowls protruding like I am a fish struggling to breathe. I am.

Slowly, I twist my head to see the girl join a group of kids from the high school. She giggles as she passes the coffees out to her friends and when they turn toward me and start laughing, my cheeks redden. The girl points a lacquered nail my way, and her grin spreads as she makes an indecent gesture with her tongue. Behind her, a boy shaped like a muscle car does the same while the others only wrap their fingers over their throats and pretend to choke to death.

Somewhere deep down, I wish they would.

I shake my head, spinning to turn my back to them and ignore the shouts aimed at me as I walk away.

"Keep running, Grim Reaper!" someone yells, the girl that nearly ran me over I assume.

"I thought they finally caged the dog," another voice joins the torments.

This one stings. I'm used to local kids making comments about me being the bearer of death, but a dog? Seriously? If they're going to try to break me, I wish they'd come up with something more original. Vulture. Terminator. The Queen of Hell, even. A dog sounds too plain for what they think I can do.

They're idiots, of course. I don't control death as they believe, I only see it happen, and even then the visions are rarely clear. Not enough that I can do anything to stop it. But it doesn't matter to any of them. No one wants to know how they die and they definitely don't want me to tell them. Christine learned her lesson the hard way.

A hard object slams against my thigh and a dull pain laces up my leg as I am knocked to the side. My eyes jerk down, following the rock drop to the pavement and roll to the middle of the street. Footsteps shuffle behind me and I don't need to turn to know the group of misfits is collecting their weapons. Rushing sounds fill the air as they hurl more rocks in my direction, and I take off in a dead sprint. Some hit me, yet others zoom by, taking down passersby as they move to get out of the path of attack. My eyes meet those of an older woman and she takes me in with pity splashed over her face. I whisper a meek, "I'm sorry," and keep running, turning the corner to hide behind a stack of newspapers laid out in front of the only bookstore in town. In the distance, I can see the sign for the flower shop and exhale a sigh of relief.

I'm so close.

"You shouldn't let them treat you this way," a heady voice sounds to my right and I spin to face it.

Standing in the wooden doorway of the bookstore, a

middle-aged man looks up at me through sparse lashes, one eye narrowed in my direction. His thick legs are crossed and in his hands; a heavy tome is sprawled open with earmarked pages flapping in the wind. The man's face darkens as he slams the book shut and tucks it between the folds of his knitted cardigan. "They're a nuisance, but they'll keep doing it if you let them."

My jaw clenches shut. "It's okay," I say. "I'm used to it."

"No one should be used to that," says the man.

He is very much mistaken. Some things you can't help but grow accustomed to. Being treated as a monster, having to be pulled out from school because you told a kid she's going to die and then she does. The feeling of drowning even though you are out of water. I am used to all of them.

The man shoves his hands into his pockets and steps aside. "You want to come in?"

I'm tempted to oblige. Weight switching from foot to foot, I inhale the musty scent of old books with greed before shaking my head. Mother sent me here for a reason, and I was already breaking my promise to her by speaking to this kind stranger. Knots form in the base of my gut when I think of the consequences if I veered off track any further. My eyes flick to the laces of my sneakers and I roll words around in my mouth before spewing them out aggressively. "I'm not hiding from those losers," I say before I could stop myself.

The man looks at me, puzzled. "Weren't you running from them a second ago?"

He has me there.

"I was running to the flower shop," I explain. "Have to run an errand for my mom."

When he watches me, I feel too seen. The man's lips twitch and a strand of grey hair falls into his eyes, which he doesn't seem to notice. "You're Elena's girl, right?" he asks.

"Uh-huh."

"I won't keep you," the man says and flips open his book again. "Tell your mother Stanley says hello."

I am about to leave when he adds, "And perhaps you're right."

Pausing, I hike my shoulders to my ears until I can feel the lobes graze against my sweater. "About?"

"Hiding is probably never the answer."

I am suddenly very aware of my surroundings and as I turn away from the man, Stanley, I am bombarded with glares. It seems our conversation drew in quite the crowd and people have stopped whatever they were doing to eavesdrop. Some huddle close together, whispering to each other while staring me down. Others have their jaws flat on the ground, trying to understand how I dared to show my face on their turf. In the corner of my eye, I see a father tug his child behind him, scolding him for getting too close to me.

I roll on my heels, bidding Stanley a polite good bye and head straight for the shop. The metal sign sways in the wind, scraping the brick from the wall and making goosebumps spread over my arms and legs. My back is ramrod straight as I push my way into the small store, and I nearly knock over a pot of plants when I come in. In the far end, a woman looks up from the counter. The first thing I notice is the short, spiky hair atop her head. The next thing I notice is the annoyed expression she shoots my way. "Can I help you?" she asks.

Hands shaking, I reach into my jeans to pull out the crumpled order slip my mother gave me. "I'm here to pick up an order," I say.

"Last name?"

"Sokolov," I respond. My finger taps the name scribbled on the form, though the shop owner doesn't bother to look down. She knows who I am. Everyone does.

Her nose scrunches until she resembles one of those puppies with too much skin and not enough meat to fill it. "You're sure you can manage carrying it all?" the woman asks. "I don't do carry outs."

Mom was right, she is a dura.

"I'm good. If you have a trolley I can use, I'll bring it right back."

She rolls her eyes then gets up with a groan and heads to the back of the shop, leaving me all alone in the forest of florals. My eyes narrow and I study the space, counting the different colors to keep myself occupied. A flash of red drags my attention and I glance to the back door, gauging how long I have to explore before the woman returns. Likely not very long.

Pushing from the counter, I walk to the flower beckoning me and read the handwritten inscription taped to the clay pot. "Poppy, thirty-five dollars."

I frown. Seems a high price for one stupid plant. Not thinking, my finger reaches for the bright red leaves and I swallow hard as I inch closer. They're so vibrant and I have the strange need to tear them off and cram them in my pocket before the shop owner returns.

"Unless you're going to buy it, I wouldn't touch it."

Twisting around, I turn back to the shop owner and yank my hand away from the poppy. "Sorry."

"I need the trolley back right away," she instructs, gesturing to the cart next to her. It is overflowing with boxes and I am sweating just thinking about hauling the damn thing back to the car. Hopefully, those kids are gone by now.

When I move to the cart, the woman shoves a pen in my face and clenches her teeth shut. "Sign for the pickup, please," she says.

I do as instructed. My handwriting is messy and jumbled on the paper and I blush, praying she doesn't notice. Mother scolds me for my poor penmanship, though despite her annoyance, it never improved. I simply don't understand why it's important. No one grades my schoolwork but her.

"I'd take the rear street," the woman suggests. "Avoid the commotion."

I raise an eyebrow. "Commotion?"

"Another protest," she answers. "Those blasted Warriors are testing my patience."

She mumbles the last part under her breath, as though I would judge her for them. I don't see why I would. Most people in town hate the environmental group calling themselves the Cherry Cove Warriors; mostly because they tend to show up when you least need them around. Constantly spewing their propaganda of cleaning up the river and getting the town to adapt a more minimal lifestyle. I don't get what the big deal is. The river had been polluted with algae for so many years, they renamed the town after it. If it was me though, I would have opted for a more fitting description. Maybe crimson instead of cherry. Or hateful. Hateful Cove has a nice ring to it. Whatever you call this place is not the point; the town thrives on the gawking tourists that swarm the shores with their painted faces and phones pointed outward to capture the true beauty of the mucky red water stretching far and wide around the town. The algae in the river is thick and dense and it's impossible to see the bottom, even if you kneel down close enough to smell it. Not an act I'd recommend unless you enjoy the putrid smells of decay and rot. It's pretty enough to look at, at least.

When the sun is high in the sky, the entire river glitters a deep red and takes your breath away, but it's most apparent in the cove located not far from the funeral home. People say the cove is the color of love and passion, I think it's the color of blood. Even in the winter, when it's frozen over, it still has a glint of red piercing the surface. Blood welling on an open wound.

They tested the algae ages ago, and when they realized it wasn't toxic, they left it alone. Now, in the summers, people gather around the cove, though no one swims in it. Except high school kids who dare each other to jump in to prove their worth to their friends. Most come out unscathed, some emerge with a raging rash covering their bodies. They wear it as a badge of honor, as if to say 'I survived the cove, can you?'

At night, when I am sure the beach is deserted, I drag mother to look at the bloody specimen. She complains the entire time, but I pay her no mind. The cove is a staple of our town and I am drawn to it. Probably because it is different like me. It doesn't quite belong, and yet it occupies the same space, regardless.

It's probably why I can't stand the Warriors along with everyone else in town. They want to take away the one thing that makes this place unique. They want to strip Cherry Cove of its identity, erase it and pretend it never existed. It's the dumbest thing I've ever heard. Our little town might not be some bustling city, but the cove does get its fair share of attention and the outsiders it brings keeps the town alive and flourishing.

Without it, we would be lost.

I bite the inside of my cheek, wrapping my cold fingers over the trolley's handle to pull it to the door. "Thanks for the tip," I tell the shop owner. "I'll be right back with the cart."

She says something I cannot hear and disappears into the back room again, clearly relieved to have me out of her store. As I pull the cart behind me, a sense of relief floods my system. Three people faced me today, and the gift did not make an appearance once. No ominous visions of death, no foretelling of endings. Maybe I'm all fixed.

My sneakers scuff against the pavement and I pick up my pace. I can't wait to get home to tell Mother about my little adventure. She'll be so proud. Perhaps proud enough to loosen the reins and let me out more often. After all, I was in town for almost a full hour and no one died.

It's like Mother says, miracles are different for everyone. Days like today are mine.

3

The sheets wrinkle under me, a mess of a bed from when I got up this morning. I should probably straighten them up, but the enormous textbook in my lap says otherwise. I stare at it in disgust. You know you hate math when you'd rather watch your mother pump formaldehyde into some poor sucker's veins than attempt solving a basic equation. My pen taps on the linen cover of the book, and while my eyes are focused on my schoolwork, my mind is somewhere else. I am still on Center Street, still at the bookstore, talking to Stanley. Still free.

A rogue smile creeps to my lips and I run a finger over the creases on my cheeks. It had been so long since I was genuinely pleased, I almost forgot what it feels like. The window shutters slam against the house and my gaze wonders, reality crashing into me. Suddenly, I'm not in town and Stanley is nowhere to be found. My meek smile vanishes, and I groan as I take in the room I'm in. Frilly curtains line the windows, tied at the base with a pink ribbon Mother cut off from a birthday present when I was six. A stuffed white rabbit sits on the sill. I grew immediately attached to the fluffy toy when Mother gave it to me; even when the ears ripped off. No matter how much surgery Mother attempted, the rabbit was never pieced back together.

Under the window, a three-tiered bookcase rests against the walls full of ancient looking tomes that demand my attention daily. When I'm not helping Mother run the funeral home, I bury myself in the stories within those pages. They offer some solitude and I often find myself reading well into the night. Reading is a welcome release from everything waiting for me downstairs, and I cannot help but cherish the time I have alone each evening.

The rest of the room leaves much to be desired, especially the floral wallpaper I absolutely despise that's starting to tear at the corners. I've asked Mother to redecorate many times, but it has never happened. Now, I'm stuck living in the room of a child with a canopied bed and stuffed animals piled in the corner.

I roll my eyes, spine shedding its shape as I attempt to find the motivation to get through today's lessons. Knowing Mother, she's likely waiting downstairs with a stupid pop quiz clutched in her hands. There's always something unexpected with her.

"All right," I say to the empty room. "I can do this."

I am still giving myself a pep talk when the doorbell rings and I hear Mother's footsteps downstairs. Jumbled voices drift toward me and I run through my inventory of memorized tones to place the visitor. The tone is unfamiliar, and I glance at my textbook once before tossing aside and tiptoeing to my bedroom door. Pressing my ear to the small crack, I listen.

"Yes, he came in this morning," Mother says.

"Can I see him?"

Strange. The only delivery we had after this morning's viewing is another body. I distinctively remember it because my stomach twisted up when I signed for the release. It was a boy from the high school, Kye, I think. I asked Mother how he died and she said it was an accident. My throat closes up when I think of him. This boy is too young to end up on one of our slabs. *Was,* I correct myself. He *was* too young.

Downstairs, Mother mutters and huffs and I wedge myself closer to the half-open door. "He is not ready for visitation yet," she says. "The family scheduled a viewing for next Friday. You are welcome to stop by then."

"I need to see him now," the voice demands. Another boy, I realize. His words come out jumbled, like he is swallowing them instead of speaking. His pain is palpable and my heart breaks for this boy, for his loss. I wonder if maybe Kye had a brother, one who can't seem to let go. "Please," he begs. I find myself begging with him.

Unfortunately for both of us, Mother is not so easily swayed. "I'm afraid that isn't possible," she says. "Have a good day."

The door creaks shut, and I crumble in my room. She doesn't have to be so harsh all the time. It's like she doesn't have a heart at all, and while I know it's only an act, I sometimes wonder if a part of my mother is broken. It would make sense for it to be so, considering the broken daughter she spawned. I push off the doorway and rush to my window, pressing my nose to the glass. From here, I can see the porch's overhang and wait impatiently for the boy to appear as he leaves. He doesn't.

I wait. Two minutes, five. Still nothing.

"Why are you still here?"

When I hear Mother close the basement door and her footsteps retreat down the stairs, I bolt. Staying light on my toes, I creep from my room, flattening against the walls as I inch toward the entrance. In my head, the theme song from a spy movie plays on a loop and I envision myself wrapped in black vinyl with a mask covering my face. Under me, the floorboards creak and I freeze in my tracks, listening. My eyes catch on the basement, and I hold my breath, waiting for Mother to pour through it to scold me. To my relief, she remains shut inside the barricade of the morgue. I glance behind me down the hallway leading to the backyard and the family room Mother turned into a viewing area, then twist around to face the front of the house. Tiptoeing past the living and kitchen, I scoot around and carefully unlock the entrance vestibule then duck inside. My breathing is shallow as I stand a foot away from the front door.

My fingers loop around the gilded handle and when I twist it, my chest constricts. Breath coming out short, I roll my shoulders and swing the front door open, gasping.

Before me, a boy's wide back blocks the rays of sun hitting the porch. His hair glistens in the light, a reddish-brown that looks almost translucent from the right angle. A stark contrast to the washed out silver of my own hair. When I was younger, I tried dying it a million times, but the color washed out in days. It seems I am forever marked by the lifeless curtains framing my face. The jacket the boy wears is embellished across his back, and I immediately recognize the emblem as the Cherry Cove varsity team. *So, you're a jock.*

"I'm sorry?" the boy asks, whirling on his heels to face me.

My cheeks grow hot when I realize I had spoken aloud. My throat is suddenly bone dry. "I said, can I help you?"

The boy looks puzzled. Muddy eyes threaded with blue penetrate me and I stumble backward, shoulders knocking against the side of the house.

"I wanted to see my friend," says the boy. "His body was delivered here this morning."

Biting the inside of my cheek, I tear my attention from his questioning gaze. "It's against the rules," I whisper.

"I don't care about the rules!"

His fury startles me, and I look up, trying to understand

what can be so urgent. His friend is gone, and he isn't getting any more gone any time soon. Why is this strange boy so desperate to see him?

"I'm sorry," he says. "I didn't mean to yell. It's been a long day." He reaches a hand out to me. "I'm Daxon. Daxon Thorn."

I stare at his outstretched arm like a complete moron. My lips tighten and my heart drops to my feet as I curl my fingers and shove the fists into my pockets. "Nastya," I say and wait for his hand to drop away. When it does, his thick eyebrows draw low, and I am certain he knows he is in the presence of the town freak.

Daxon's lips peel away, and my knees knock. "I know who you are."

Of course, you do.

I am about to tell him to leave when he takes a step forward and shoves his face so close to mine, I can smell the coffee on his breath. "Think you can sneak me in?"

"W—What?"

He nods to the door. "To see Kye. Do you think you can get me past your mom?"

It is impossible to stop myself from laughing. Getting anything past my mother is never an option; the woman is a walking lie detector, and even if I could somehow manage to get Daxon inside, I wouldn't dare it. I don't disobey Mother's rules and I definitely don't sneak boys in. That is another girl's life.

I clear my throat again to rid it of the sand gathering

there and back away from Daxon. "Yeah, not really an option around here."

He looks defeated. Shoulders sagging, he takes a deep breath and runs a hand through the hair I cannot stop staring at. Instinctively, I reach for the hood of my sweatshirt and tuck loose strands of silver inside. "You should probably go," I say.

"Please, Nastya," Daxon counters. "It's important."

"Why?"

"Because I don't think it was an accident."

The porch closes in around me. Brick walls drag across the wooden slats and press into my skin, and I am forced to hold my breath to keep them in place. Daxon shifts his weight and a ray of sunshine slams into my eyes, making them water. I blink and part my lips, but no sound comes out.

What does he mean?

Death is always an accident in Cherry Cove. It is why Mother is so adamant on staying in the stupid town, because even with how I'm treated by the locals, it is the safest place to be. There hasn't been a murder in the cove in, well, ever.

I staple my senses back together and glare at Daxon. "Not possible."

"It is," he says. "I know Kye and I'm telling you, it wasn't an accident."

My brain hurts as I try to recall the details on the report

I read this morning. "Your friend died in a car accident. Accident being the key word here."

Daxon shakes his head. "No."

"Yes," I argue.

"No," he repeats. "I was with him that morning and he was bragging about his new car. His parents got it for him for his seventeenth birthday, and he was so excited to finally drive the damn thing. We were going to meet up and drive around in the afternoon."

"That doesn't prove anything," I say, yet I am starting to doubt myself.

"The car was brand new!" Daxon exclaims. "There was nothing wrong with it, and there definitely wasn't anything wrong with the brakes. Whatever happened to Kye, it wasn't an accident. Kye was the most careful person I knew, and there is no way in hell he would risk pissing off his parents. Something happened to him, and I need to find out what."

As he continues to glower, my entire body freezes over. I can feel my bones shatter and soon, I am nothing but a shell of a girl. Daxon is wrong, he has to be. If he wasn't, it would be the sheriff standing here on our porch instead of this sad boy. Kye's body came in as all the others, no investigation, no signs of foul play. Another corpse amidst many.

"Listen," I say, fighting against my every need to keep him here longer. "You're upset and I get it, but there's nothing I can for you. It's like Mom said, come back on

Friday with everyone else and say your good byes. I'm sorry."

When he falls apart in front of me, I have to turn away. His face crumples and he watches me with muted anger, as if he is waiting for me to change my mind. I do not. Cannot.

I watch Daxon stomp down the stairs and walk down the driveway, his figure shrinking as he disappears from my line of sight. Around me, frigid air nips at my face and even with him gone, the walls of the house are still tight against my body. I try to clear my head, but Daxon's words repeat in my mind. I can taste them on my tongue.

Not an accident.

Could it be?

I shake my head, refusing to let his brand of crazy overtake my own. I have enough to deal with today, starting with the damn math lesson. My heart lays heavy in my chest as I sneak through the door and crawl up the stairs, shutting the world away. Somewhere out there, Daxon's grief is painting Cherry Cove a new shade of red and I fall on my bed, tucking covers around me until I am in a cocoon of fabric. My eyes flutter and the bed sinks under my weight as I work to steady my breathing. Eyes wide open, I focus on a spot on the ceiling and after a while, it starts to look an awful lot like Daxon's face. I groan, tossing the covers off me and sit up. How am I supposed to concentrate on schoolwork when all I can think of is some lunatic town boy?

Head spinning, I reach a shaking hand for the textbook

and flip it open. "Head in the game," I tell myself. "Forget him."

I do not and as I groggily read the book in my lap, Daxon sits on the edge of the bed and watches me work. His eyes are blank and his chest rises and falls as he breathes in the dusty air of my room. Every once in a while, I glance at him, forgetting everything I read moments ago. My visions spots and when Daxon opens his mouth to scream, I shut my eyes. When I open them again, he is gone and I am all alone. Somehow, alone starts to feel much more lonely.

4

A branch hits the window, jerking me awake. My eyelashes stick together, sleep still dripping off them and coaxing me to lay back down. I rub my face and rise to sit. At the foot of the bed, the textbook is open with the pages crinkled from my foot kicking them while I slept.

Mother is not going to be pleased I passed out studying again.

Taking one look at the book, I stand and groggily make my way to the bathroom down the hall. Downstairs, the grandfather clock we inherited with the house chimes, and I pause. How is it midnight already? My feet are light on the floorboards as I shuffle into the bathroom and close the door slowly behind me. Washing my face, I keep my eyes on the sink to avoid catching a glimpse of my ghostly reflection in the ornate gold mirror; no one needs to see this creature right now. When I feel more like myself, I scurry out and head downstairs.

The house is eerily quiet and sharp shadows crawl over the walls as I walk down the stairs. This late at night, they look like thick bars, which is more fitting than I'd like to admit. On either side of the landing, two doors block me in, and I try to gauge my options carefully. Mother is already sleeping, so it is only me in the house of death and while there isn't much to do in the form of entertainment, I am still unsure of where to proceed.

"Food or work?"

Wetting my lips, I turn my back to one door as though its presence insults me and head for the second. As soon as it opens, a chill rushes up my spine and I reach my hand around for the hooks on the wall outside. My fingers wrap around thick wool and in seconds, I am wrapped in one of the sweaters Mother keeps at the entrance to the morgue. I guess her meddling comes in handy after all.

This late at night, the basement is an ice box and my toes curl as skin touches concrete. I roll on the balls of my feet, floating toward the morgue like I am drawn to a flame. At the bottom of the stairs, the basement opens up to a wide box with every wall painted a jarring shade of white. Metal shelving units line the walls, each stuffed to the brim with filing boxes of past patients. It's what Mother calls the dead. Patients. Like they came in for a standard checkup and never left. The rest of the basement is cut in half by a thick wall with two large windows on either side of a steel door. The place where Mother and I spend most of our time. The morgue. Beyond the frosted glass, I can make out the shadow of a gurney and my stomach pitches violently. There is only one other person here with me and I bite my tongue, chewing on it like a medium-rare steak as I try to swallow down guilt. My body temperature drops when I round the corner, pulling on my cardigan as I take in my project for this sleepless night.

Kye.

I stutter-step toward him, eyes glassy and blank as if I am the one lying under plastic. Swallowing the lump in my throat, I pull the zipper, letting the stiff fabric split open to reveal the face of a boy I never knew. His eyes are closed, dark hair parted to one side. Shaking, I hover a palm over his face and waist. Kye doesn't speak, and I am relieved by the silence, grateful the dead are playing dead for one night.

Despite being out of the cold chamber, there is a chill rising from the body and I wonder how long he'd been lying here. Mother must have embalmed him just before heading to bed for him to still be this cold. Low skin temperature is not optimal for painting, but I am determined to get the job done. Maybe if I get a head start on this, it will win me some brownie points for when I tell Mom I didn't finish my homework again tomorrow.

My brow knits and I cast one final glance at Kye. "Let's get you cleaned up for your big day on Friday."

I chuckle at my own pathetic joke, then shake my head. Even the dead deserve an ice breaker.

It takes me longer than usual to fill the metal bowl with water, and I am annoyed with myself for how many times I check it for warmth before finally settling down. Kye doesn't care about this nonsense and yet, I want to make sure he gets the best treatment possible; for Daxon. As I run the wet cloth over his chest, I pretend he is in a spa and not on my slab. A low melody escapes me, mimicking the sounds of waves crashing to shore. Once in a while, I pause to inspect him. He seems happy enough. I continue.

I am about to turn him over when something catches my eye. My gaze lasers in on the glowing spot in Kye's thick, curly hair and I grit my teeth as I reach for it.

"What is that?"

My arm is shaking, and I have to take deep breaths like Mother and I practiced while I dig around Kye's hair to pull the object out. It is soft against my skin, fragile and warm; a stark opposition to the rest of Kye.

"What the hell?" I whisper, pinching my fingers around the tiny red petal to bring it up to my eyes. Fumbling, I swivel the lamp at my side toward it, pointing it at the petal as one would a flashlight. My breath leaps from my mouth, hanging in the air in a puffy white cloud before vanishing. My back hits the back wall and the thick handle of the cooling chamber behind me jabs my shoulder blades. I groan. "A poppy?"

A thought tugs at the rear of my mind and I cannot

quite place my finger on it. Daxon said his friend died in a car accident, at least it's what the sheriff's report read. And Kye's body showed all the standard injuries following a car crash. Bruising on the chest, lacerations, slight swelling of the skull. Nothing out of the ordinary. So why am I so shaken up by this stupid petal?

My grip on the flower tightens until I am all but crushing it in my fingers.

"Where did you even get this?"

Poppies are not indigenous to Cherry Cove. Our soil and weather does not allow for an optimal growing environment, not to mention the legal gray area of growing poppies in your own backyard. Opium is no joke, kids. It especially isn't one in a town like Cherry Cove, where rules and regulations are basically a way of life. The only poppies I've seen are the ones I read about in books back in my two-month period of being obsessed with gardening. Those and the small plant I recently saw in the flower shop.

Somehow, Kye doesn't strike me as someone who is big on gardening.

"Did you get these for someone? A girl maybe?"

I wait for him to respond and am instantly deflated when he doesn't.

My mind reels, thoughts slamming into each other as I work to place the pieces together. The plant I saw in the shop was expensive, too expensive for a teenager to buy. And everyone knows roses make for better gifts, anyway. Besides, even if he did somehow manage to get his hands on a poppy, why would this one loose petal be buried in his hair?

Could it be from the crash site?

I curl my fingers over the petal and push away from the gurney. Nostrils flaring, I stomp to the walnut desk in the corner of the room and push file folders aside until I find the one I am looking for. Across the tab, a label with Kye's name is tacked on with a paperclip and I flip the folder open, scanning the police report with hungry eyes. My jaw rests on my chest and the back of my neck pulses as I run my index finger over every word.

"Where did they find you?" I ask. Flipping through the pages, my aggravation grows and I am all but snapping when I finally see it. "Route fifty-seven, across from Mill Creek."

It doesn't make any sense.

The place is completely desolate. An industrial wasteland with nothing around for miles. There is barely any life on the route; the area covered in concrete and abandoned buildings that once housed the only factory in town. Back when Cherry Cove still thought a modern way of living was the answer to a thriving town and decided to open their very own cheese factory. From what Mother told me, the place closed down fairly quickly and remained a running joke for years. "Why cheese?" she asks. "Why not something else?"

No one knew why, and no one bothered to ask. These days, it didn't seem to matter, and as soon as the cove morphed into the tourist trap it was today, everyone forgot all about the abandoned monstrosity at the edge of town. Everyone but Kye.

I peel my fingers apart and glare at the red spot in the center of my pale skin. The petal is darker now, wilted from the faint heat of my skin, and I wince as I flip my palm and watch it fall on the table.

I should leave it alone, I think.

But I don't.

Instead, I flip through more pages until I see Kye's family records and known associates. Names leap off the paper and rush into my thoughts and I struggle to memorize them. There are so many. Whoever Kye was, he sure was popular. I spot a few names of kids I recognize and my heart drums against my chest as memories of their torments rush my system. In seconds, I am five again, crying on the swings while those morons hurl insult after insult my way. Somewhere in the distance, Mother is cussing out a teacher, threatening to sue the entire school if they don't rectify the situation. They don't. Obviously.

My lungs contract and I am wheezing over the file folder with my hand clutching my chest. My neck twists, and I turn my head to peer at Kye, trying to place him in the crowd of monsters in my mind. I don't. Relief laces through me when I decide Kye wasn't there. He wasn't one of them. I'm not sure why the thought relaxes me, but it does, and I do not look a gift horse in the mouth.

"You didn't deserve this," I whisper. "Whatever happened to you, you didn't deserve it."

The words slither on my trembling lips and my eyes widen. *Daxon was right,* I realize. No matter what the sheriff's report says, something isn't right about Kye's death. The report doesn't add up.

Darting my eyes between the gurney and the poppy petal, I turn my attention back to the list in front of me and find another familiar name with a phone number next to it. My head is spinning and droplets of sweat roll down the arch of my back and I reach for my pocket to pull out my phone. With my pulse hammering in my ears, I type out a string of numbers, choking on the saliva pooling in my mouth. My entire body convulses as I build up the nerve to type out a message. *'Hey. It's Nastya. From the funeral home. Are you up?'*

I am holding the phone so tight, the plastic clings to my skin. A little blue bubble appears on the screen, and I hold my breath and wait for Daxon's response to pop up.

'I'm up. I'm always up.' he responds. *'What's going on?'*

I take a moment to compose myself, then think about my answer. What *is* going on? I am not sure yet, but at this point, I am on a path which will not allow me to turn around.

"Say something, stupid," I scold myself.

My vision blurs at the edges as I type, and I press my hips into the edge of the table to keep from melting on the floor. My muscles swim under my skin and every bone in my body feels like broken glass. My shoulders shake and when I finally grasp the courage to press the send key, I am a block of ice.

'We need to talk,' I type out. *'Can you meet at the cove in a half hour?'*

5

The cove is beautiful tonight. Rays of moonlight wash over it, twinkling across the surface in swirls and casting a lighter shade over the water. From my spot on the rocky shore, it looks almost clear now, with only hints of pink peeking through. All around me, rocks jut out at odd angles, blocking me away from the rest of the world. Beyond the shore on either side of me, trees cram close together and rustle in the light wind. On the other side of them, Cherry Cove sleeps. The rancid smell of the river is almost gone now, blocked by the coolness of the evening air. I relax. This late at night, it is only me and the cove and I am finally able to let my guard down. My neck is stiff as I look out into the distance, eyes drifting past the copse of shadowy trees and high up to the sky. Tomorrow, when the sun comes out, this place will be filled with townspeople and tourists. They will waddle along, skipping from rock to rock to get as close to the red water as possible without falling in. Some will come in groups, others will bring a book to read in a more or less secluded spot. It will be chaos.

But not tonight.

Tonight, the cove belongs to me only.

My lips twitch and I lean back on my elbows and begin counting the stars. It is an impossible task and yet my favorite game to play out here. When I was only a child, Dad used to bring us here well past my bedtime and we would lie back on the rocks, much as I am doing now, and count stars together. He told me stories of each one, painting the stars as though they are people. I remember listening to him for hours, inhaling the adventures of the stars until my eyes grew foggy and my lids too heavy to stay awake. Dad never stopped talking, not until I was asleep and sprawled over his arms as he carried me back to the car to drive us home. I don't recall much of my father besides the crook of his nose and the ridiculous cowlick at the back of his head that never seemed to settle down. Yet, I can picture those nights as if they happened yesterday.

It's strange how some things stay with you for no reason at all.

My elbows dig into the rock and my skin tugs against a sharp corner. I swat at the rocks, clumsily rolling over and pushing up to sit. Behind me, leaves rustle and heavy footsteps near. My head jerks backward, eyes adjusting to the darkness of the surrounding space until I see the person closing in on me with ease.

"Sorry I'm late," Daxon says. His hair is unruly and his blue eyes gleam amidst the night. They draw me in, and I tremble as he approaches. *Running rivers,* I think. *His eyes are nothing but water and air.*

I shiver, violently pushing myself to get a grip. "It's fine," I say. "I haven't been here long."

This is a lie, but I don't want him to feel guilty over leaving me waiting. Daxon is a stranger, and strangers do not owe you their guilt. At least, it's what Mother says.

When he draws closer, I scoot to the side, giving him ample space to sit. My chest tightens when he chooses a spot facing me, and I am all too aware of his eyes following my every move. My nerves drum against my belly and I avert my gaze, turning to lock my attention on the cove. In my periphery, I see Daxon's brow crease, and I wonder what he's thinking.

I don't have to wonder for long.

"It's nice here at night, huh?" he asks.

"I come here a lot," I admit. "When no one is around, it really is a very different place."

"People don't give it enough credit," he says, picking up an empty plastic bottle from the ground someone left behind. "Makes you wonder if the Warriors have the right idea to clean this place up."

"Maybe," I say. "Maybe not."

A light wind blows passed and I pull on the drawstrings

of my hoodie to tighten it around my face until only my eyes and nose are visible. My teeth chatter, frigid air rolling down my throat as I take a deep breath in. In front of me, Daxon isn't the least bit bothered by the cold, and I let my eyes wander over his open variety jacket to trace the ridges of his chest and stomach. He is built of stone and muscle, an extension of the landscape we are in—hard and solid like a wall. His jaw is locked, and the sharpness of his face is almost jarring until I catch a glimpse of his eyes again. How can one person be rigid and soft at the same time? I don't understand it.

Daxon crumples the bottle with his hands and sits it next to him. "So why did you want to meet up?"

Here we go.

"I believe you," I say.

Daxon loosens a breath. "For real?"

"Yes."

Carefully, I reach into my pocket to pull out the poppy petal I tucked into a Ziplock bag for safekeeping. It's almost unrecognizable now, a brown speck in the universe disintegrating before my eyes. I can see the confusion on Daxon's face when I hold the bag up to his face and grin like an idiot. "What is it?" he asks.

"A poppy petal. I found it in Kye's hair when I was..." My words fade into the cool night air. "Doesn't matter. The point is, it doesn't make sense for this to be on him."

"Where the hell did Kye even get poppies?" Daxon asks. "I thought they were impossible to find in these parts."

"They are," I confirm. "Very rare and very expensive. I checked the inventory of his car and there was no mention of poppies anywhere. So, the question is, why did your friend have it?"

Daxon's chin jolts out and his nostrils flare. "That's not the only question," he says.

I feel as clueless as I must appear. One eyebrow quirked, I swallow hard before speaking. "What's the other question?"

He smiles. "Why did the poppy make you change your mind?"

I am unsure how best to answer without sounding foolish. There is no concrete reason for it; I simply chose to believe him. A part of me knows how insane his claims sound, and his grief is thick enough to paint a clear picture of a person lost. Yet, he is not, and I am sure of it. Something about Daxon makes me want to help him, give him some peace so he can smile again. Scrub his mind clean of Kye's death. Maybe it's because I cannot place him in my memories that I feel this way. No matter how hard I tried, I can't recall Daxon Thorn; not in any part of my childhood. He was not one of the kids that tormented me in school, and in the few times I've left the funeral home, I've never encountered him. His absence from my life beckons me in. We are similar; both ghosts to each other. Both lost. My throat is suddenly very dry and the thread holding my hoodie together digs into my skin as I fidget with the plastic of the bag. Leaves rustle in the background, their whispers fogging my mind until I can no longer hear my own heart beating. My eyes narrow to slits and I sink into the rock beneath, begging my body to relax.

"I don't know why," I finally answer. "I get the sense you're right and the sheriff missed something."

"Hmm."

"I sound crazy," I say.

I'm greeted with another smile, this one stingy and small. "No, not crazy. It's—" he considers his words, weighing them on an invisible scale to gauge their importance. "—People talk. About what you can do."

"That's not what I meant," I say, cheeks flushed. "Whatever you heard, it's not true."

I am lying again, and it is scary how easily it comes to me. Anyone else would have chalked up my paranoia around Kye's death as a teen with a wild imagination. And if it was anyone else in the position I am in now, it would have made sense. But it isn't someone else. It is me and I have learned a long time ago my intuition is not to be messed with. When it comes to death, I have a different palate than the rest. Maybe in a way I am telling Daxon the truth; after all, I didn't foresee his friend's death, not the way I do with all the others. Still, the feeling I have deep in my gut now bears the same frequency; there is a truth buried here, one no one else can uncover but me.

"So, what do people say exactly?" The words bubble out and even if I wanted to stop them, I wouldn't. I need to know, if only to gauge how much I can trust the boy sitting before me. "You can tell me," I say. "It won't offend me at all."

"You sure?"

I nod blankly. I am not sure at all.

The woods creep in on us as Daxon rearranges his weight to sit more comfortably, and his long legs stretch out in a straight line between us. I stare at the soles of his sneakers, memorizing every speck of dirt in the rhombus pattern etched into the rubber. "They say you can tell when someone is about to die," he says. His voice wavers like he is afraid he can hurt me with them. "And you see dead people."

A laugh escapes me, and I clamp my hand to my mouth to stop it. "Sorry," I say, "but that's really dumb."

"Which part?" Daxon asks.

Touché. "The seeing dead people part."

"And the other?"

I wish to argue and tell him everyone is wrong so badly, it stings. Instead, I gulp cold air and face him head on. "This part's true. I'm a freak."

He is quiet for a long while. His eyes remain locked on mine, but he cannot see me. Daxon's mind is elsewhere as he considers what I said and as he sits there unblinking, I contemplate running away. Beyond the trees, the low hum of a car zooming by echoes toward us, and I rub my hand over the hairs standing upright on my arm.

This is not going well at all.

"You're not a freak," Daxon says, surprising me.

I laugh. "Of course, I am. Didn't you hear me? Everything you heard is right. I have this thing, this curse, and there is nothing I can do to get rid of it. What am I then, if not some freak of nature?"

He grows silent again and I shrink in my oversized clothes.

"I don't know what you are, Nastya," he says. "Whatever it is, I'm glad you have it. I'm glad it made you believe me."

My throat is sandpaper and when I swallow the saliva pooling in my mouth, it does nothing to quench my thirst. I want to reach out and grab his hand, tell him I'm on his side even though no one else is. I want to be for him what others have never been for me. This is a brand new feeling for me, this urgent need to help someone who isn't Mother, and I embrace it to the fullest. Helping Daxon fills me up like a bathtub and as I float inside myself, all I want is to figure this out for him. To find out what happened to his friend before the boy I'm coming to know disappears. I can see him clearly now, but for how long? Grief has a strange way of erasing the best parts of us and I can already sense the Daxon I met is not the Daxon he used to be. Whoever this new Daxon is, I do not want him to change.

"It wasn't an accident," Daxon says.

"I know."

Near to us, the cove whispers and both our eyes shift to the water. I search the surface, mind traveling into the depths while my body remains on the shore. When I was little, I used to beg Mother to let me duck in late at night when we came here. It never happened. Mother is as weary of the water as everyone else in town, but not me. I crave to see what lays within the crimson deep. How many treasures are hidden on the bottom, I wonder? How many secrets buried and lost? The cove is impenetrable, a fortress, and the things hidden inside it are for the river alone.

"You know, when my mom sat me down to tell me about Kye, I didn't even cry," Daxon says, tearing me away from the water. "It's like I didn't believe he's gone. I still don't. Every morning, I still wait for him to text me with some stupid joke he saw online. And I wait. Nastya, I wait every single minute of the day."

"I'll figure it out," I say. "I'll find out what really happened to Kye so you don't have to feel like this anymore. I promise. It won't make the hurt go away, but it might help."

Shoulders sagging, he crosses his legs, resting his chin in his hands and looks at me through hooded eyes. "Thank you."

Blood rushes to my face and my vision falters for a moment. It is enough to jolt me back to where I am and what time of night it is. Mother will be waking up soon and I cannot let her find me missing, I can't afford to be grounded right now, not if I plan on following through with the promise I just made to Daxon. Pushing away from the ground, I start to rise and am about to say good night when Daxon does something I don't expect.

His hand reaches for me, wrapping over my wrist and pinning me in place. His skin is hot against mine and my body recoils from the touch. It has been so long since anyone but Mother touched me, I am spinning. Dots dance under my lids and my vision falters. The night is gone and bright lights explode around me as I crouch on the rock with my arm still in his grip.

"Nastya?" Daxon asks.

I cannot answer.

My bones creak and my veins sizzle. In my mind, the sound of rushing water fills me to the brim, and I snap my eyes shut to keep myself from falling over. When I open them again, Daxon is gone and I am alone at the cove. Muffled sounds of cars in the distance fill my mind, and I whip my head from side to side, trying to adjust my eyes to the darkness. In the air, voices speak in hushed tones, but I cannot see anyone else around. This is wrong. Night covers the cove but there is too much commotion, too much life, around me. It is never this loud here in the night.

I gasp, shaking my head to free myself of the vision, but it is of no use. I understand exactly what this is. There is no fighting fate.

Goosebumps spread over my legs as I strain my neck to face the water. In it, Daxon wades and sways, his gait unsteady as he fights to make it back to the shore. His eyes snap open like he can see me and the terror behind them tears me apart. My focus shifts and I am standing next to him, tears falling from my cheeks and landing in thick drops into the water below. Red, bloody water.

I dare to look down, a scream trapped in my chest. Daxon's body twitches and the scent of iron fills my nostrils. My vision narrows with a singular purpose and falls on Daxon's leg where blood pours in waterfalls. It blends into the river, staining the bottom of my hoodie, and I am so close to fainting, I do not have time to blink. I feel a stabbing pain in my side and my lungs collapse under my ribs. Prying my lips open, I try to breathe but air is hard to come by. Liquid pours down my throat and I dry heave to clear it. Inside, I can feel the flow of my blood slow, my pulse disappearing. My body riles and twists and I blink my lids rapidly, understanding the vision all too well. I am dying. No, not me. Daxon.

The light disperses, Daxon's shape wavering before me until I am looking at a different version of him. The version I am with right now. His face is twisted up as he tries to figure out what's happening. His fingers are on my wrist, and I yank myself away, shoving my hands into the front pocket of my hoodie.

"Nastya? Are you okay? What just happened?"

I turn my head and wipe the cold sweat from my neck. "Nothing," I croak out. "It's nothing. I'm tired, I need to go."

Daxon calls after me as I run away. Feet pounding the rock, I let his voice fade away and burst into the trees, not bothering to look back. My muscles pulse and branches hit my face as I run, but I don't let it stop me. I have to get home. I have to get somewhere safe where I can fall apart. I have to get as far away from Daxon as I can before what the vision I had tears me into pieces.

Breath heaving, I keep on, my thoughts racing to keep up with my legs.

Daxon is going to die, and I cannot change it.

There are no windows in the palace,

Only mirrors and deceptions.

Thick, heavy waves crash into the walls;

Lolling her back to sleep.

She cannot.

Will not.

There is much work to be done and she rages within the cage she occupies.

Her fingers trace the veins of the flower;

So red and fresh it is unbearable to touch.

She grins.

Soon, she whispers.

She will hear us soon.

She will come.

6

"Nastya?"

Mother's low voice startles me, and I miss a step, my knee hitting the hardwood with a pang. A dull ache laces up my leg and I wince. "Go back to sleep, I'm getting some water."

From her bedroom, the rustling of sheets drifts down the upstairs hallway and I stay unbearably still until she quiets down. My shoes are packed in mud from the forest, and as I press them into my chest to keep the dirt from falling on the carpet, my heart races. If she saw me like this, there'd be no amount of lies to get me out of getting grounded. Not to mention how she'd react if she knew I was sneaking off in the middle of the night to meet a boy by the cove.

I tip toe toward my room, eyes catching a glimpse of my

reflection in the bronze mirror on the wall. A girl I don't recognize watches me intently. She is all sharp edges and bite, dark streaks caking her garish face like the markings of war. My bones ache from running and I run my fingers through my hair, trying to untangle the mess in the mirror. It is no use.

Pulling a knot of silver free, I sigh and rush for the bedroom so fast, wind all but howls at my back.

My hands tremor as I strip myself of the filthy leggings and hoodie and let the clothes drop in a pile next to my bed; my armor coming undone. The room is dead quiet, and in it, every breath I take vibrates against the walls and sends me into a deeper spiral. Lids heavy, I shut my eyes, praying to anyone who would listen for a peaceful night. As always, my prayers fall into the darkness and vanish and I am soon wide eyed and full of panic with the vision I had replaying in my head like a catchy song. All I see is the blood and Daxon's empty expression. I feel his absence as though his death had already happened, even though I am certain he is safe at home.

It is never clear how long until my visions come to be, though from experience, they manifest almost instantly. As instant as death could manifest. Sometimes, it could take weeks as it did with Christine, others mere hours. My throat closes up when I recall the time I predicted the end for one of the couriers delivering our mail. The man's heart gave out before he even had a chance to leave our driveway. I remember Mother ushering me inside and telling me to stay upstairs while the paramedics strapped him to a gurney and wheeled him away. After they left, she brought me tea and cookies and talked non-stop about some show she had been watching she thought I'd enjoy. Her behavior baffled me, still does to this day, and I never understood how she could be so pragmatic about things; bringing me food and warm clothes and acting as though I had a bad case of the flu and didn't just witness a man die in front of me. But that's Mother for you—sweeping things under the carpet and moving on is a specialty of hers.

Lying on the bed now with Daxon's death on my mind, I wish I had some of her strength.

I clamp my teeth down on my tongue hard enough to draw blood.

"Who would do this to you?"

In my stomach, knots twist and turn, snakes crawling over my organs and driving nausea up my throat. I don't know Daxon at all, and yet the vision unsettles me. From what I've seen so far, he doesn't strike as the type of person who would have enemies; certainly not ones who would want him dead. So why is this his fate? What is he hiding?

Mother says everyone has secrets, no matter how perfect they might seem on the outside. This is her way of making me comfortable with the life I was handed, but she isn't wrong. No one is perfect, not even Daxon Thorn. Whatever secrets this boy holds are going to be his undoing, and I can't help but wonder if perhaps this one time, the future might not be set in stone.

"Don't get involved. It is not your business." I recite Mother's instructions until I am numb and unable to move. "He is not your problem."

But he is, isn't he?

For all I know, if Daxon hadn't come to see me tonight, everything could be different for him. Maybe I'm the reason he ends up dead; maybe I don't foresee death at all. Maybe I deliver it.

I flinch and sink into the covers, refusing to let dark thoughts penetrate my heart. Death doesn't require a chariot; it arrives as it pleases, and there is no stopping it from coming to your door. Even if I wanted to help Daxon avoid the tragic end waiting for him, I am powerless to do so. The last time I tried to change the outcome of my visions, I ended up becoming the pariah of this wretched town and I'm not falling for it again.

My knees slam together. "Stop thinking about him!"

Outside, the wind trills and branches crash into the window like fingers tapping on glass. My own fingers dance on my shaking leg, and I growl under my breath, realizing it will be a long while until I can forget Daxon Thorn. If ever.

I'm not sure why that is.

There is nothing special about Daxon. He is only another boy—albeit a cute boy—in a town full of them. Yet, I cannot shake the way he makes me feel, like I am not who I am. I'm being foolish. A few years ago, Mother and I watched a documentary about a rescued poodle that refused to let anyone touch him, even when they bribed him with food. The shelter kept him in a separate room and when people came to pick out a new pet, he was never on the list. One day, a little boy got separated from his parents. They spent hours looking for him and finally found the trouble maker in the room housing the poodle. They said when they walked in, the boy was sitting next to the cage, spewing random facts about his life, his tiny fingers shoved into the holes between the bars. To everyone's surprise, the poodle didn't snarl and bark as he usually did. Instead, he pressed his nose against the boy's fingers and occasionally licked them to tell the kid he enjoyed his stories. When the workers asked the boy why he wasn't afraid of what was clearly a menace of a dog, he shrugged. "He wants a friend," the boy explained. And a friend was exactly what the poodle got when the family adopted him. According to the documentary, the boy and the dog had been inseparable since, and the poodle followed him everywhere without so much as a sound.

I am embarrassed at how much me and the stupid poodle have in common. Both of us so eager for someone to talk to.

Combing my fingers through my hair, I roll over to grab my journal from the nightstand and place it in my lap. The worn leather is soft against my skin and my shoulders sag when I unravel the cord binding the covers and flip the book open. Wayward handwriting fills its pages and I'm lost in the memories locked inside. I hadn't written in what feels like forever; tonight is as good a night as any to start again.

Testing the pen, I am about to mark my entry when something catches my eye. In the back of the journal, a photograph I had long forgotten is buried, its corner sticking out far enough to cause me grief. I yank it out and my heart shatters instantly.

The photograph is so old, I almost don't recognize myself. Still, there I am, wide eyed and cheerful and grinning toothily. My silver hair is even lighter here, tied into two small buns atop my child's head. At my side, Dad crouches. His thick-rimmed glasses slide down his nose and his blonde hair is coiffed into a dramatic side part, cowlick and all. Dad was quite the eccentric person; one of the things I loved most about him. In the picture, I am looking straight ahead—probably at Mom, barking orders—but not him. He only has eyes for me.

I pinch the skin at my neck and burrow holes into the image with my thunderous gaze.

"What do I do, Dad?" For a moment, I think he winks. "Traitor."

I shove the photograph back in the journal and slam it shut. It truly doesn't matter what Dad would want me to do right now, he is not here to guide me. I know what Mother would say if I told her about my vision. *'You have no bearing on fate.'* She'd said it enough times that the sentiment is burned into my mind like a law I am unable to break. Death comes for all of us, and even though I see it a mile away, I cannot interfere. It is not my place. I am not the answer.

Then why do I feel like this time, I might be?

My cheeks are crimson, and my throat is bone dry, the answer crashing into me. Because I don't want him to die. I want to save Daxon from whatever horrible thing is coming for him. I want to protect him from the monster that wants to erase him from my life. I want to give fate the middle finger and laugh as I defy it.

Daxon's eyes flash before me and I press my back into the tufted headrest. Head pounding, I swallow the acid trapped in my throat, though the burn never quite goes away. The room spins around me, colors fading to black as I close my eyes and shut out the thoughts racing through my head. It is some time before sleep finally comes for me, and when it does, I don't fight against it. An image of blood filling the cove is the last thing I see.

7

"Pass the salt, please," Mother says, her arm stretching over the round dining table in anticipation. I push the shaker her way.

"This stuff is bad for your heart, you know."

"Life is bad for your heart," Mother bites back.

She's not wrong.

I gulp down the rest of my cold coffee and refold the napkin in my lap while she watches me. Mother is no fool; she knows something is up, even if I'm trying my hardest to act normal. She edges closer and wrinkles her nose. Her lips look to be drawn on her face with a fine-tipped pencil. "What's going on with you today? You seem off."

I cannot tell her I have never been *not* off.

"Nothing," I say. "I didn't sleep well."

"Oh?"

My knees shimmy under the table and I avoid making eye contact with her. My mouth has other plans though and before I know it, I am spewing words I wish to swallow whole. "Why did you send Daxon away?" I ask. "All he wanted was to see his friend."

Mother's face gives nothing away, and if she is surprised by my question, she doesn't show it. "Daxon?" she asks, arching a perfectly manicured eyebrow.

I dig my nails into my thighs. "The boy who came by yesterday. I heard you tell him to leave."

"And you know his name, how?"

"I went out on the porch, and he was still here," I answer. I don't dare to tell her about our rendezvous at the cove last night. I'm not a complete idiot.

A coffee cup slams on the table and Mother gapes at me. She isn't angry, but she certainly isn't pleased. I ready for a lecture, struggling not to roll my eyes. "We have rules in place for a reason, Nastya," Mother chides. Right on cue. "Seeing a loved one before they had been prepared can do more harm than good. I feel for this boy, this Daxon. I'm not heartless."

"But?"

"But it is best he sees his friend at the viewing," she says, her voice husky and low. "It will be easier this way."

I choke back a laugh. "Easier for whom?"

For a while, we are both quiet. Mother plays with the handle of her cup while I stare down at the bowl of apples on the table, my plate still full of the breakfast I do not want to eat. I can't tell where we go from here. Mother does not budge on rules, and when she makes her mind up, you can be sure there is no turning her around. She is a horse with blinders on and I am strapped to her back and forced to follow the direction she walks in. Everything we do is based on her instructions and while deep down she only wants the best for me, I am tired of the journey I didn't sign up for. Her ways are not my ways and more than anything, I wish I could explain it to her.

How come I never do?

When Mother finally speaks, the answer is clear.

"You cannot talk to him again," she says. "If something happened, if you see something you shouldn't, we both know how he would react. Do you want the imbeciles to show up here with pitchforks? Is that your plan?"

In my core, shame bubbles to the surface and I gag on its moldy taste. I want to fill her in on the vision, about how it made me feel, but I can't move my lips. For years, my mother gave up everything to protect me from the people who wanted me gone. She fought for our home, for our place in Cherry Cove, because she understood that no matter where we went, it would always be this way. I would always be an outcast, someone to fear. All she wants is to shield me from heartache, and there is no life in which I can fault her for it. Despite her strict ways, she loves me.

More, I am indebted to her.

Without her, who knows what the town would have done to me. Best-case scenario, they'd chase me out and delete me from memory. Worst case, I'd end up on a slab downstairs right next to Kye.

I shudder.

"Sorry," I choke out through clenched teeth.

"Promise me you'll not see this boy again," Mother says.

My fingers cross under the table. "I promise."

My response seems to satisfy her because soon, she is going on about some gossip she heard from the mailman. Her eyes sparkle with mischief and I am once again confronted with the trickster side of my mother. I try to put the pieces of her story together, but my brain refuses to cooperate. The Warriors are getting in the mayor's way, I think. The information is as relevant to my life as college applications and I tap my foot lightly, urging myself to stay quiet while she talks.

"Isn't that insane?" Mother asks. "I swear, the people in this govniuchiy place get crazier by the minute. I mean, come on! Leave the damn cove alone and move on with your life. It's only a river."

"It isn't though, is it?" I ask.

"Pardon?"

I clear my throat—tight and full now—happy to be back to our usual breakfast banter. "The cove, I mean. It's not only a river. It makes the town what it is, defines us. Kind of a big deal, if you ask me."

"Well, exactly!" she exclaims. "They can clean it up all they want, but in the end, it won't do anyone any good.

Those Warriors have a one track mind. It's like they can't see the bigger picture."

Her words make me flinch as I consider them. Out of the two of us, I am quite familiar with seeing the bigger picture and I wonder if Mother knows how much her stories affect me. Every morning, she tells me news of the town, trying to coax me into thinking I am a part of this wretched place as much as anyone else. What she doesn't realize is she is doing the exact opposite. The more I hear, the more evident it becomes that I will never fit in here. Or anywhere. The table is sturdy under my palms, and I push against it, letting the wood secure my balance. "I'm sure it'll blow over," I say. "Usually does."

"No kidding," she says with a huff. "I swear, one day, that damn group of hippies will find a way to get what they want, and we'll all suffer for it. Good on Renee to keep them in check all this time."

Renee Kim, Cherry Cove's mayor, is a good friend of my mother's and she speaks fondly of her almost every day. I can't blame her for it. If it wasn't for Renee, we wouldn't have the funeral home or even a place to live. She was the one who helped Mother transfer the mortgage after Dad left and though I had never spoken to her directly—for obvious reasons—I appreciate everything she's done for us. Mother says Renee is our first line of defense against the hillbillies. Her words, not mine.

"Hey, Mom?" She stills in her seat and looks at me. "Have you heard from Dad lately?"

A fermented expression crosses her features and shadows creep behind her hazel eyes. "Nastya," she says. "I haven't spoken to your father since the day he left."

"The day after my surgery," I add.

"Correct. Why are you asking this now?"

I have no idea. Biting my lower lip, I face her. "I found an old picture of him last night and it jogged some memories. Don't you think it's odd he never bothered to see me? Especially after the surgery. It's weird."

My mother's face falters, and her bangs sit so low on her forehead, I am having trouble making out her eyes. She's angry, I have no doubt. "Not everyone is meant to be a parent," Mother says. "Some people think it's what they want, then they realize they bit off more than they can chew. Your father is one of those people. He wanted everything to be perfect, and when it wasn't, he bailed. That's not someone you want in your life, trust me."

"I guess," I mumble. "Still think he could have called at least."

"Alexei could have done a lot of things. But he didn't. You need to accept it and move on."

I suck in a shaky breath. "Like you did?"

"Exactly like I did," Mother says. "What? Am I not enough for you?"

She's teasing, but there is a hint of hurt in her voice as it wavers. "Oh, trust me, you're plenty."

I shoot a half grin her way and am relieved when she returns it. Mother and I have an understanding; as long as I do what she says and don't ask too many questions, we get along fine. It's when I start digging that she pulls away and I hate when it happens. Every day is another reminder of how deeply I need her, and we are both painfully aware of it. No matter how much I wish Dad was here, she's the one forced to carry the burden of my existence. All alone. I watch her posture as it slumps in the chair, memories of Dad likely drowning her while we sit here. I hate myself for being the one to have caused her grief. She doesn't deserve this, like she didn't deserve to be left behind to deal with a sideshow daughter in a hateful town. My hands shake as I stack my cup on my plate and stand up.

"I'm going for a run," I say. "Want to join me?"

Mother shakes her head. "Too much to do. You have fun though."

As I clear the table, she watches me with hawk eyes, nostrils flaring.

"I better not catch you with that boy, Nastya. I mean it."

I stay quiet. She waits for me to agree, to make more promises, but I am a locked vault. There is too much I already hid from her, too many lies that should have never been. If I tell Mother I will not see Daxon, it will only be another to add to the list. Because it's one promise I can't keep, at least not until I get his stupid face out of my head.

I will forever see Daxon Thorn, even if it is only in my dreams. But Mother doesn't need to know it. No one does.

8

The trees are silent today, thoughtful, and as I walk through the dense woods, I am very aware of the acute loneliness in my heart. Above me, sunlight creeps in through the branches and makes the morning dew glitter in diamond-lit brilliance. It must have rained last night because the fresh smell of foliage permeates my senses with each clumsy step—the forest rushing to greet me.

Dusting a patch of dirt off a crusty old stump, I lower to sit and crane my neck to peer through the trees. From here, I can see the outline of the funeral home as it looms on the horizon and my stomach turns. Somewhere inside, Mother is going about her day. I can picture her stoic stance while she organizes the viewing room to her liking. Her eyes narrow and her brow knits with each scrape of a chair leg across the tiled floor, and when she stands back to inspect the room, I can feel her agitation as though it were my own. I swear, she spends more time prepping for viewings than she does with the actual bodies; an unusual trait for a morgue facilitator. But it isn't unusual for my mother. No matter how tough she tries to act, I see right through her. Giving those left behind a proper good bye is the only thing keeping her head above water. I know this because I have inherited her prudent heart.

It is also how I know she hated sending Daxon away. She must have.

Peeling my eyes off the house, I dig the toe of my running shoe into the ground to scruff up the soles. I've been pretending to take morning runs for months now, hoping my lack of coordination and loose muscles would not give me away. I'm not sure how it started, but one day, I spoke the words aloud and had no choice but to follow through. Squeezing myself into the only pair of running leggings I own, I didn't even bat an eyelash as I walked out the door with Mother's watchful eyes on my back. During the first few weeks, I think I even ran a little. Until I realized running and me do not mix. Each morning, I left the house with every intention of doing the thing I claimed to do, and every morning, I ended up here. Sitting on some random stump in the midst of mute trees and frozen air. A part of me is upset about the small untruth, but there is no guilt in me today and as I recline, digging the fat of my palms into the wood, I let my bones relax.

This is so much better than running, anyway.

My head dips backward and the hood of my sweatshirt rolls away, exposing the bright locks to the world. They are happy to be free and in moments, unruly knots line my shoulders and I feel the breeze of the morning wind on my scalp. My body wavers, mimicking the movement of the trees until I am one with the forest. Deep in the foliage, birds sing, their daily gossip washing over me as I stare off into the woods.

I'm not sure why I never tell Mother where I go each day, this is not something that could upset her. Maybe it's because I like having the time for myself; one small secret she isn't privy to. Ever since the visions started, I became an open book. A room without a door. I don't so much as sneeze without Mother knowing about it and having this small moment that doesn't belong to her feels like a victory. It likely isn't but at this point, I don't much care.

Thighs flattening, I stretch my legs out in front of me and take a deep breath. My throat is full of sand, and I wince in a sad attempt to clear it. Around me, leaves rustle and my brain fogs as memories overtake me.

I am not in the woods anymore.

Blinking, I struggle to clear my vision, but it is of no use. Before me, the cove comes to life, red water bubbling like an overflowing cauldron. The scent of iron fills my nostrils and my lungs contract as I hold my breath to keep it out. Blood is everywhere. I am everywhere.

A familiar voice screams at my back. I flinch. My head

jerks from side to side, trying to spot Daxon in his final moments, but all I see are blood coated rocks and crimson waters. Dots swarm my vision and I work to wave them off with little success. My ears perk up, listening intently to isolate Daxon's agonizing cries from the sound of cars zooming by somewhere beyond us. There is so much noise, I cannot concentrate. My head spins and my legs buckle as I fall to my knees. Searing pain rips through me when bone meets ground and I am crawling in circles, clearing a path for myself amidst the river of death. Urgency thrums through me and deep down, I am not far from joining Daxon in the darkness awaiting him. I steel my gaze.

Curling my fingers, I claw at the rocks. Pushing away the pool of blood I'm trapped in. My teeth rub against each other until I can feel chunks break away and slip down my throat. In the corner of my eye, a bright red dot draws my attention and for a second, I forget the mess I am in. With titanium resolve, I force my body to move and inch closer to the tiny speck on my left. My jaw hits the ground when I am near it.

"How?" That is all I can manage to utter.

Beneath me, the blood disappears, and my vision clears instantaneously. I was wrong; it isn't blood at all. At least, not all of it is.

My breath wavers as I reach out trembling hands toward the broken poppies lining the rocks. There are so many of them, I can't count them all. They burst in waves from the stone, reaching toward me as I reach for them in return. Poppies. Poppies everywhere.

The trilling call of a Cedar Waxwing pierces my ears, and I close my eyes against my will. Prying my lids open, I am breathless and covered in sweat as I recover from the vision. My body shakes uncontrollably, and my heart is pounding against my chest.

I'm back in the forest. I'm safe.

Daxon isn't.

The knees of my leggings are brown and wet, and I stop myself from thinking of excuses for Mother and focus on the vision. In all my years, the visions had never been so uncertain. They most definitely had never tricked me before. Why did I not see the poppies when I touched Daxon? Did I jump to conclusions from my own fear of keeping him safe?

None of it matters right now. I can flog myself with questions later.

My shoulders hike up to meet my earlobes. "Poppies," I whisper to the trees. "I saw poppies."

My heart aches as I realize what I must do. I cannot stay away from Daxon Thorn, not anymore.

Whatever happened to Kye is somehow connected to my vision. The poppies are the answer, and while this should relieve me, I'm still in the dark. What use is it to have answers to questions you don't know to ask? The boys are tied, their deaths tethered, but I do not see how. Worse, Daxon's death is still unclear. No matter how it happens, the poppies in the vision are a clue, and I must follow them if I have any hope to save him.

"There is no way to sway death from your door," I remind myself.

I do not listen.

This time, I will beat death back with a baseball bat if I have to. I'm going to stop Daxon from dying, even if it's the last thing I do in my pathetic, useless life. My spine straightens until I am a stick of a girl and I twist on my heels, facing the funeral home with the eyes of a lioness. As I turn, I suck in a cool breath between my teeth and glare at the figure bouncing from foot to foot on the front porch of the house.

Daxon.

My steps falter and I stutter-step down the narrow path leading out of the forest and toward the driveway. I am so close.

Not close enough.

As I break through the trees, the front door swings open and Mother steps out to greet him. Her jaw is set, and she holds a stack of paper under her arm, looking Daxon up and down. I halt in my tracks.

In the sky, the sun ducks behind a cloud and casts me in shadows as I stand frozen and watch. Mother is furious, and though I cannot hear what she is saying, I can read her expression perfectly fine. She doesn't give Daxon a moment to speak before she slams the door in his face. Dust kicks up around his sneakers and I notice his posture change before me. Defeated, he hesitantly turns around and makes his way down the rackety steps.

If I stay put, I can avoid him, though I do not wish to do so.

Gathering myself as best I can, I tense my neck and take a step forward. The branches snap around me and the sound carries toward the driveway, forcing Daxon's attention my way. His blue eyes clear as he meets mine, and I continue to march forward against my better judgment.

When I finally close the distance between us, my arms are crossed. I scout the windows, to make sure the blinds are still shut and there is no chance of Mother seeing us. "Hey," I say sheepishly. "Sorry about her."

"Yeah, she's a bit much."

I scoff. "You have no idea." My fingers claw at the zipper of my sweatshirt. "You came back."

"Uh-huh." Daxon nods.

"Why?"

Sapphires burn into me as he tilts his chin and looks up through hooded eyes. "I want to help you figure out what happened to Kye."

Not a good idea.

"Um, it's fine. I got it," I stutter.

"I'm not asking," Daxon says, his voice stone cold. He must sense my discomfort and forces a crooked smile to his lips. "I *need* to help you. Please."

I try to fight him on it, but instead the only thing that comes out is, "Why?"

"It's my fault," says Daxon. "He was coming to pick me up. I told him it was an emergency."

"What kind of emergency?"

His mouth thins out. "It doesn't matter. The point is if I didn't call him, he would have never been in the car. You don't owe me anything, but, please, let me do this. I can't sit around and wait for some damn viewing. I need to do something."

My eyes land on the front door and bile rushing up my chest and throat. I cannot let him in, can I? Red fills my vision. "Do you have a ride?" I ask.

Daxon points to a shiny black truck at the end of our driveway.

"Good," I say, starting to walk toward it. "Let's go."

I hear him jogging to catch up with me and cold sweat licks the back of my neck.

"Where are we going?" Daxon asks.

I do not turn to face him. "Route fifty-seven. We need to check the area where Kye's car crashed."

"What are we looking for?"

How do I tell him I don't have the slightest clue? I shrug and pull the passenger door open and climb in. Before closing it, I steal a glance at Daxon. He's confused and I cannot blame him. I am too.

We can be confused together.

The truck roars to a start and as we drive off, the funeral home gets smaller and smaller until I cannot see it at all. My body sinks into the leather seat, and I press my temple to the window, head hitting the glass with each bump in the road. Daxon keeps his eyes straight ahead the entire time, and I am grateful for his silence. Unlike Mother, he seems to trust me implicitly, though he really shouldn't. I am keeping so much from him and even though it is for his own good, I wonder how long until the truth breaks free.

Shaking the worries away, I focus on the road before us and let my thoughts float over the sprawling farmland on either side. Outside the truck, the wind howls and carries us closer to our destination. My eyes turn to Daxon and when he looks at me, I blush. "So, you want to tell me what you think we'll find there?" he asks.

"Anything," I answer.

For once, I tell the truth. I have absolutely no idea what I hope to find at the crash site, but anything is better than nothing. The entire thing feels like I am grasping at straws and as I rest my head back on the window, I realize I'm fine with not having all the answers yet. I will build an entire hay bale if it means I can save the boy sitting next to me.

And saving him is precisely what I plan to do.

9

Route fifty-seven is as close to the end of the world as one can get. The road stretches far and wide and on either side of me and unclaimed fields threaten to overtake every inch of ground between them. My hair whips in the wind and I am growing restless from having to tuck in the unruly strands every few minutes. To make matters worse, I am frozen solid and in the rush of leaving, didn't remember to grab an extra layer of clothing for the trip.

"This place is definitely lacking," Daxon says, drawing the words from my mouth. "Where do you want to start?"

I turn around, eyes scanning the abandoned factory looming at our backs, then twist to face him. "The sheriff's report said they found the car over there." I point a blue finger to a dip in the road ahead. "We should check there first."

He follows me without question, and it throws me off. Daxon should be afraid right now, much like everyone else is. Any second now, I will feel the familiar sting of harsh words and my skin crawls while I wait for the hit to come. When it doesn't, I am unsure if I am relieved or scared.

"It should be right around here," I say. Not far from where we stand, black tire treads swerve across the pavement before disappearing into the side ditch. My gaze flashes to the drop and I pause. "You sure you're all right to be here?"

I don't know why I didn't bother asking him before. This can't be easy for Daxon, and I'm an idiot for dragging him out here without considering his feelings. My throat is tight when I look at him to gauge his expression.

"Let's get this over with," Daxon says, skirting around me. He drags his feet across the pavement, nearing the ditch with sloth speed. At the edge, he glances at me with dead eyes. "You coming?"

I nod and follow him down.

Tall, dry grass flogs my legs as we skid down the hill. In our path, some of the grass is broken beyond repair and vertigo overtakes me. I make a poor attempt at not imagining Kye's car flipped over in front of us. Though the car had long been hauled away, the memory of what happened here hangs thick in the air and my feet are cemented to the ground in its wake.

Daxon looks around, his brow furrowed with disdain. "See anything yet?"

I do not.

"Maybe this wasn't a good idea."

Daxon crouches, his fingers dragging over the earth with care. He is quiet for a while, and I notice his breathing grow long and heavy, his chest rising and falling as he tries to keep himself together. When his shoulders start to shake, I look away.

One step at a time, I walk backward to give him a few moments alone. My arms press into my side, and I keep them prisoner for fear I might reach for him. I want to comfort the sobbing boy in the field, but it would not do him any good. The last thing I need is another horrifying vision to dampen this already soaked day. My foot hits a loose rock and I stumble, twirling my body like a cat to land on my knees. Hands breaking the fall, I groan, studying the scrapes on the soft parts of my palms. Blood wells on the surface and I gag in my mouth.

"You okay?" Daxon yells out from somewhere behind me.

I swallow hard. "Yeah. I'm fine."

Brushing the blood and dirt against my leggings, I start to straighten out and halt. To my right, the hill scales up to meet the road, a wave of beige blocking me from the world. The grass is sparser here, and it's easy to see anything that might not belong in the wild landscape we're in, which is exactly why I have no trouble zeroing in on it.

"One of these things is not like the others," I whisper, reaching for it.

I pluck the wilted petal hungrily, raising it up to the sunlight. It is so thin, I can make out every vein as the rays of light shine from behind it. Not so thin I don't know what it is.

"Daxon?" I call out. "Come look."

The ground thunders under me as he runs to my side. His chest bumps my shoulder and I suck in a breath when the heat of his body penetrates the icy wall I erected. He is so close, and I am so undone. "What's this?" Daxon asks, his breath brushing the top of my ear. It smells of peppermint and coffee. "Is it another poppy petal?"

"I think so," I say.

"Where did you find it?"

I point to the rise in the ditch, and he is there in seconds. Daxon's movements are no longer careful and, as he scours the grass, he resembles a feral creature searching for food. Dirt kicks back behind him and I gather some courage to inch closer to the boy tornado. My arm stretches, thumb hovering a mere inch from his cheek. I do not dare to touch him, but he can feel my presence and it is enough to make him stop. Twisting, he looks up at me with an untamed glare. "There's nothing else here. That's the only one."

"It still shouldn't be here," I offer. "If there's a poppy in this field, it must have come from Kye's car. There's no other explanation."

"No explanation at all."

"I know." I scowl. "Let's keep looking."

We stay in the ditch for hours, turning over every rock then venturing so far out into the field, I cannot see the road anymore. Above us, the sun sits on a different trajectory and panic fills my body when I realize how long I've been gone. If Mother hasn't called in the calvary yet, I'd be surprised. I prepare myself for the scolding I'll likely get when I return and jog up to Daxon, who is picking at a patch of dirt a few feet away from me.

"We should probably head back," I say. "I don't think we'll get anything else here."

He looks like he wants to argue but doesn't. "Okay," he says. "I'll drive you home."

As we crest the hill, I shrink into myself. What a waste of time. While it's true coming here was a hunch, I was still hopeful to find at least some clues in this stupid place. Now, that hope is gone and there is a hole in my gut the size of a canyon. A chirping sound echoes from the truck as Daxon unlocks the doors and starts to climb in. I dredge after him, eyes on the road and the tips of my running shoes as I walk. Each step forward leaves less of the tire treads from Kye's crash in my path and as the black markings vanish, my heart shatters.

My eyes are still on the road when I notice it.

The rest of the pavement is gray and dusty, an uneventful stretch of road unlike any other in these parts. Except this one spot. It is shiny, almost reflective in the sun, and I stammer when I make out the shape of a boot mark on the worn out road. How did the cops not see this? I look around, noticing more footprints on either side of the road and in the gravel. Probably the sheriff's and his crew. If they deemed Kye's crash an accident, it would make sense no one bothered to check for prints. I don't know much about police investigations, but I do know the cops in Cherry Cove are not exactly gumshoes, which isn't surprising considering that crime isn't exactly high in these parts.

My nose itches and I follow the direction of the mark to see another take shape not far from it. I follow them, discovering one faint footprint after another until I'm on the opposite side of the road with the ditch we climbed out of in my sightline. Here, the prints on are more pronounced and there are more of them. As though someone was here a long time, pacing. Waiting.

The grass rises high before me and I know if I were to need a spot to stay out of sight, this one is perfect. My skin pricks and I kneel, studying the area. Soft steps boom closer to me, and I glance up to see Daxon towering over my folded figure. His arms are placid at his sides and his legs burrow into the road, but it is his eyes I notice first. Eyes wide with worry and staring directly behind me.

I spin around, nearly losing my balance, and my mouth gapes. Something is very wrong here.

In the patch of dirt surrounding me, strange symbols are carved into the earth, each one connected to the other to form a clumsy semi-circle made entirely of etchings. They are unlike any symbols I know; jagged lines and swirls that seem to make no sense at all. One stands out. A triangle with swirling lines on either side of it meeting in the middle. I toe at it, dust settling into the dug out lines and over my shoe. In the center of each symbol, a crimson petal lays embedded in the ground, soil gathering at its edges.

My mouth is dry, and I smack my chapped lips together, rubbing sandpaper skin until I'm numb. "What is this?"

Daxon shrugs. His hands fumble in his pocket and he pulls out a cellphone to snap a photograph of the symbols.

The corner of his mouth curls up and he watches me with a Cheshire grin. "I think what we have here is a lead," he says.

In my gut, I fear for what he might mean.

Ghostly hands stretch toward her and beckon her forward.

She hesitates.

It is not time yet, my children.

Above the palace, night swallows her realm and buries her deep. Deeper. Deeper.

One palm pressed to slick glass, she swallows air and water; and death.

So much death.

She is made of it entirely.

One step.

Two steps.

Three steps; she walks.

At her feet, snakes hiss and slither, and their bodies writhe against her own.

She looks around.

I will miss this place, she thinks.

A forked tongue slides across her ankle and she smiles, sharp teeth pointed.

She will miss the serpents most of all.

10

The funeral home is too quiet when Daxon's truck finally pulls into the driveway. It's not exactly a hub of activity on a good day, but it still seems much too silent for my liking. All the shutters are drawn in and not a light is lit within. Mother must be downstairs.

"What's with the snakes?" Daxon asks.

It takes me a moment to realize he's talking about the sign above the porch. "I don't know," I respond. "Dad had it made when he bought the place. Something about serpents being guardians of the dead or some other nonsense."

Though he is smiling, his eyes are blank. "That's different," he whispers.

It is indeed.

I fumble with the door handle and start to crawl out when Daxon reaches for me. Instinctively, my back pancakes against the leather seat and I twist my body into an uncomfortable position to put some space between our bodies. The idea that I resemble the two snakes slithering on the sign is not lost on me and I force myself to breathe, tongue squeezing the top of my mouth. Daxon must realize my discomfort because his hand hangs in the air between us for only a second before he pulls it back to rest on the steering wheel.

My cheeks burn.

"Think we can meet up later?" He doesn't look at me when he asks. "We should see if we can figure out what those symbols mean. If you're up for it, of course."

"I am," I blurt out a little too quickly. "I'll have to ask my mom first."

He grins, hands still clutching the wheel. "I'll text you later."

As I climb out of the truck, his attention on my figure makes sweat roll down my back, soaking my clothes. At least I resemble a runner now. I laugh under my breath; there is no way Mother will buy my story when I've been gone all morning.

Behind me, gravel scrapes as Daxon rips out of the driveway and wind hits my wet back. My shoulders shake. I climb up the stairs, twisting the knob so carefully, it barely makes a sound. My head swivels to scan the hallway and when I'm certain I'm alone, I exhale. At the end of the hall, the door to the basement is shut and I run up to test the handle. It's locked. Strange.

"Mom?" I yell out into the murky house.

There is a rustle upstairs, followed by cursing whispers. "I'm up here!" Mother yells down to me.

Chest thrust out, I roll my shoulders and saunter up the wide staircase to follow her voice. It's odd she isn't working. Mother is always working. More rustling drifts toward me when I reach the landing, and I trace their path to her room. The door is wide open, light pouring into the hallway in streaks of gold. Inside, Mother sits at the base of her king-sized bed surrounded by photo albums torn open. Photographs line the dusty rose carpet, and my eyes widen as I take it all in. Mother's room is a mess, even by her standards. Snippets of newspapers and crumbled Post-it notes crowd the space and there are boxes stacked in every corner. The small writing desk propped under the window facing her bed has so much paper on it, I can't even make out its shape.

I tiptoe inside, pushing a box atop the plush ottoman by her bed to make room to sit. "Um, what's going on here?" I ask.

"Spring cleaning," Mother says.

I snort. "It's summer."

She tears her eyes off the photographs in her hands. "I'm a little late."

A rawness pulls at my heart, and I glance the room once over. For the life of me, I cannot recall the last time Mother did any sort of cleaning at all. Picking up her mess is my job, and I'm a little hurt she chose to take this away from me. It's a foolish thought, one I tuck away for later dissection as I watch her shift to sit cross-legged on the floor. The morgue's white coat is wrinkled on her one side, and I notice ink stains on the frayed edges of the sleeves. I tilt my chin down to get her attention. "Shouldn't you be getting ready for Friday?"

A scowl is all I get back.

"Fine," I say, resting my chin in my hands. "So why the sudden need to clean?"

Mother's eyes blink twice as she shoves one photograph in my face. "Remember this?"

I lean in to inspect the image. How could I forget? I swallow once, twice, but the lump thickens in my throat as I run my gaze over the tiny girl in the photo. Her silver hair is loosely braided, and she beams up at whoever took the photo with pride, one chubby finger pointing at the white bandage around her neck. My hand reaches to retie the silk bandana covering my scar. "The day after the hospital," I bite out.

"You were so proud," Mother says. "Telling me you're going to keep the bandages forever to show how brave you are. I didn't have the heart to tell you otherwise."

"You didn't tell me a lot then," I counter.

A darkness passes behind her eyes, but it is gone before it settles. "If you're referring to your father, Nastya, I think we both know why I couldn't tell you."

"I can't believe he left," I tell Mother. "No phone calls, no letters, nothing."

At my feet, Mother turns the photograph over and reads the date jotted on the backing. Her head tilts, and she chews on her bottom lip while memories of that horrid day flood her system. It was hard for both of us. Dad leaving. Harder for her, I think. Though she is right; I do understand why she didn't tell me he left right away. Mother—disorganized as she is—is calculating to a fault. She needed to wait to tell me until she was ready and had a proper plan in place for our future. I don't fault her for it, though sometimes, I wish she trusted me more. Enough to be honest when honesty counted.

"Your father was never good with good byes," is all she tells me.

This is how it goes. I ask questions about him, and she brushes it off with simple, tied with a bow sentences. Her explanations leave little room for arguments and by this point, I am so used to my head hitting brick walls, I brush the pain off and keep going. Arguing with Mother never leads to anything good, so it makes sense to keep the peace between us. We are all each of us has left. I pick up a pile of pictures from the box beside me and straighten the corners until they are a neat stack in my hands. "I want to go to the cove tonight," I say.

Mother's eyes flash green. "Sure. How about after dinner?"

"I was thinking of going alone."

Her fingers relax and the photographs drop to the floor in a heap of lost worlds and secrets. My spine is rigid, and my tongue flips over in my mouth as I trace the backside of my teeth with it. Mother stares at me and I stare right back until we are statues in the bedroom. She is waiting for me to change my mind and I am waiting for her to yield. Both of us are about to be sorely disappointed.

Mother drums her fingers on the carpet and says, "Oh?"

How typical of her to give me nothing to grasp on for argument.

"It's not a big deal," I tell her. "We can't do everything together all the time." *Especially when the thing I want to do is see Daxon.* I leave that part out.

"I don't know, Nastya," she says so quietly I almost don't hear it.

"Please, Mom," I beg. "I need this."

While she considers me, I count to ten in my head to calm the racing of my heart. I should have told her about Daxon, I should have been straightforward. Hypocrisy is not a characteristic I wish to have, but she would never understand. This isn't the same as all the half-truths she told me; it's different. I know if I told her what I really planned to do this evening, she would never approve it. Would likely stalk outside my bedroom door until I fell asleep. Mother is overprotective to a fault, and I desperately need a break from her shackles.

It's only one night, I decide. I almost convince myself.

"Have you finished the essay you have to write this week?" Mother asks.

I mumble a soft, "yes," under my breath.

"Good. You can go then."

"Thank you!" I yelp, but she holds her hand up before I can say anything else.

"Only to the cove and back," she instructs. "No going into town and no sneaking off past the cove. Got it?"

"I got it."

"I mean it, Nastya," Mother chides. "I don't want you getting involved with the town's business. It's bad enough I have to worry about stalker boy, I don't have the time to deal with you too."

I find that hard to believe. Mother has been dealing with me my whole life. "To the cove and back," I repeat.

Mother's long legs unwind and she kicks the photographs as she awkwardly climbs to stand. Taking in the room, she purses her lips and blinks fast. Then peering down at me says, "Will you look at this mess? I really don't know how you put up with me sometimes."

"I'll clean it up. You should get back to work."

As she leans down to press a kiss to my head, the smell of her perfume spills into my nostrils. Lavender and honey, like a potent bath bomb hitting a full tub. I close my eyes, stretching my neck to get the most of her affection while I have it. My toes curl and I breathe her in, drawing closer. Closer. Closer. Panic swarms the back of my lids and I fight the urge to pull away. The gift has never shown me Mother's death, but that doesn't mean it never will. And when it happens, I am not so sure I'll survive it. Crisp air slaps my hair when Mother pulls away and turns to the doorway. My bones leave my body and I slump down on the ottoman, peeling my eyes open to watch her leave. She pauses, glancing my way over her shoulder. "Your scar is showing."

I reach for the silk on my neck, fingers meeting flesh. Making quick work of it, I untie the bandana and refasten it in place until I am once again hidden. When Mother walks away, I let her words engulf me.

'Your scar is showing.'

I scoff. Better my scar than my lies.

11

Daxon's house is further than I realized and by the time I get there, it's pitch black and I'm breathless from the walk over. The sweat-soaked layers of the sweaters I'm wearing cling to my skin, and I waver as I climb the winding stone steps leading up to the small Victorian home. On either side of me, wild bushes reach for the moonlight and their leaves tickle the sliver of flesh at my ankles when I pass. Rolling my gaze over the house, I can't help but draw my arms closer to my body. There is nothing to distinguish Daxon's house from any of the others in Cherry Cove; in fact, it looks so similar, it's like I never left the funeral home. The front door is centered on the porch and two large bay windows frame it. Lights twinkle through the deep navy curtains and I feel as though the house is watching me. Waiting.

Low, jumbled voices creep through the darkness and I hear plates clinging against each other inside. They must have only now finished dinner.

My heart skips.

There are people inside. Real people.

I'm not sure why I'm rattled; of course, someone other than Daxon would be home this late in the evening. Yet, my arm still shakes when I reach for the doorbell.

The voices quiet down and I glance over my shoulder, gauging my chances of escape. There is no time for me to hesitate because by the time I turn back, the door swings open, and I am bombarded with piercing yellow light streaming onto the porch. Before me, Daxon's wide shoulders silhouette the entrance as he leans against the wood frame to greet me.

"You made it," he says. His voice is different somehow; husky and dangerous. "Let's go upstairs."

I let him step aside before crossing the threshold and hold my breath. Unlike the exterior, the belly of the house is a stark opposite to the funeral home. For one, it doesn't smell like someone doused it in bleach and chemicals. There is also the matter of the front hallway, which is non existent. Daxon's home is modern and open to the point of discomfort. Like someone ripped out the guts of the house and tossed them aside. To my right, a massive sectional blocks off what I assume is the living area while on my left, the most precise kitchen I've ever seen takes up more space than is necessary. Oyster colored cabinets span an entire wall, perfectly matching a light granite countertop uncrowded by appliances and unwashed plates. This is nothing like home.

Daxon catches me staring and says, "My room is this way." He gestures to a strange-looking glass staircase with a frown. "We'll have more privacy there."

Worry sets in. I don't understand why we need privacy when, from the looks of it, no one is here but us. "Aren't your parents home?" I ask.

Daxon nods. "They're in the library," he answers. Because, of course, this place has a library. The Thorns seem intent on flaunting their wealth and what better way to do it than having your own private library. I bend my spine and try not to let my jealousy come through.

"Oh, sure," I say. "Lead the way."

As Daxon jogs up the stairs, I stay alert and linger behind him. My feet clamp down on the glass and while I try to keep my eyes straight ahead, they refuse to cooperate. Each time I glance down, my head spins and I imagine the steps shattering under my weight and sending me crashing down. When we reach the landing and my sneakers land on the marble floor, I jump for joy inside.

Daxon is pointing again, his stone-cold glare focused on a room down the hall from us. I sincerely hope he isn't gunning for a career in tourism because his delivery could use some improvement. "My room is right over there," says Daxon, marching us toward the door. Framed photographs hang on the walls, and I slow my pace, studying them intently. Each one is almost the same as the last; an image of Daxon in between his two parents, a few showing him holding up a shiny trophy with his lips pressing tightly together, one of his parents with a fluffy golden retriever. If I had to describe Daxon's parents in one word, sturdy would be a good choice. They seem like the type of people that have their act together, the ones with everything planned out to the detail. Daxon's dad is tall, much like his son, with the same red-brown hair and eyes that see right through you. Darkness seems to wash over both of them, and I can feel it seep through the glass. His mom is lighter in appearance, slim and dainty. So much so, she is almost invisible standing next to the burly man at her side. I note the wide, unoccupied space between them, then to the ball of golden fur at their feet. "You have a dog?"

"Had," Daxon corrects. "Rover. He died last summer."

"I'm sorry." I run to catch up with him.

Not making eye contact, Daxon turns the knobs and opens the door. "It's fine. He was old."

All thoughts of Daxon's childhood pet vanish when I enter the bedroom. It is, well, something else. A gargantuan bed takes up most of the space, the covers tucked in tight at the corners. Above it, three floating shelves stretch from one side of the wall to the other and the same style of trophies I saw in the photo battle for space atop them. There is a small glass desk with what looks to be a state-of-the-art office chair tucked into it and a stack of unopened textbooks rising high in its center. Near the bed, a built-in wardrobe system with mirrors for doors stands obnoxiously tall and I roll my tongue over the back of my teeth when Daxon isn't looking.

His room is plucked out of a high-end hotel. Just as intimidating and just as lifeless.

"This is," I start to say, but Daxon cuts me off.

His hair falls over his eyes when he looks at me. "It's whatever," he says, steel in his voice.

We stand there in silence while I wait for him to explain. When no explanation comes, I shrug and hiss out an awkward sigh. "So, you said you wanted to talk about the symbols?"

"Right, yes. I've been doing some digging."

"And?"

By the look of him, I already have my answer. "And I got nothing," Daxon says, proving me right. "There is literally nothing online about any symbols matching the ones we saw. I only spent an hour or so checking, but you'd think there'd be more to find."

"Odd," I agree. "Maybe you're checking the wrong sites."

"Maybe," Daxon says. He leaves me in the doorway and plops down on the bed, legs kicking out in front of him to stretch across the floor. "So, your mom really let you come over?"

The tone of his voice jars me, and I roll back on my feet and cross my arms. "Sort of," I say. "I didn't tell her where I was going."

Daxon chuckles and runs his fingers through his hair. "I

guess she doesn't want you hanging out with some creep who's stalking his dead friend's body."

"No, it's not that. Mother is—" I try to think of the right word, "—protective. It's nothing personal."

Standing is suddenly akin to falling and I pick at a scab on my hand absentmindedly, then move toward the chair by the desk. It swivels smoothly, not like the old piece of junk in my bedroom, and as I lower into it, I am convinced this is the best chair in the world. Daxon watches me from the bed with narrowed eyes. "Can I ask you a question?"

"Um, sure."

He looks uncomfortable, his forehead creases over his bushy eyebrows until the lines are red from the pressure. "What's it like? When you see people die, I mean." When I don't answer, he adds, "You don't have to talk about it if it's weird."

"We can talk about it," I say. Though, I do not wish to discuss it at all. "It's strange. Kind of like a dream but different. I don't usually see what's going to happen exactly, it's more of a feeling I get. Bits and pieces of what's to come."

"Is that what happened with Christine Solar?" he asks.

A growl vibrates my chest. "How do you know about her?"

"Kye told me. He said you told her she's going to die and then the next day, she did."

For a dead guy, Kye sure talks a lot. I bow my head and clutch my stomach, anything to keep from looking at him as I try to explain the worst day of my life. "Christine was my best friend," I say. "We were always together, so much so, we even dressed alike. It was only a few weeks after my surgery, and I was so excited to go back to school. Christine was waiting for me at the front when Mom dropped me off with a stuffed bear in her small hands. Everything was normal. I should have known then it wouldn't last. When I first saw her death, felt it, I was hysterical. I kept crying and babbling like a maniac and screaming at the teachers to help her. I didn't understand the visions then. I really thought someone was going to hurt her."

"But they didn't, right?" Daxon asks. "Kye said she got hit by a car."

I nod. "It didn't matter. The damage was already done, and everyone blamed me for it. Or the kids did. I got bullied constantly. I still remember crying to my mom after school every single day about the Hell they were putting me through. She pulled me out and started teaching me herself."

"Kids are assholes."

"They are," I say. "Adults are worse. After what happened to Christine spread through town, no one wanted anything to do with me. Parents refused to let me near their children, and I became the pariah of Cherry Cove. They acted as though I was the moron driving the car that killed her."

From the bed, Daxon watches me intently and blood rushes to my face and neck. Tugging at a loose thread on my sweater, I watch it unravel and say, "I don't kill them, you know." I'm sure this doesn't need explaining, but for some reason, I have the urge to clarify. "It doesn't happen all the time, the visions, I mean. Lately, they barely happen at all."

My voice shakes when I say this, and I am instantly reminded of the blood in the cove. The vision burning in my mind and so much clearer now that I am in Daxon's room.

Daxon shrugs. "I never thought you did. Some people say otherwise, but I never believed it. Do you hate it?"

"That's a stupid question."

"Do you though?"

How can I possibly answer him? I evaluate my options carefully, feeling the rock at my back and the one pressing on my chest. "Sometimes I do," I answer. The truth of it hurts and my eyes are dry and red when I peer at him. "I think I mostly hate being alone all the time. My mom isn't keen on having people around, so for the most part, it is only me and her. Every day. Every single day."

"It must be pretty lonely," Daxon whispers into the warm air between us.

I smile. "For the most part, yes."

To my surprise, he doesn't fumble with his words. Doesn't say any of the things Mother often says when she is trying to convince me my life isn't as bad as I know it to be. Instead, he rolls his sleeves up and digs his feet into the floor, solemn. "Now *that* I can understand."

I flick my eyes over his pristine bedroom. "I highly

doubt it." My head nods to the shelf of trophies and I smirk. "You seem pretty popular to me."

Daxon sighs.

My happiness vanishes.

"Don't let those fool you. Popularity and loneliness are not one and the same." He sucks in a breath and the air rushes from my lungs. "Kye is, was, my only real friend," he says. "He was the only one making things bearable around here."

Behind his eyes, the waves are turbulent and loud, and they buzz in my ears as his gaze cascades over me. I hate the attention and when he doesn't turn away, I do the job for him. Craning my neck, I peel myself away from Daxon and focus on the open door. "You have a nice house," I mumble. It is the only thing I can think of to say. "Very stylish."

"It's all Mom," Daxon says. "If she had her way, the entire house would have been knocked down so she could build it from scratch to resemble the homes she obsesses over. I swear, the woman spends more time doting on magazine photos than she does anything else."

"And your dad?"

As soon as the words leave my lips, I feel their wrongness. The mood shifts in Daxon at the mention of his father, and my fingers itch to unravel the mystery that is Daxon Thorn. He sits uncomfortably straight and the strained muscles in his thighs are visible through his jeans. Every inch of him seems to be working hard not to move.

"I try to stay away from him," says Daxon. "He's a bit of a bastard."

"In what way?"

Though his body relaxes, I can still see the tension in his neck. "In the way fathers never should be. The way that hurts."

Understanding crashes through me and my heart slams into my ribcage. My mind wanders back into the hallway, and I focus on the photographs of Daxon and his father. I am immediately threatened by a man I never even met. My head pounds and I scan Daxon's exposed skin for bruises, but there are none there. At least not any I can see. Noticing my staring, Daxon tugs the sleeves of his shirt over his knuckles and tilts his head to the ceiling. "It's not so bad," he says. "You get used to it."

"How can you?"

"I just am," says Daxon. I search for encouraging words, but he cuts me off, sparing me the embarrassment of blurting out the wrong thing. "The day Kye died, he was on his way to get me. He was the only other person I ever told about my father. That day was especially bad. I don't even remember what happened now or how it started, but I remember getting into it with him and it got out of hand. Mom kept crying and yelling, but it didn't matter. It never matters to him."

I blink. Once. Twice. Three times.

"Anyway, that's why Kye was in such a hurry. I called him and told him shit was going down and he dropped everything to pick me up." He sucks in a heavy breath. "Sorry I lied before. About why he was in the car, I mean. We weren't going for a drive. He was coming to save me from doing something I'd regret."

"Doing what?"

"Whatever I had to."

He drops the conversation and my forehead slams into the wall he erects between us. A dreadful need to know more crushes my bones, but I do not follow through. Whatever Daxon means, he doesn't want to discuss it and I owe him to stay out of it. I owe him so much more than this small task; his life, for starters.

My clumsy fingers reach for the phone in my back pocket and I whip it out like a show performer. "Want to see what else we can find about these symbols?"

Daxon agrees and before I know it, we are at the base of his bed with fingers typing furiously on the keyboards of our phones. We do this for hours; exchanging any bits of information that might help while Daxon takes notes in a lined notebook.

We find very little. Nothing, to be honest.

Daxon is jotting down notes when my phone chirps an incoming message. I look at the screen, nerves bubbling on my skin.

"It's my mom," I say. "I should head back, it's getting late."

When Daxon walks me downstairs, I avoid sneaking glances at the pictures on the walls for fear of making eye contact with the man who created the boy I am trying to save. Mr. Thorn's presence is in every inch of the house now, and I feel it on me as I take uncertain steps toward the front door. Somewhere in the heart of the home, a door slams and I jump, scurrying to keep up with Daxon. In the back of my mind, I picture the man in the photographs, Daxon's father, rushing from behind us with his fingers tense and stretched toward our throats. I bristle.

Standing in the doorway, Daxon asks, "See you tomorrow?"

"Sure."

As Daxon closes the door behind me, night envelops my body and I sway from side to side with the wind. Behind me, the porch light goes out and darkness swallows me whole.

I do not leave.

12

Mother gives up after the fourth text message. It's surprising I manage to convince her I'm all right without her stomping in the middle of the night to drag me home. In her defense, she has no idea where I am.

The backyard of the Thorn residence is a slight improvement from the neatly manicured facade facing the street. Not by much, but it's better than nothing as far this place is concerned. At least the rear of the house has some character. There are no carefully positioned stone pathways here, and the shrubbery encasing the lawn is overgrown and looking like a new pup in need of a haircut. Ivy spans one side of the fence, reaching greedily for a brand new shed in the far corner. Across it, panels of carved rock burst from the ground and water trickles down them and into a long basin running the length of the yard. I roll my eyes and dig my heels into the grass, standing stock still in the shadows.

I should probably leave; there's no telling what the Thorns will do if they find me creeping on their premises this late at night. Every sensible part of me urges for escape, and yet I do not move a muscle.

From here, Daxon's bedroom window is in clear view, and it draws me like a flame.

I have to make sure he keeps breathing tonight. More so now I know his home is not the safe haven a home should be. No matter what Mother does, how deeply she digs her claws into my life, she has never laid a hand on me. A thought flitters in my mind and I stop dead. What if Daxon's father is the one to kill him? Is he the danger hanging over Daxon's life? I shake my head. No, it can't be. If Daxon's dad is the reason I had the vision, then how does it explain what happened to Kye or those symbols we found? It can't be him.

My breaths are shallow and painful, and each time I open my mouth, I can see frozen air linger before me. I shiver, too cold to care anymore. My lashes flutter and I trace the smooth backing of the house to the second story, eyes glued to the pane of glass separating me from Daxon.

He is still at his desk as he's been since I left and found myself back here. He never looks out, never notices me, and while I should be glad for it, I somehow am the opposite. A part of me wishes to be seen.

The stupid part, I'm sure.

Daxon purses his lips and tosses a pen at the computer screen, groaning. It is only now I realize he is searching for more clues on the symbols and having as much luck as we've had thus far. None, to be specific.

How strange it is that there is nothing to lead us forward with this. It's almost as if someone scrubbed the entire world clean of those signs laying idle in the image folder of Daxon's phone. Was it only a coincidence we found the symbols at the crash site? Kids playing jokes to scare each other off?

Or is there something else?

Something we are not seeing?

My finger presses to unlock my phone and I quickly lower the brightness to make sure I don't send Daxon a beacon giving away my position. I scroll the thread of our messages, finding the photo he sent after he dropped me off. My eyes grow as I zoom in on the image, inspecting the rough drawings in the dirt.

"What are you?" I whisper, bringing the phone close to my face. "Who drew you?"

The symbols won't talk, but I have to admit I feel better for trying. At this point, hiding in the dark like a creep and talking to a picture is surprisingly comforting.

"There is nothing secret in this world," I remember Dad saying. "Everything can be found, you simply have to know how to look."

How do I find out more when I don't know what I'm looking for, Dad?

My vision falters and I click the phone off and shove it back in my pocket. At the window, Daxon seems to have given up and as he rises from the desk, I hold my breath. His shoulders block the light until he is silhouetted against the glass. I bite the inside of my cheek. When Daxon walks away, the weight on me drifts off, and I sink into the fence I'm propped against. Wood planks flatten against my back, and I shake my head to clear the exhaustion seeping into my body. I'd been standing in one spot for so long, my legs are numb and tingly. Stretching my toes in my sneakers, I slide down to sit. My palms graze the freshly cut grass and I close my eyes, letting the blades tickle my skin.

Around me, the air thickens until I am swimming in molasses and struggling to move. My limbs slacken at my sides, and I fight to peel my lids apart. No matter what I try, they stay closed, and I am shrouded in darkness.

I want to scream, but no sound comes out.

Images form behind my lids and fear grips me as I realize what they are. The vision. I am reliving the vision.

Why?

As my mind tries to make sense of what's happening, my heart is long gone. I ache to be free of this and I snap my lip shut, internally begging for the vision to go away. But it doesn't listen.

Death does not like being told what to do.

Suddenly, I am no longer in Daxon's backyard. My feet are drenched, and water rises up to my ankles, soaking the jeans I am wearing. The water is muddy and when I take a closer look, I realize it isn't water at all. It's blood. It's the cove, and it's full of blood. Spinning, I tread through the disgusting cocktail of doom and try to make my way to the shore. I yearn for the rocky beach in the distance; I'm so close. The river feels even more frigid now and I tense, icicles forming on my eyelashes. My head swivels and I look around, eyes disoriented from white particles falling all around me. Snow. My hand reaches for it and then I hear it.

Daxon screams.

My head jerks to the side as I scan the beach for him. Like last time, I am blind to everything but the night and the flood of poppies scattered on the rocks.

Heart pounding against my chest, I fight the anchor of the surrounding water to get to shore. My foot slips and I tumble forward, hand shooting out in front of me to block my fall. Then the water is everywhere. Blood is everywhere.

I can taste it on my tongue and in my throat. Tangy and foul, like meat left out in the sun too long. I retch.

My feet find balance and I manage to uncurl myself until I am standing again. I am certain I'm crimson in shade everywhere the blood touches my clothes. Bile rises up my throat and I swallow it down, praying to keep my senses about me.

Another scream pierces my ears and I whip my head up, jaw slapping the water's edge.

Stranger.

A girl stands on the beach, hair the color of ravens dipped in ink. Her lips are painted bright red and dark circles line her eyes as she watches me. Blood covers her hands.

Panic races up my arms and legs and I stop splashing in the water to take her in. The girl wears no emotion, but one side of her lips is drooping, making her look sinister and cruel. She takes a step in and for the first time, I notice the knife in her hands.

I start to scream but she moves before I can part my lips and then she is running. Faster. Faster. Faster.

She is at the edge of the beach in moments, wading into the water toward me. I push away and crawl backward to put distance between us, but no matter how hard I try, she doesn't ease up. Gaining momentum, the girl closes in, the knife's tip pointed to the sky. Despite the pitch black surrounding us, I can see the glimmer of silver clearly. It reflects off her deep brown skin; a spotlight on an enemy stepping up to the stage.

I gasp.

The light from the knife dips to the left side of her breast and a small patch catches my attention. I recognize the logo. A fork and knife with a small sailboat in their center. The back of my heel hits a hard surface in the water, and I lose my balance. My body crumbles and soon, water is everywhere. It devours me whole.

Wind whips at my face and chaps my lips; I jerk my eyes open. High above me, the golden light of Daxon's room streams through the window and I slump when I feel the wooden fence at my back. The vision is gone and I'm back in the Thorn's backyard, albeit a little more flustered than I was when I left it. A little more torn apart.

A headache careens behind my eyes as I replay the vision, right up to the end. Hope flares in my chest. "Cherry Cove Diner," I whisper into the night.

The logo I saw on the girl's shirt is burned into my mind as I rise off the ground and tip toe through Daxon's backyard. Glancing up, I see him at the desk again, buried in notebooks with the screen of his laptop illuminating his solemn face. He looks destroyed and I wish I could take his worries away. Daxon might not see it yet, but the dead end we hit is no longer. The symbols we found might not reveal how Kye died, but I am certain the vision had given me an opportunity. I saw the person who's going to hurt Daxon. Better, I know exactly where to find her.

13

"You've been running a lot," Mother says as she watches me lace up my shoes. Her morning kasha is cold in the bowl in front of her. "Training for a marathon?"

I let out a whistling laugh. "Trying to soak in the sun before the weather flips."

My hasty voice waves a red flag, and I silently pray she doesn't read through my act. In my sporty attire, I look the part well enough, but the only running I'm planning on is to the marina and back. To the Cherry Cove Diner. This early in the morning, there shouldn't be many people around with kids at school and the adults running this asylum busy with work and chores. Luck allowing, I should be in and out of the diner in under an hour, which gives me plenty of time to scope the place out and hopefully, find the girl I saw in the vision.

My fingers clamp up around the laces for a moment. What am I going to do if I find her?

I can't report a crime that has not yet been committed, even if I do think it ends in Daxon's death. And it isn't like I can threaten her to stay away from him without sounding even more crazy than everyone believes me to be. I suppose I can go undercover, or whatever it is people do in those silly cop shows Mother watches. Maybe if I get the girl to open up to me, I can find out why she has it out for Daxon and stop her from doing whatever she has planned.

Assuming she'll speak with me in the first place. From experience, I am going to bet she'll keep far from the harbinger of death like the others.

The sun beats at my skin as I maneuver the small streets leading to the docks. I keep a steady pace, somewhere between a brisk walk and a slow jog. Sweat pools on my top lip and I don't wipe it off against my better judgment. Might as well make the exercise story more believable for when I get back home.

As suspected, there is almost no one at the marina when I arrive. A few boats still linger in the distance, knocking against rusted walkways to the steady flow of the river beneath. I spot a few local fishermen loading up for the day and slow my stride to avoid getting noticed. They carry on with their banter, oblivious to my intrusion on their lives. One man must say something funny because I soon hear boisterous laughter roll down the docks toward me. Their voices glue together into a chorus as they slap the comedian on the back, exchanging pleasantries before continuing with whatever task they busy themselves with. They have a long trek ahead of them and it's not surprising they're here this early in the morning. With the river's waters polluted, they must venture further out to fish and some leave for days on end. Weeks even. To be a fisherman in Cherry Cove requires quite the dedication and even from this far away, I can see the lot of them wear their profession with pride. Their shoulders tight and rigid, their chests puffed out to greet the rising sun. Water warriors, Dad used to call them. I can see what he meant now.

To everyone else in Cherry Cove, this is nothing more than a normal weekday. To me, it feels like a trap. Any second now, one of the men will spot me lurking on the docks and their demeanor will change. Any joy they may have felt will vanish to be replaced by worry and fear. Their faces will blanch, and they will exchange uncomfortable looks, wondering which one of them I came for.

The more I think about it, the more I realize how little people change as they grow older. Before, I assumed adults get wiser and less superstitious, but this isn't the case. Not in Cherry Cove. Here, the older you are, the more you fear the things you cannot explain. Sometimes, I'm not sure which is worse, the kids tormenting me and calling me names or the adults that cross the street when I near them. Both hurt the same.

The men turn their backs to me, and I take the chance to run past them and turn the corner to the narrow passage leading away from the boats.

At my back, the call of the river grows more and more silent as I widen the distance between me and the docks. The passage I am on cuts through the trees, and I slow down, knowing I won't run into anyone here. Most locals steer clear of this route to get to the marina shops and opt for the main road instead. I am not most people though, and it suits me fine. If I stay on track, I'll come out right behind the diner and avoid walking in the front door. Back when Dad was still around, he used to take me to the diner every Saturday and I vividly recall him refusing to use anything but the back entrance. He was so adamant about it, the owner kept the server entrance open all hours of the day to make my father happy. This was the kind of influence dad had in this town. Wherever he went, people went out of their way to make him happy. Not because he carried any weight in their lives, but because he treated everyone with kindness and respect; treated them as friends.

I miss him.

The trees part and I jog up to the building, rounding a dumpster with the lids open. The smell of warm garbage wafts up my nose and I heave, taking quick steps to get around the monstrosity. How Dad and I kept our appetites after marching through here is beyond me.

As I expected, the back door is propped open with a doorstopper and light chatter drifts from within the diner. I can count a handful of voices, most of which I'm sure are the workers, and when I step over the threshold, my eyes slide to the front door. I can see it clearly. A wide metal frame, a small bell adhered to the top, an open sign holding on for dear life on two suction cups. Exactly as I remember it.

My stomach rings itself out as I make my way down the corridor, passing the bathrooms and the swinging door leading to the kitchen. In my periphery, I spot two employees hunched over the retro bar table with a pile of receipts between them. My eyes are glued to the mosaic floor tile when I pass them and slip into a booth furthest from the wall of windows in the front. Other than me, three patrons take a table each, all of them preferring the window view so they can watch the street outside. From the booth, I can make out a few of the other shops making up the commercial street of the marina and I scan them quickly, eyes peering over the top of the laminated menu I am using as a shield. The bait shop is already booming with traffic, not surprising considering the time of day. The other two shops, a convenience store and a small tourist trap with cheesy Cherry Cove t-shirts in the window, seem less populated. The lights are still low, and I don't see one person walk in for a good ten minutes.

I turn my attention back to the menu, even though I already know what I'm going to order.

My mouth dries.

"What can I get you?" a disinterested voice drags me from my thoughts.

I tilt the menu enough to appear welcoming, yet not enough to make eye contact with the server. "The tuna salad sandwich, please," I say.

"You want coffee with it?"

"Yes, please."

The server clears his throat and I catch a glimpse of him briefly. He is in his thirties with long blonde hair tied at the nape so tight, his skin is taut at the edges. A crisp white uniform covers his wiry frame, and my eyes travel over the logo on the right breast pocket. A cartoon boat with a fork and knife on either side of it. The same logo I saw in the vision.

The man clears his throat again. "I'll get you the coffee then Ally is going to take care of you after, okay?" he asks. "I'm on break in ten."

I nod, smiling.

As the server turns away from me, I realize he never once looked down to see who I am. His back retreats while mine sticks to the ripped brown leather of the booth. A few minutes later, the server returns, just as uninterested, and pours me a cup of coffee. It is the color of mud no matter how much creamer I add, and I find myself stirring the coffee more than drinking it.

Time moves slower in the diner, always had, and I finish reading items off the menu four times before my tuna sandwich arrives. The plate clinks against the glass tabletop loud enough to draw a customer's attention to me. I sink down, tightening the strings holding my hood in place.

"I wasn't sure what you wanted for condiments, so I brought the entire fleet." The voice is light and airy, soft against my skin. I turn, ready to thank the replacement server that no doubt hates being stuck with me while Mr. Bored-to-tears goes on break, and my face drops.

It's her.

The girl leaning one hip against the table is none other than the possible murderer from my vision. Today, her features are not quite as grim as I remember, and her soot-colored hair is pulled into a tight ponytail. Strands of it jump out in random spots, making her look carefree and uninhibited. She digs more of her weight into the table until she is almost sitting on to my sandwich. Unloading the stack of condiment bottles on the tray she holds, the girl wipes her brow and grins. "I'm Ally," says the girl. "If you need anything, call me over. Enjoy the sandwich!"

She twirls around, the table breathing in relief when she lifts off it. I hold my hand up. "Actually," I say, drawing her attention, "can I get another coffee. This one—"

"Tastes like acid dipped in gasoline?" Ally asks with a smirk. "That's the house specialty. Afraid the next one won't be any better. You want me to get you an iced tea?"

I try to think of something to say to keep her near me longer. I don't need to think for long. "Hey, I know you," Ally says. "Your mom runs the funeral home, right? The one near the cove?"

"Um, yes," I whisper.

"Sweet! Is it creepy as hell?" she asks. Ally glances side to side then says, "The funeral home, I mean. Is it like haunted?"

"No," I respond, though deep down, I'm not sure if she might be right.

Her face drops, and she picks at her nails, looking me over a few times. Eyebrows kissing, Ally leans over the table and her ponytail brushes up dangerously close to my food. "So, you like, get to see dead people and stuff?"

I frown. "It's a job like any other."

"Uh-huh, uh-huh, uh-huh. Have you touched a dead body before?"

Mischief floods her dark eyes and when she leans further in, I can smell her perfume in the air. She smells of strawberries and roses; not the scent I would imagine fits the killer she is. Oblivious to my awkward glaring, Ally pouts her lips and clicks her tongue. "I haven't seen you around school," she says. "You a junior?"

"I'm not sure," I admit shamefully. "I'm kind of home schooled."

The briefest recognition flashes across her face and my nerves shatter as she cocks her head to the side to get a better look at me. Any second now, she'll figure out who I am and make an excuse to leave. I will be left alone; the bill dropped off casually to signify it's time for me to go. Or maybe she'll wave my entire meal to get me out of her hair. Any second. Any damn second.

Ally smiles; beams, really. "Sweet! I wish I could be home schooled."

"I'm Nastya," I say. Then add, "Sokolov."

"Ally Singh."

She stretches out her hand for a handshake, but I let it hang between us. "You seriously don't know who I am?" I ask. I should probably keep my mouth shut, but the words pour out without a filter.

"I know who you are," she says. "But it's weird not to introduce yourself to people. Rude."

What is happening here?

Ally doesn't seem to care one bit about the darkness that follows me, nor is she acting like someone who's afraid for their lives. Not the way most people do, and for the life of me I cannot spot a hint of discomfort in her. The opposite, actually. Ally seems almost excited to talk with me. My head hurts trying to figure her out. I didn't expect to walk into the diner to find the girl from my vision waiting for me with a bloodied knife in her hands, but I certainly didn't think she would be so... nice. Ally doesn't strike me as someone with one bad bone in her body, let alone a murderer. Was I wrong, and she isn't the one after Daxon?

Outside the diner, a commotion draws her attention and I follow her gaze to the door. A crowd of people start to gather near the windows and they're all peering inside with open mouths and eyes wide as moons. I shudder thinking it might be me they're interested in.

It is not.

Every person is facing the same direction, and it's nowhere near my booth. I stretch out to see better, noticing a small television mounted on one of the walls with a news channel on. On it, two newscasters sit rigidly straight behind a shiny table with images of the sun projecting behind them. I squint to read the captions, but I'm too far away to make them out.

"Hey, Marcus!" Ally yells out. "Turns it up, will you? Give the people what they want."

Behind the counter, a sphere of a man mumbles harsh words under his breath and clicks a button on a grease covered remote beside him. He narrows his eyes, then stomps away and out of my sightline. The sound from the television fills the diner and though it's still difficult to make out what is said, I hear the words 'eclipse' and 'phenomenon' repeated over and over.

"You heard about this yet?" Ally asks.

I shrug.

"Some big deal eclipse is happening next week. Everyone is all about it these days." She tucks a pen behind her ear and bites her bottom lip. "You'd think a celebrity is coming to town. Stupid."

How come Mother never mentioned an eclipse? My eyes dart between Ally and the crowd outside. They look like zombies; pressed up against the window so tight, I think the entire wall might give way. "They're really into it, huh?"

"Like I said," Ally whispers. "Idiots."

My tuna sandwich is too soggy, and I push the plate

back and forth on the table aimlessly. My brain is foggy, and my shoes click against each other as I try to unite the image of the Ally I had in the vision with the girl standing next to me now. No matter how hard I attempt it, I cannot make the connection. The two are oil and water. Lifting the bun, I inspect the damage the dripping tuna unleashed while I left it alone.

"Gross," Ally says. "Want another one?"

I battle against myself. "The bill is fine."

"Sure thing."

She starts to walk away, then stops. "You got plans tomorrow?"

If she knew me, she'd know how laughable her question is. "No," I answer. "Why?"

"Wanna hang out?"

The bun disintegrates in my grasp and the tuna juice soaking it runs down my wrist. "Sorry?" I ask. "You want to hang out? With me?"

The mischief is back on her face now. "Yes, you. I have the afternoon shift tomorrow right after school, so say, six?"

This might be the strangest day of my life. No one wants to spend time with me, and they certainly don't try this hard to do so. There is something off about Ally, and it isn't only the fact she might be a killer hiding in plain sight. She is a different breed, I can feel it in my bones. I should decline her invitation and run back home immediately. This is the smart move here. Instead, I let her question linger for a few moments. As far as I can tell, I have two options;

forget I ever met Ally or do what I came here to do: find out what her connection is to Daxon and stop her from hurting him.

Time to put on your big girl pants. Daxon's life depends on it.

I wipe my fingers on the napkin and place a twenty-dollar bill on the counter. "Six sounds good. I'll meet in the back by the dumpster."

14

Somehow, there is less air in my room now than yesterday. The walls have also moved in a few inches and are getting dangerously close to the table at which I sit. My feet drum against the baseboard and I push my spine into the chair until the middle plank of the backing is flush against me. On the table, my calculus textbook lays unopened and my eyes strain to focus on the rigid letter spelling out the title. Everything is small in insignificant now, and I wonder how I managed to spend so much time in a room clearly too small to fit me.

I push back, the chair legs scraping the floor, and walk to the half-open door. "Mom?"

There is no answer from downstairs. She's likely still in the morgue and I have half the mind to join her, if not for any other reason than to get a change of scenery. Ever since the diner this morning, I'm unable to concentrate on anything that matters. Or used to matter. Schoolwork seems pointless right now.

Why would I even care about calculus when Daxon's life is on the line?

My stomach rings itself out as Ally's laugh runs through my thoughts. One more sleep until I see her again and I can't get the ominous longing in my chest to subside. Is it wrong to be excited to spend time with a possible killer? I'm sure it is, though it doesn't stop the anticipation from tapping its fingers on my heart.

I am a fool.

One that might get herself nice and dead before the day is over tomorrow.

Catching a glimpse of the textbook's spine, I groan and push the door open. A pointed toe shoe peeps from below the door and I follow the leg it's attached to all the way up to mother's face. She must have snuck in while I was daydreaming. When I jump back, startled, she says, "Getting some work done, I see."

I shrug. "Taking a break. Where were you?"

"Basement," she answers.

When Mother isn't working, she is preparing for the work she will have to do later. It's a never-ending loop. I had come to accept that if I want to share this life with her, I must do so surrounded by dead bodies and covered in the stretch of decomposition. I let go of the handle and allow her to push her head into my room. She looks around, inspecting my room as though she's looking for intruders. That's Mother for you; constantly waiting for the other shoe to drop.

"Are you working all night again?" I ask.

"Looks like it."

I try to recall who's gracing the funeral home this week, and my mind draws a blank. "Who's on the docket?"

"The four car collision from last week," Mother says. "We have to release the bodies tomorrow, so I'm trying to get all the paperwork done in time." The rear of her hand slides up and down the doorframe when she looks at me. "I feel like I haven't seen you around for days."

In her tone, I can sense she's not simply stating facts. Mother is digging for information and if I'm not careful, she'll see right through my perfect daughter act. I make a poor attempt at straightening my features and meet her eyes, burying my weight into the soles of my slippers. "Trying to get ahead on homework," I say, so sickeningly sure of myself.

"I need some help with the laptop later. The program you installed is glitching again."

I sigh dramatically and roll my eyes. "You messed around with the settings, didn't you?"

Mother looks far from innocent, and it makes me laugh. The woman can never follow instructions and one of these days, she's going to crash the only computer we have in the house with her fiddling. I crane my neck to check the clock on the wall behind her. "Give me an hour or so and I'll come down."

"Wonderful. You hungry?"

"Not really," I admit. Then say, "Have you heard about this eclipse thing?"

For a moment, the color washes from her face and the hair on her arms ripples. She swipes at it, eyes on everything in the room but me. "I read about it in the paper the other day. Why?"

"No reason. Thought maybe we can watch it together." I put on an indifferent expression before she questions me further. "Might be fun," I add.

With few words, Mother agrees and leaves me to my studies, mumbling in Russian under her breath as she stalks off. Her steps rumble down the hallway and I shut the door, locking it. My back is still to the window when a loud pang ricochets off the glass and I spin around to face the sound. It is eerily quiet now, so much so, I can hear the wind outside even with the window closed. Another pang alerts my attention and I rush to the opposite side of the room. My nose presses into the glass and my breath fogs the pane.

Panic settles into the depths of my soul.

Outside, Daxon stands with a handful of pebbles in his hand. His hair ripples in the breeze and the thin polo he wears sticks to his chest as he aims for the window. He catches me staring and stops, waving his arm.

I unlock the latch and wind the small handle to crack open the window. "What are you doing here?" I call out.

"I found something," he answers. "Can you talk?"

Wasting no time, I turn from him and make my way downstairs, triple checking for Mother as I slip out the back door. Twigs crunch under my feet, the unruly mess of our backyard swallowing me while I walk. The silk scarf at my neck flaps against my skin and I tuck the edges into the neckline of my sweatshirt, pulling the hood on over my hair. When I round the side of the house, my stomach pitches violently.

"Ever hear of a phone?" I ask, closing in on Daxon.

He ignores my snide comment and pulls out a notebook. "Come look at this."

Doing what he asks, I press closer. I am nothing if not an obedient soldier with years of training under Mom's iron fist ruling. I loathe it. Oblivious to my low growls of protest, Daxon flips the pages of the journal and points a finger to the cream paper. "See this?" he asks. All I see are scratches of ink vaguely resembling the shapes we saw on the road near the crash. "I found them."

I have no idea what he thinks he found. My raised eyebrows signal him to explain, and he does so briskly. "It took forever, but I found a site with some research on old myths," Daxon says, his words almost resembling song. "Everything from Greek Gods to the tooth fairy. It's amazing how much is out there, really." He jerks his head, brown waves flipping to one side. "At first, I thought it was another fan site, but then I found this. The symbols! Nastya, I found the symbols."

"No way," I whisper. My toes swell in my slippers, and I am suddenly very aware of my decrepit appearance. Was this truly the day I decided to wear the oldest, most hole-ridden outfit I owned? It was. Of course, it was. I dig a finger into one of the holes in my leggings, pulling them apart even more.

Relief floods me when Daxon doesn't notice.

"What did it say the symbols mean?"

There is a twinkle in the hollow of his eyes that wasn't there before, and I try not to pay attention to the heat in my belly when I notice it. "There wasn't much," he admits. "But it seems they stem from an ancient myth about some Goddess of Winter. Marzanna, I think." He double-checks his notes while I take a few strenuous breaths. "Yep, that's it. The website said she's a Slavic deity and is believed to bring death with the winter season."

I tear the notebook from his hands; studying the symbols and the few rough notes scribbled on the page. "Anything else?"

"No. It's a start though."

"At least we know where to look now," I agree.

A flash of gray burns into my periphery and I swallow hard and tuck my hair back into the hood. My cheeks flush as Daxon's crooked mouth grabs my attention. "You shouldn't hide it," he says.

"What?"

"Your hair. You shouldn't hide it."

I exhale. "I hate it. I tried to dye it so many times, but

nothing works. I'm damned with this colorless mane forever."

"I think it's pretty," Daxon whispers. "Unique."

And there's that word again. I hate that word. People flaunt it as though it is a shield, a solemn promise to separate one from the herd, but when you try to fit in as much as I do, unique is a danger. You cannot be invisible if you are unique. You cannot fade into the shadows.

To spite him, I shove more of my hair into the hood and smirk. Daxon laughs and I am displeased he finds me amusing. I am not a funny thing. If Daxon only knew the truth, he wouldn't think so either. My heart wrenches when I remember the vision predicting his death and I pool into a puddle of a girl in the pristine bedroom. Daxon's agonizing scream tears through my psyche, and I am paralyzed. No, not a funny thing at all.

"You all right?" Daxon asks.

I'm tempted to tell him about the vision, to come clean with everything and hope he leaves me alone for good, yet I do nothing. I don't move and I don't breathe; I stand there like a complete moron and stare at the stain of coffee on the toe of my slipper. Numb.

Blazing heat warms my cheek as Daxon traces a finger over it and I jump away from him.

"Sorry," he says, neck red and blotchy.

"It's fine."

Words and thoughts jumble together, and I fight to think of words that sound remotely sane. How do I explain the last decade to him? How do I make him understand that even by being here, he is putting everything mother, and I worked so hard to contain at risk? Before I could make an even bigger fool of myself, a page in the notebook Daxon brought catches my eyes and I pause. Drawings dance before me, blurring into one gargantuan mess of ruffled thoughts. I trace a finger over them, stopping on one in particular.

"Oh, yeah, that one came up a lot in the article," Daxon says, catching me staring obsessively at the symbol. "Nothing about what it means."

"It looks like—"

"Snakes, right?"

My mind races and my feet pound the ground as I turn to run, rounding the corner to face the front of the house. Before me, the porch looms upward, a border containing the dead and the two women destined to care for them. My gaze trails up the wood, past the front door and all the way to the awning. To the funeral home sign and the two snakes intertwining over the words.

Daxon slides to a stop beside me. "Makes sense," he says. "The snakes, I mean. Goddess of death, snakes, funeral home. Didn't you say your dad put the sign up to represent death?"

I nod.

"Strange, isn't it?"

"What is?"

He glances from the symbol on the page to the sign. "How close you are to this whole thing."

Dryness coats my throat and makes words hard to come by. My focus stays on the sign, though my mind is elsewhere. I am at the cove again, treading blood and fighting to stay above water. My lungs are paper-thin and my bones ache, and somewhere in the distance, all I hear is Daxon crying out for help.

I snap myself out of my daze, turning to Daxon as I slam the notebook shut and shove it in his chest. "You have no idea," I whisper.

He doesn't hear me.

What is a dream if not a memory?

A long-forgotten thing, tucked away and hidden.

A reflection.

She knows of dreams too well; has tasted them too often.

This is not a dream.

The ground rumbles and tears at the seams.

She stretches long; fingers and toes pointed. Talons out.

For years she has searched for her;

Centuries of unanswered calls drowned in the waters that bind her. Until now.

The earth shakes once more, and she vibrates in response.

Under her flowing body, cracks appear, glimpses of a new world. A new home.

Soon, she will awaken.

Soon.

Though not quite soon enough.

Freedom can never come as quickly as she wishes,

Though it will come, nonetheless.

It will come for them all.

15

"Never trust a line cook," Ally roars. Her cheeks are red and puffy, and her eyebrows are so close together, they look like one thick line. She slams the back door of the diner shut, then opens it again in a huff. "You owe me ten bucks, Leo!" she yells, louder this time, then turning to me, "Ready to go?"

I scale the side of the dumpster I've been crouching next to. "Is everything all right?"

Ally scowls. "Sort of. Spoiled brat refused to swap an order, and I got stuck picking up the bill for a table," she explains. "This place sucks."

Ally tugs at the ratty hair elastic holding up her hair and crams it into her jean pocket. A thick, shiny wave of black waves roll down her shoulders and she shakes them out, blinding me as the setting sun reflects off her locks. The uniform she had on yesterday is gone and instead, replaced with the shortest cut-offs I've seen and a top that can only be described as an oversized headband. Every curve of her body is out for the world to see, and I am baffled with how proudly she dons it. Meanwhile, I am decked out in my standard inconspicuous outfit, and as I stand beside her, I can't help but notice the differences between us. It is enough to make me want to run back home.

Ally nods to the small path between the trees. "Let's go this way."

"What's this way?" I ask.

"Anywhere that isn't here."

It's as good an answer as any, so I follow her in. As we walk, Ally types on her cellphone, rapid-firing messages like she's in a race to finish. Her face rotates through expressions, and I get whiplash from watching her. I tuck my hands into the pockets of my shirt, pinching the fabric between my fingers. "I take it you're not a fan of your job?" I ask.

She glances up from her phone. "It's the actual worst. But money is money, so I have to do it."

I cannot relate, having never had a job to compare her situation to. Unless you count the funeral home, which I don't. Mother doesn't exactly pay me for helping her, and even if she did, I'm not sure I'd care for it. Money is not exactly a priority when your life is contained to a four-thousand square foot box.

Around us, the trees grow denser, and I realize she is

leading us away from the docks and into the wooded area spanning the edge of the shore. Light streams through the treetops and the footpath we're on is rough and untamed, unbothered by human feet. The muscles in my legs tighten as I battle the new terrain, though at my side, Ally strolls through the woods with the ease of a wild rabbit. Hopping over dead branches and bouncing her hair like a furry tail.

"Seriously," I say, "where are we going?"

She slows her pace. "Just walking around. I figured this place might be better than the street. No people."

For a moment, fear grips my heart, but I soon realize what she means, and it's replaced with shame and worry. We are not in the middle of nowhere for anyone's benefit but mine; Ally doesn't want me near the others, likely too embarrassed to be seen with me. The tendons stand out on my neck. Her taking me out here to kill me would have been a preferable scenario.

"Um... I..." I stammer.

Ally waves a hand in my face. "Don't even stress it," she says. "This town is full of idiots, so I figured you'd want to stay away. Must be rough having to deal with all their crap."

I stop mid-stride. "Wait, what?"

"You know," she says, "the rumors those bastards spread about you. It's pathetic, really. I honestly don't even get how you put up with all of it. If it was me, I would have told them to shove it a long time ago."

There's a massive flaw in her logic, and I try not to laugh out loud. To 'tell people to shove it' as she so delicately phrased it, I would need to talk to them in the first place. Not a day has gone by when I didn't wish to fight back, to prove to the town how wrong it is about me and vomit every thought I have back into it. But it would involve getting close, maybe even touching people. It would involve the possibility of seeing death. I can never risk it.

"It's not so bad," I lie. "You get used to it."

I am all too aware of how often I have said those same words in the last week and the more I think on it, the more I despise myself. Ally's eyes soften and a look akin to concern crosses her face. A memory of her blood-coated hands blocks my thinking, but I don't let it fester. There is no trace of vindictiveness in Ally, and either she is very good at hiding her murderous side, or I was wrong. I hope it's the latter.

She leans her shoulder against the trunk of a tree and tips her chin down, having to stretch her neck to watch me from the tall vantage point of her height. "So, I didn't want to pry," she says. I sense a 'but' coming.

"You're wondering if it's true," I say. "The rumors about me."

Ally doesn't reply, her curiosity lingering between us.

"It is. Most of it."

"Nice," she whispers.

"Not exactly."

She wants to ask more of me, and I struggle to stay silent. Strangely, Ally makes me wish to tell her everything. It's different with her. Not the way it is with Mother or even Daxon. I worry I can't lie to her quite as easily, and the thought sends streams of panic through my chest. Perhaps Ally is a murderer in disguise and her darkness is akin to my own somehow; like we are both entwined in death and aching for release. No matter how different Ally and I are, I have the distinct feeling we are also very much the same. Both alone and both ravenous. Somehow, I guess if I open my mouth to speak, I will not be able to stop.

What is it about her?

I don't want to find out.

A flap of wings sounds in the distance followed by the scurry of small paws, and I stop to listen, burying my shoes into the earth. "How come you're not scared?" I ask.

Ally snickers. "Of you? Girl, please. I'm like twice your size."

"Doesn't stop anyone else," I say.

"Well, it should. Don't let those morons get to you. If anyone gives you trouble, you come to me, okay? I'll make sure it's the last you hear from them." She cracks her knuckles in false bravado. "Besides, you're pretty much the only one in this town not cut from a cookie cutter. My kind of people. Besides, us girls have to stick together."

Leave it to me to be the type of person a possible killer would be drawn to. Can Ally smell the death on me? Is that why she isn't afraid? I tip my head to the sky to watch a flock of birds pass through then glance to Ally, my eyes instinctively lowering to her long fingers and expecting to find a knife there. There isn't one and I am both elated and perturbed by the idea. A part of me wishes she would out herself and get this entire charade over with; kill me where I stand then move on to Daxon. Again, things don't add up. As Ally checks her phone again, I realize she is more in danger than I am. She's the one trapped in the middle of the woods with the girl who communes with death.

"Subject change time!" Ally announces, pocketing her cellphone for the millionth time. "Did you hear about the kid that died?" I bite my lower lip and she latches onto the movement with greed. "What am I saying? Of course you did. Tell me you didn't see the body?"

The question is suspicious, but I chalk it up to Kye's death being the highlight of excitement in the sleepy town we call home. It isn't often someone young gets taken, and when they do, people can't stop the news from spreading like wildfire. Everyone knows everything in Cherry Cove, and I am sure Kye's name passed many lips lately. Ally is as curious as the rest of them, and I can't blame her from grilling me for information. When it comes to death, you're better off going straight to the source.

I balance on the balls of my feet and look around. "It's sad," I say. "How he died. I'm sorry for his parents." Then add, "And friends."

"Yeah, he was popular for sure," Ally says.

"You knew him?"

"Everyone knew Kye. Or they knew of him," she answers. "Him and the other guy he was usually with were like the kings of the school. Never talked to either of them, but they seemed nice enough."

So, she isn't friends with Daxon. Interesting.

"Did you ever see him get into a fight with someone? A bad breakup maybe?"

Ally arches a crisp painted eyebrow my way. "Nope. Wait, why? Do you know something?" Her lip curls back from her teeth. "Girl, spill. I want all the drama."

For someone who doesn't enjoy gossip, Ally is surprisingly interested in Kye's death, and I wonder how much of it has to do with what she might be planning for Daxon. How much of this is a trick to get to him through me? Except she doesn't know about Daxon and I, so what is her angle? I shake my head and adrenaline caves up my spine; not having all the answers doesn't prove anything. Ally is involved in Daxon's demise, I know so because I saw it. Invisible strings pull at my heart as I try to unravel the vision once more, yet nothing new comes to light. They're all wound tightly together; Kye, Daxon, Ally. I simply don't know how.

I run my tongue over the back of my teeth. "The sheriff said it was an accident."

"But you think otherwise," she says.

The answers I should give her run through my mind and I reach for them, trying to grab hold as though they are a life raft in a storm. They slip through my fingers, slick and wet, until I'm sinking and can't breathe. Ally watches me, waiting.

And I tell her everything.

As I speak, revealing what Daxon and I discovered, she doesn't move. Her shoulder stays glued to the tree and her chest barely rises when she quietly gasps as my story unfolds. The pull to share this with her is strange. Perhaps I am tired of lying, or perhaps some part of me refuses to believe the vision was right. I can't come to grips that the only person who pays attention to me, other than Daxon and my mother, is anything but decent. The woods settle down while I speak, and my heart punches my ribcage with every word. Sentence by sentence, I wash Ally with the sordid details of my life until she is covered in them.

When I am done, her mouth opens and closes, no air escaping.

"One hell of a story," she finally says.

"It's a hunch," I tell her. "I'm probably crazy and looking for mystery where there isn't any."

Ally flashes a wicked smile. "I think those symbols you found say different." She pushes from the tree and whips around me, storming further into the woods. "Come on," she demands.

"Where are you going now?"

Ally glances at me over her shoulder. "We're going to find out more about this Marzanna. I have an idea."

"*We*?" I ask, baffled.

"Yeah, we," she says. "You don't actually expect to sit this one out, do you?"

"I did."

Then why did you tell her?

"Don't be weird," Ally says. "This stuff is right up my alley. Dad says I have the nose of a hound, so if there's anything to find, I'm your girl. Now, let's get a move on before they close."

"Who?"

"The library," she says. "They have a killer occult section."

As Ally skips through the trees, I follow her. Not because I'm hopeful she will help me get answers, but because I can't escape her gravitational pull. Whether or not I like it, I am caught in her orbit and there is no way out now. When I made the choice to walk into the diner yesterday, it was all over for me. I brought her in, and I have to keep her close. I am not sure if it's for Daxon's sake or my own, but whichever it is, Ally is here to stay. At least until I figure out how she's connected to all of this.

We dash through the woods, jogging to pierce the foliage leading us forward. Around us, the wind howls and I swear I see a flurry of snow in my periphery. Each time I turn to check, the air is clear, albeit cooler than usual. The season is about to turn, winter's rabid fingers quaking in the darkness and waiting for the sun to depart so it can come out to play. For a moment, I remember Daxon mentioning the Goddess of Death and Winter and I can't help but shake. If one follows the other, we are not far from death grazing our doorsteps. A few months at the most, I reckon. My pulse drums a steady beat and as we burst through a thick corpse, feet hitting pavement again, Ally stops to look at me.

I wait for her to tell me she changed her mind, that she wants nothing to do with me and to shower me with insults as she walks away. Instead, her neck flushes and she crosses her arms, pushing up the cleavage of her chest so high, it nearly touches her chin. “So,” Ally says with a wink. “How hot is Daxon from up close?”

16

There must be a leak somewhere because as we huddle at the far end of a long library desk, all I hear is droplets hitting floor. Drip. Drip. Drip. A symphony in my ears. At the chair next to me, Ally has two books open and is comparing passages with frustration steeling her features.

She huffs out another long groan and someone shushes her from deep within the musty stacks behind us.

My eyes wonder.

The last time I was here, the Cherry Cove Library looked very different. Gone are the dusty old chairs that used to crowd the reading room like it was a garage sale. The piles of books on the floor are no more, replaced with neat, sleek tables of steel and wood with slots to deposit whatever tome you're reading into when you're done so some poor sucker can come collect it at the end of the day. Even the small windows I recall have been ripped off and a wall of glass sits between me and the small playground outside. There are no children there; there were never children there as far as I can remember. One of the swings hangs on desperately on a single chain and rust engulfs the seat in an eery shade of brown.

Why would they bother updating the interior and leave this monstrosity outside?

In the belly of the library, a book gets slammed shut and I jump in my seat. Right. No one comes here for the view. I shift my focus to Ally, who seems to be in a more cheerful mood and slide the book in my hands across the table. "This one is going to the loser pile," I say.

The loser pile is what Ally decided to call every book we search which doesn't give us what we're looking for. It is a fitting title, though I am aggravated with the size of it. So far, we've come up with exactly nothing and the irony of getting no information in a building full of it is not lost on me. I am surprised we managed to slosh through so many books in little under an hour, even if they did all end up in a discarded pile on the table.

Unlike me, Ally is a fast reader, and she's been tearing through pages since we sat down. It is impressive. *She* is impressive.

"Thanks for nothing, loser," she says, mocking the innocent book. "You're lucky your friend isn't quite so useless."

She pats the open page in front of her.

"You got something?" I ask.

She meets me with all her teeth. "Sort of. It has some notes on your Marzanna, but this one here," she says and flips the second book around. "Look for yourself."

Feet numb, I draw the book toward me with shaky hands, closing it to inspect the cover. The spine is muddled with age and it's hard to make out the inscription with the gold foil rubbed off. "Lost myths of Eastern Europe."

"Page forty-seven," Ally instructs.

Dust thickens the air when I flip the book again and find the page she mentions. I am immediately entranced by the words and my eyes run across the page, foot tapping on the tiled floor below. Whatever Daxon found on the website is a joke compared to what I'm reading right now. There still is not a massive amount of information, but it's more than a few sentences, which is a huge improvement as far as I'm concerned. My head throbs.

"Marzanna, Goddess of Winter and Death," I read to Ally as though she hasn't already memorized the entire passage. "Is said to defeat the weakened sun in the fall and rules over the earth until spring. She is presumed to bring death in the form of freezing and starvation. That's ominous."

"No kidding. Check out this part," Ally says, circling a short paragraph in the book with the pencil she had stashed behind her ear. I am one hundred percent sure she's not supposed to do that. "They say she lives in some mirror palace under the water and can only be reached by a bridge.

Wait, hold on," she exclaims and turns the page over. "Yep! Here it is. Kalinov Bridge."

"Where's the bridge?"

"Nowhere, I think. It says it's a mythical bridge leading to the mirror palace."

"Not creepy at all."

"Right?" says Ally. "And the mirror palace sounds awful. Who in their right mind would want to see themselves from so many angles?"

"What does this mean?" I ask. "Nav?"

"Ah, yeah! It's what they call the underworld, or this book does at least."

She slides her chair across the yellow carpet and hops to stand. "Hang on, I'll be right back."

I watch her disappear into the rows of tomes at my back and slump down in the chair. Sweat collects on the folds of the silk scarf at my neck and I loosen the knot threatening to choke me until cool air greets my skin. My body aches, dull and paralyzed, as I turn to the book once more. For a moment, I idle, then type a message on my phone and press send.

'I might have more for us.'

Three blue dots appear on the screen as Daxon's response lingers. *'Anything good?'*

My lips lift from my teeth. *'Maybe.'*

A hefty paperback crashes to the table and I flip the phone over before I have a chance to see how Daxon responds. A hand opens the book in a rush, Ally's. I arch to glance her way, but she is oblivious to my presence. There is a sheen of light in her dark eyes and for a brief moment, I forget she is not to be trusted.

"I knew the name sounded familiar," Ally says. Whatever she finds on the page seems to satisfy her because she is bouncing from foot to foot beside me. "So, still not much, but it's the same here. Nav is apparently a place containing all the souls of those who passed. And it's basically a hell hole guarded by giant serpents. Geez, who wrote this stuff?"

"Someone with too much time on their hands," I reply. My gaze locks on her and I realize she's no longer staring at the book. Mouth open, Ally watches me with care, eyes zeroed in on my neck. My hip bones tense under the table when I remember I forgot to retie the scarf. I am splayed open for all the world to see. I am bare.

"What's that from?" Ally asks, pointing at my scar.

"Battle wounds," I say mockingly. "I had surgery when I was a kid, thyroid problems. I'm fine now but stuck with this mess forever."

Her face contorts. "Sick! I like the swirls."

"Swirls?"

She reaches for my neck, and I pancake against the chair backing. "The way it's shaped like a rope," Ally explains. "I like it."

Glaring at her, I trace the rough skin with my finger, following the pattern. I reach for my phone, clicking the camera on and turning the screen to face me then lower it to my neck. She isn't wrong. My scar is shaped like a rope. It's funny, I never noticed it before. When I reach the tip of the scar, bumping into a hardened ridge, my legs tremor. Heat blazes behind my eyelids and I cover the scar with the palm of my hand. My thighs cool and I am shivering in my skin.

Where Ally sees a rope, I see something different. A snake.

I'm forever marked by a serpent, and I didn't even realize it. Half of me expects the bridge we read about to rise from the ground and swallow me whole; to drag me under to where the snakes guard the palace of mirrors.

My focus shifts to the book, and I can't help the frown lines forming on my forehead. I imagine myself in the realm of Nav, soul drifting down the bridge while my body lies on the operating table and men in white coats and masks slice me open to dig around. Their faces blur together and disappear, replaced by a long, never-ending bridge. My feet hit its hard surface and I pump my legs, running away from the gargantuan snakes on my tail. One wraps around my ankles, dragging me down. My chest hits the bridge first and a searing pain rushes up my body. The serpent winds itself over me, a forked tongue reaching for my neck.

I blink my eyes, shaking my head to clear the nightmare I manifested. It's all in my head and I'm ashamed of letting it get to me. Nav is imaginary, I tell myself. It is not real. There are no snakes, no bridge, and no mirror palace.

Your scar is just a scar.

On the library table, a sketch draws me in, and I reach for the open book greedily. It feels familiar about the drawing, and it doesn't take long for me to realize it bears an awful resemblance to the symbol Daxon and I found on the road, the same one he later drew in his journal over and over. A triangle with two swirling lines on either side that meet at the tip.

"Did you read this?" I ask Ally.

She shakes her head. "Not yet. What's it say?"

Reading as quick as I can manage, I scan the text. My face is ashen in seconds and my chest bobs up and down as I heave over the book. Next to me, Ally's breathing slows, and I feel warm air tickle my forehead. "Though it has never been proven, there are those who believe a near death experience can mark those that visited the realm. On their return, their connection to the land of the living is severed, making them a conduit for departed souls."

"What the hell?" asks Ally.

I don't answer. My vision floods with black and my hand drops from my neck to clasp the edge of the table. Nails digging into the wood, I close my eyes and count to ten, replaying the passage in my head. "Making them a conduit for departed souls," I whisper.

Every vision I had since I was a child runs through my mind and I'm dizzy from their intrusion. Am I a conduit? Did I die in the hospital? Is it why I can see death before it happens? I reread the paragraph again, concentrating on the description of the people said to have visited the realm of Nav.

Are there others out there like me?

My phone vibrates on the tabletop, and I catch it before it plummets to the floor. Clammy fingers gripping the case, I press it to my ear. "Hello?"

"Where are you?" Mother's voice is concerned on the other end.

"Running," I say. I ignore the confused look Ally gives me. "What's wrong?"

There is a pause, followed by a frustrated moan. "I need you home, please," Mother says. "We got another one and I need your help to get it ready."

"Sure," I respond. "Who is it?"

"The dura from the flower shop."

Fumbling with the buttons, I lower the volume before Ally has a chance to hear my mother trash talk the dead. My eyes refocus until I can see the flower shop owner's face clear as day. She still has the same scowl on she had when I was last with her, and I have no doubt it will be the first thing I see when I get home. Cherry Cove is starting to feel like a deadly game show I cannot escape. Sucking in a breath, I keep my tone low and say, "I'll be back soon. Does it say how she died?"

"I don't know, Nastya. A heart attack. Why does it matter?"

As I hang up, I think of the woman I met in the flower shop. She was a stranger, someone who despised me like everyone else, yet I can't get her face out of my head. Mother is wrong because how she died does matter. It matters to me.

If I am truly what the book said—a conduit for the departed—then every body passing through the funeral home is my concern. I never took the time to think about it, but it's so obvious to me now. I am the last step between the dead and their afterlife. Intertwined in their fates in so many ways. Bound to them.

I bid Ally an awkward good bye and rush from the library, taking the back alleys and forgotten trails that lead me to the funeral home. My body is numb when I reach the front porch, and I let my eyes roam past the roof to the sign looming over my head as relief floods my system. Two snakes eyes glare back at me from above.

This is where I belong, with the dead and the lost. This is where I'll always belong.

I walk up the creaky steps, turn the handle and slip inside. A withering smile lingers as I shut the door behind me and let the darkness of the house drown out my skin.

I am a serpent girl, and I am home.

17

Bubbles of soap flood the steel table and I wipe them off when Mother isn't looking. Everything is wet. The table, the woman's body, my wrinkled apron. I breathe into the mask on my face and heat rushes up my nostrils. It feels as though I am on fire.

In face of me, the flower shop owner lies stock still and I keep my gaze locked on her while Mother drains the blood from her body. I never like this part. My stomach turns and I tell myself to focus on the woman before me instead of on the lunch threatening to come back up. Her hair is the color of fresh earth, cut short and spiked at the top with remnants of yesterday's gel. It too will be clean soon. Though her eyes are forcibly closed, I can still see them; though in my mind, they are vivid and blue and not the placid gray they are now. I turn downward, settling on the woman's hands crossed over her abdomen while Mother pumps embalming fluid into her veins. It is a lengthy process, and I am numb by the end of it.

"Final wash then get some color on her face," Mother instructs.

I nod weakly, reaching for the water basin, but she stops me. "Don't waste too much time," Mother says. "She's going straight to burial."

"There's no viewing?"

"Guess not."

She turns her back to me, cleaning up her station while I scrub all remnants of our presence from the woman's body. By the time I finish, she looks like she had gone through a dishwasher, sparkling clean. At my back, I hear Mother's footsteps retreat as she leaves me to finish the job. It is so quiet, I can hear the hair twitch on the back of my neck.

I hate it when she leaves me alone with them.

Legs glued to the floor, I twist at the waist to wheel the makeup cart closer and begin loading the airbrush gun. The woman's skin is flawless, and I wonder if she took great pride in her appearance when she was alive. Back in the flower shop, she didn't strike me as someone vain, but then again, I didn't know her intimately. Though judging by the lack of family members lining up to say good bye, I doubt anyone did.

I shake a bottle of flesh-colored ink and turn to her. "I'll make you look great," I whisper. "I promise."

For the first time, the body does not speak back.

The gun sputters and I spray the paper towel on the cart before pointing the tip at the woman's face. Suddenly, I am embarrassed I didn't bother to check her name. Mother was so keen to get her ready, that it completely slipped my mind. I put the gun down and walk to the table, looking for the woman's file in the midst of all the others. I am halfway through the stack when a gust of wind blows past my shoulder. I shiver.

The morgue is cold, even by morgue standards.

My eyes widen as the wind howls in my ears, and I tighten my hold on a random folder, fingers leaving dents in the paper. There are no windows in the basement and the door is closed shut. My back is rigid as I turn, bile eating away at my esophagus.

My head spins and I try to make sense of what I am seeing.

There, right where I left her, her corpse lays stiff on the table, but it is not right. No longer are her arms crossed, nor her mouth closed. Instead, she is on her side, one arm flailing over the edge of the table with her lips parted in a silent scream. I shudder.

"Hello?"

I'm not sure what I expect in return, but it isn't this. The body jerks, legs bicycling once before slamming down on the table. The hit is so hard, the makeup cart shakes and rolls away. My butt presses into the side of the wooden table as I teeter backward. Goosebumps race up and down my arms, and my feet are caked in sweat inside my sneakers. Thoughts racing, I try to remember everything Mother taught me about the dead, cataloging strange reactions to formaldehyde as I go. Nothing comes to mind. As far as I can tell, there is no way in fresh Hell a dead body should be moving. Not this long after expiration.

A finger curls toward me and it almost looks as though the shop owner is beckoning me forward.

I stay uncomfortably still.

A few seconds pass and then she's flapping around on the table again, taking violent hits to her head. She is so close to the edge, I gasp as her chest flips over. Then she is falling. Down. Down. Down. All the way to the concrete floor.

A loud thud fills the morgue and I all but climb atop the table, papers and files crunching under my weight. The body doesn't move now, yet I am horrified all the same. Her ashen skin takes on a new shade of empty, one akin to fog floats over her in a thick mass. I follow the fog's traction with narrowed eyes. It rises high above the woman, twirling in a tornado before me.

The movement is so fast, I barely have time to register it. In mere moments, the fog is gone, and a very different entity takes its place. I cannot describe it, though if I had to, I would say this is none other than the woman's ghost. The shape in front of me bears a light resemblance to the dead body splayed across the floor, only with the features missing. In all the places one would expect to see human orifices, there is only darkness. Her eyes, her mouth, her nose, all black as night. The apparition wiggles, and if I wasn't so afraid, I would laugh. A dancing ghost is the closest thing to comedy in a morgue, I wager.

Foggy fingers stretch toward me, then move to the ghost's throat. They pass right through, then try again.

"Are you trying to talk?" I ask.

The sheer blob shakes again and waves its long limbs.

"What are you saying?"

There is no answer from the ghost, but I assume it is difficult to speak without a mouth; or a life. Easing my fingers from the desk, I inch toward it. Every step is agony and I pause a few feet from the apparition, keeping a safe distance. It cocks its head to the side, then stretches out and down, forcing me to look at the woman's body on the floor.

I take one more step in.

The fog swirls over the body, somehow moving it until the woman's head falls to the side. As I stand dumbfounded, the fog drifts toward the makeup table and knocks a bottle of ink over. The container shatters on impact, glass flying in every direction. I scream silently, dropping to all fours and crawling toward the mess to tidy it up before the corpse gets covered in makeup. When I reach the woman's body, the fog floats away and hovers over my head. I feel the breeze of it in my hair like the leaves of a weeping willow grazing grass.

Swiftly, I gather pieces of glass and push them aside, then look at the woman. Her head is still tilted, so much so,

I have a clear view of the side her neck. There is a speck of red from where the ink landed on her, and I curse under my breath as I reach for the bright dot. My finger rubs at her skin, and I shudder thinking what would happen if Mother were to walk in right now. She'd think me crazy; huddled on the floor over a dead body with my sticky fingers on its neck.

I glance to the door and continue to rub at the ink that refuses to budge when it dawns on me.

The spot on the woman's neck is not makeup.

It's an incision.

My nostrils flare as I lean in to inspect it. The cut is not one of Mother's. "What's this?"

Above, the fog whirls maniacally, making my hair whip around my face. My stomach lurches and I battle the urge to retch. A deep, unmeasurable sadness overtakes me, and wetness gathers behind my eyelids. Pain, I realize; I am sensing her pain.

No, that's not quite it. This is so much worse than pain.

The room spins and I can't keep my vision clear as everything blends into itself. Fluorescent bulbs flicker overhead, and I blink to match them, keeping my gaze on the fog. It covers everything in sight. My heart thunders and drops to my hips as images flood my system. Flowers fill my sightline, so bright and so red I know what they are immediately. Poppies.

In my mind, I see the woman and she is so alive, I can almost touch her. There is an unreadable expression on her face and her lips part as she starts to speak. She screams instead; a wail so high pitched, my eardrums pulse like they might bleed. A sharp prick at my neck causes my legs to buckle under me. I press a palm under my ear, right where I felt the pain. When I bring my hand up to face me, a drop of blood rests on my skin.

Nausea engulfs me and I am so weak, I don't think I can stay awake. My eyes flutter slowly, sleep calling me into its embrace. I fight to stay lucid, biting the inside of my cheek until I taste blood.

Then the pain is gone, and the vision disperses, a new one taking shape.

I am at the cove now, watching red water glisten in the dark of night. On the shore, I see the shop owner, though she is not herself; not fully. She is half human and half fog. Her legs float above the ground, taking her away from me and into the river. I reach for her and as though she could feel me, she turns her head. Her face falls and tears fill her eyes. She moves her lips over and over until I can make out what she says.

"Find him."

The world spins, and I am thrust away from her and from the cove. My back hits a hard surface and my bones rattle in my skin. I clamber to get up, light piercing through as my sight returns. I'm standing next to the stainless steel table; a woman's corpse lying on top. Hands crossed at the waist, mouth and eyes shut. I inch my face closer to her, seeing the red dot on her neck as if for the first time. It is so small, no one would pay it any mind, but I know it is there, and I know it's bad news.

"You didn't have a heart attack, did you?" I ask the corpse.

Upstairs, something drops, and I hear Mother curse violently.

Picking up the makeup gun, I begin to apply light strokes to her skin until the dot is gone. As I finish preparing the body, visions of the cove and the shop owner fill my thoughts. I have no idea what happened, but she's trying to lead me to the truth. Whatever landed this poor soul on the table was not accidental, and she needed to reveal the truth to me. Whoever landed her here, I correct myself.

Someone did this to her and I have to figure out who.

"I'll find him," I promise. "I'll find him, and you can be free."

The bark of the tree stump I sit on pulls on my leggings and I shift my weight, catching a string on the wood and pulling it out. I tear at it with my finger, stretching it so far, the string cuts my skin before I pull it out. My eyes stay glued on the funeral home peeking through between the trees. The porch light is on even though its not night yet and I can already see bugs twirling around it in a tornado.

"She's not there," says Daxon.

I lower my gaze to the earth then twist to face him. After I finished prepping the body, I had to get out of the house. It was between the trees out back and the cove and considering mother's obsessive warnings about dinner being almost ready, I didn't dare venture to the water. The plan was to get some fresh air and clear my mind of the vision. The plan was to be alone.

The plan failed.

As soon as I got to my usual spot in the woods, the funeral home taunting me from a distance, I couldn't stand it. My thoughts raced and a headache formed in the back of mind. I didn't want to be alone, I realized. But I also didn't want to be with Mother. That only left one person and when I called Daxon to meet me, he didn't hesitate. Sitting here now with him beside me, I'm wondering if he regrets the decision. I haven't said a word since he got here.

Daxon glances from me to the porch and says, "Your mom. It's who you're watching out for, right?"

I bite my bottom lip. "Uh-huh."

"She keeps a tight leash on you, huh?"

"It's not her fault," I say defensively. "She's trying to protect me."

Daxon's arms shoot out in surrender and his smile makes me buckle back. "I'm not saying it's a bad thing. I wish my parents cared enough to be overprotective. Or my mom at least."

"Do you get along with her?" I ask. I don't bring up his father.

"We're okay," Daxon mumbles. "You know, I used to wonder what she'd be like if he wasn't around. What *we'd* be like. Better, I think. Though, knowing my luck, we'd actually be worse."

I try to slow my breathing and fiddle with the corners of the scarf tied around my neck. It suffocates me and I pull on the knot, loosening it enough to breathe but not enough to show any skin. "I think the same thing about my dad," I offer.

"How long has he been gone?"

"Long enough," I say. "Since after I had my surgery. I ask Mom about him all the time, but she constantly changes the subject. I think it hurts her too much to talk about him."

Up ahead, the porch light flickers and the bugs disperse, returning as soon as the beacon is lit again. I scan the driveway, then tear my eyes away from the house and focus on a single tree before me. It's thinner than the others, spindly and sickly looking, and the branches are long and pointed, not one leaf growing from them. I like this tree, I think. I like the way it refuses to give up. I like the way it craves to exist. Beside me, Daxon scratches his head and sighs. "If it helps, I wish my dad would leave."

"Maybe he will," I say.

"I doubt it. Even when school's done and I can finally move out, I'll never be free of him."

"If it helps," I repeat his words, "at least you can leave."

He chuckles and my cheeks flush, heat spreading through my body like a furnace.

Daxon stretches his legs and crams the tips of his fingers into the pockets of his jeans. The zipper of his jacket cuts against his chest and strains to keep his body contained. I wet my lips, jerking my head away before I dare reach for him. "So, these symbols," Daxon says. "Any clue what they mean?"

I shake my head. "No. But I don't think it's a coincidence we found them."

"Me either. You think the book was right? They're some kind of markings for people who died?"

I almost forgot I told him what Ally and I discovered in the library and when he mentions it, I wish I hadn't. For once, I'd like to have a conversation with Daxon that doesn't involve the symbols or the Goddess or anything to do with Kye. I wish we could keep talking about our lives, but I know this can't happen. Both of us are in too deep, too close to death now to discard it. Too trapped.

Resting my chin in my hands, I slouch and loosen a breath. "Is it weird I hope the book's right?" I ask.

"What do you mean?"

"If it is, it might mean I'm not the only one with these visions. Maybe if there's others like me out there, I can find them. I'd have to leave Cherry Cove to do it, I know, but it's something to look forward to. Leaving here, I mean. And not being a freak anymore. Or not being a freak on my own."

"You're not alone," Daxon says. I notice he doesn't correct me on the freak front. "You have your mom, and me."

And Ally.

"Who cares what the other idiots in this town say? I think it's pretty amazing what you can do."

"It's really not," I whisper. "It's actually freaking terrifying."

"But you're different."

I swallow hard. "Thanks for reminding me."

"No, I meant in a good way. You're not like other people, not in Cherry Cove, and not anywhere else. I don't think you realize how great that is."

I'm pretty certain he would change his mind if he knew even a sliver of what the visions are like. Or what it means to live with them every day. He doesn't, which is why he says, "I wish I could be different."

"You are," I say. "Maybe not the way I am but you are different. Being here right now is proof enough for me. No one else would dare it."

"I guess I don't believe being afraid gets you anywhere."

But you should be afraid, I want to tell him. You should be more than afraid of me and the things I see. Instead, I only say, "We can be not afraid together."

"Sounds like a plan to me," Daxon agrees.

The porch light flickers again and this time, I hear the front door slam against the frame. I yank my eyes from Daxon and watch Mother look around, searching for me. Her kitchen apron is covered in some type of oil and her hair is tied high above her crown. She scowls and I take it as my cue to move. "I should get going," I tell Daxon. "Thanks for coming by."

"Any time," he says.

As we part, Daxon hangs back to leave after I get home to avoid Mother spotting him, I have the incessant need to linger. I take my time walking to the house, pausing every now and then and arguing with myself to keep going. The trees part and usher me toward the funeral home and my mother, toward the gloom of being locked away. With each new step, Daxon's face is erased from my mind and by the time I reach the front door, I can no longer feel him in the crevices of my brain. I peer over my shoulder to the woods and wave, then I shut the door behind me.

18

I spin the straw in the smoothie tumbler in front of me while Mother slices vegetables for a salad. She is humming a song I don't recognize, and it is so off beat; I doubt it's a song at all anymore. More of a repetitive buzzing sound than music. Taking a sip, I gag when the unblended parts of the smoothie jab at my throat on the way down. Mother catches me put the tumbler down and stabs the knife into an innocent red pepper. "Finish it all," she instructs. "You're starting to look pale."

"How is that different from how I usually look?"

"Drink the damn smoothie, Nastya."

I follow her command, slamming the tumbler hard on the table when I am finished.

"What is going on with you today?" Mother asks.

"Nothing," I say. "Tired."

"It's all the running. No matter what they say, exercise will kill you. I stick by it."

I am certain she means every word. Mother has not performed any exercise in as long as I've been alive, even before whatever happened to her leg. You'd think it would have some effect on her health, but as far as I can tell, she's a workhorse with a heart stronger than the rest of the town combined. Definitely stronger than mine. Behind her, the kitchen shutters slam against the house in random intervals and my stomach plummets with each hit. The weather is turning, I think. Soon, the leaves will fall from the trees and frostbite will cover every inch of Cherry Cove. I miss the summer already.

"I think I'll go to the cove again tonight," I say, tapping the straw against the wall of the tumbler. "Unless you need me."

Mother continues prepping the salad, but her eyes flash to mine briefly. "Alone?"

"Obviously," I answer.

Black irises watch my every move as Mother reads my expression. This is new to her; this version of me, the Nastya who dares to leave the funeral home and venture out without needing her protection. Though she doesn't stop me, I sense the longing in her every day when I leave. She is kind enough to give me space, despite how much it costs her. I pray the price she pays is worth it. Maybe if I find out what happened to Kye and keep Daxon from dying, it will be.

Probably not.

Nothing is worth the miles of distance I put between my mother and me.

I rinse the tumbler and plop it atop the mountain of dry dishes in the rack and head to my room. Behind me, tuneless humming resumes and my knees weaken when I reach the top landing, the sound of broken words fading into the house. In my pocket, my phone vibrates and I cut my eyes toward it, noticing two unread messages. Panic flutters in my hips as I scroll through them. One from Daxon and one from Ally. Both saying the same thing.

'Can you meet tonight?'

Teeth chattering, I reply with a time and place. The cove, seven pm. Same reply, copy and pasted twice; one for the victim and one for his killer. Both leave an empty space in my chest where my heart should be.

THIS IS A BAD IDEA.

Bits of gravel lodge in the crevices of my boots and I kick at the ground, sending bits of stone into the water. It doesn't splash, only shivers a little like it is laughing at me from deep within its sternum. I roll my hips out and kick again, then turn to Daxon. "She's almost here."

"Who are we meeting again?"

"Ally," I answer. Nerves swirl on my tongue and my head spins. Why did I invite them both here? To the cove of all places. The same place I know will be Daxon's downfall at the hands of the girl we now wait for to arrive. It seemed like a good plan at first; put them together, and let fate play its course so I can stop whatever Ally has planned. If she even does. My plan is solid, it is the implementation of it that frightens me. What if I can't stop her? Worse, what if all I'm doing is speeding up the inevitable by pushing them together against all odds?

No matter now. I must stay the course.

Daxon shrugs beside me, his hands buried in his pockets. "And Ally is..."

"A friend."

I'm not entirely sure if this is a lie, so I try not to think about the guilt pushing its way into my chest. Is Ally a friend? I want her to be, but it doesn't mean much, no matter how badly I wish it. Though I haven't found a connection between her and Daxon yet, the vision still stands and I can't discount it. I've misread the warnings before, and it cost me everything. I will not let any harm come to Daxon, even if it means losing Ally. My chest tenses. I have only known her for a short while and the thought of not being near her tears a hole through me. One I'd rather not have to fill with someone else.

"I thought you're not allowed to have friends," Daxon says.

My cheeks puff out as I suck in breaths and for a

moment, pointed rage fills my stomach. At least, until I realize he means no harm with his words; he is only stating the obvious truth. "I'm also not allowed to meet boys at night, but here we are."

Daxon laughs. I hear another sound and my toes curl in. Behind us, rocks crunch under incoming feet and I don't turn around, knowing it is Ally without even seeing her. The lilac scent of her perfume fills the air around us, and I study Daxon's face as she steps near where we stand by the shore. There is no recognition in his eyes. He watches Ally with the curiosity of a Golden Retriever, head cocked to one side and jawline set, nose pointed in her direction.

Slowly, I turn.

"This place is even creepier at night. Why did you want to meet here?" She plops herself beside me, facing Daxon.

I swing my arms over the river. "No crowd this time of night."

"Right." She nods, then locks her gaze on Daxon. "If it isn't Daxon freaking Thorn."

My heart races as I wait for Ally to pounce on him. Widening my stance, I get ready to stop whatever attack she plans, a low growl hanging on the edge of my lips. When Ally stretches her hand toward him, I stand stone still. Her arm dangles in front of Daxon and to my utter bewilderment, he takes it, shaking it lightly. "Ally, I take it," Daxon says, letting go of her hand. "Good to meet you."

"Oh, we've met," she responds.

Daxon scratches his head, confused. "Really? I don't remember."

"You wouldn't. We don't run with the same crowd, but I've seen you around."

"Ah," Daxon says with a grin. "Glad we get to meet properly then."

"Not as glad as me."

Not caring if he sees or not, Ally winks at me and bites her lip. "Definitely hotter up close," she says. My face takes on the red color of the water. "So, what's the plan for tonight?"

This was it.

I peel my eyes off the two of them, turn myself inside out, and try to get my brain to stop worrying. So far, there is no indication Ally means Daxon any harm and while I should be relieved, I am full of pins and pointy objects. The visions are never wrong, yet they feel off. If Ally is truly the reason for Daxon's death, why does their occupying the same space seem so natural? No anger, no confrontation, only a sense of peace and belonging. At my feet, the water laps the shore in agreement.

I don't think Ally is the killer, though I have been known to be mistaken.

My heart sinks when I remember the day Christine Solar died. I was convinced some evil entity was after her, shadowy fingers reaching for her life and waiting for the right opportunity to latch on. In the end, there was no malice in Christine's death. The poor kid simply didn't look both ways before crossing the street, and I felt like a jerk for months. I didn't interpret the vision well then and I wasn't interpreting it any better now. Whatever danger is coming for Daxon, I still don't know what it is. What I do know is there is a very good chance the glossy-lipped Amazon Queen might not be it.

"Um, hello?" Ally's voice rattles my brain. "You good, girl?"

Far from it, actually. I shake myself awake and peer at her, then whisper, "Sure. Do you want to fill Daxon in on what we found in the library? I told him most of it, but I don't think I got all the details right."

I FORCE MY SHOULDERS DOWN OVER AND OVER UNTIL the tick in my neck stops pulsing. Ally's story takes on new colors as she describes Marzanna and soon, I find myself entranced in her words as though I am hearing them for the first time, as though I wasn't there when we discovered the truth of the Goddess of Death. She does a much better job at putting everything together and the eccentricity of her performance makes it hard to look away. I wonder if Ally might have a future in theatre. She'd like that, I think. Watching her now, I realize why she is impossible to stay away from. Ally is infectious. Alive. And everything I wish to be. She is the kind of friend I always wanted and never got to have; the type that doesn't care what others think. She reminds me of Christine a little, and I smile, thinking that if

Christine never died, it might have been her here tonight putting on a show for Daxon. That it might have been her making me feel like I am not a freak.

When Ally gets to the part about other death seers, she glances my way briefly. Daxon's gaze follows hers and I shrink in the heat of their attention. Cold sweat chills my lower back and I play with a small rock on the ground aimlessly.

"Sounds like you were right. Might be others out there like you," says Daxon.

I tip my chin to my chest. "We don't know for sure," I say. "It could mean anything."

"Doesn't sound like anything to me."

"Me either," Ally adds. "But can we take a second to talk about the damn snakes for a second? Anyone else find that weird? I mean—"

She goes on, but I'm no longer listening. My vision spots and I sway to the side, a familiar headache careening behind my temples. Another vision is coming. Not now. Please, not now. My tongue laps my teeth, and the inside of my mouth feels like I swallowed a lit match. I breathe in through my nose and start to count down when I see her.

Mere feet from where Ally and Daxon sit, the shop owner's ghost lingers over the water. Her feet are completely covered, the wetness having no effect on her rippling body. The fog surrounding her in the morgue is faint now, and I can make out her features clearly. She looks so real. So alive. Her body quivers as she lifts an arm and stretches out a finger to Daxon. My entire soul breaks into pieces. I snatch a stone from the ground and run my thumb over its rough edges to give myself something to do. Anything but fall apart. "What are you saying?" I ask.

"Nastya?"

Daxon's face takes on a worried expression as he jerks his head from me to the cove. He cannot see her, yet she is there all the same. "Nastya, what's going on?"

"Yeah, girl," Ally chimes in. "You look freaky."

"I... I..." I mumble.

The ghost's lips peel from her teeth and the darkness within pours out. It crawls over the ridges of her chin and neck, covering her in blackness. My legs shake as I fight to stand, but I cannot move. The tiny rock in my hand is soft and when I glance down, I see a bright red poppy in its place. I rub my fingers until it disintegrates and falls to the ground. Where it lands, the rocks shimmy out of the way, creating a direct path from me to Daxon. A silent scream hangs on my bottom lip and I watch as more poppies sprout from the ground to line the path. They grow higher and higher until I cannot see anything but them. Eyes wet, I push off the ground and stomp my feet over the poppies, but they only continue to bloom. Their pollen covers every part of me, wrapping me in a cocoon of red that crawls up my body. I can smell them as they cram into my nostrils.

Wheezing, I twist on my heels and turn to run. Hands grip at my legs and I am not sure if they are Daxon's or Ally's; or neither of them at all. My bones creak as I kick at whoever is holding me and burst into the water, wading toward the shop owner. She floats further out, and I follow. A blanket of ice covers my legs and the further in I walk, the more anchored I feel. There is no turning around now.

It's me and the river and the ghost of a woman scorned. A woman murdered.

Behind me, shouts rise, and I hear splashing as my friends rush in after me. I paddle onward. The shop owner's grin widens and when she ducks into the water, I do not hesitate. My lungs fill with air, and I close my eyes before dropping into the river. The world disappears with me.

19

"Get her head!"

I make out the muffled words and force my lips apart to yell out. Instantly, the mistake of my actions crashes into me, and I am gulping buckets of water. My lungs burn and I gag on the river water rushing into my mouth. Legs and arms wailing, I jerk my body in so many directions, I'm not sure I'm whole anymore. Thin fingers claw at my hair, and I whip my head away from them, elbow meeting soft skin.

"Ow! She freaking hit me!"

"Get her head up!"

The water is so dark and deep, I can't make out who is talking and while there is no danger from the helping hands clawing at me, I still fight. I need to get upright. I need air. I *want* air.

My feet slip and slide across the eel-like river bed, and as I struggle to lift one leg, I'm yanked back down. Ankle rolling, I am sucked under with so much speed, whatever hands were on me fall away into the darkness, leaving me alone again. More water pours down my throat and I am certain there is no escape now. My body writhes in agony and I wrestle the urge to shoot upright, ducking my head deeper into the murky cove. My hair spreads around me, mesmerizing me with its silver sheen as I sway from side to side. I watch the strands glide in the turbid water while I wait to die.

A new pressure digs into my shoulders and suddenly, I am no longer alone in the darkness. In front of me, clear blue eyes pop open and Daxon's face comes into focus. His cheeks puff out and he motions down with his hand. I follow his direction to my shoes, one of which is securely tangled in a patch of seaweed lining the bottom of the cove. My legs shake, but Daxon's hands grip my shoulders tighter, forcing me to look at him. He shakes his head, holds up one finger. *Wait.*

Against everything in me, I still.

Letting go of my shoulders, Daxon dives to the base and tears at the seaweed. In moments, my leg goes flying up, kicking him in the chest and catapulting him away from me. I scream and horror crawls its way up my body as the bubbles of my final breaths burst before me. Heavy, unyielding pressure builds at my temples and my brain begs to implode. Someone shoves two hands under my armpits, and I am soaring upward, head breaking the surface of the water as I fly to freedom. My throat gurgles and I cough hard enough for bile to make its way up from my stomach to my mouth. Retching, I continue to kick and wail my arms to stay afloat as another grunt sounds at my back.

"Stop punching me," Ally commands. "I'm trying to help here."

I barely hear her. Every part of my insides burns, and my bloodshot eyes fail to focus. All I see is water. The rancid smell of the cove pushes up my nostrils as I empty out half the river back into it.

Mother once said I am not a dainty creature and tonight proves it. There is nothing remotely fluid about my poor attempts to breathe without throwing up. My hair hangs in wet, knotted strings down my forehead and cheeks, and traces of mascara run down my face. I rub my hands over my eyes, pulling away a sooty black mess, and turn to Ally.

"I got you," she says.

Swinging away from her, I examine the river for any sign of Daxon. My heart beats against my ribcage when I can't spot him and panic laces through me, slicing into my flesh like knives. "Where's Daxon? Did he come up?"

Ally shakes her head. "He's still down there."

Jerking myself free of her, I'm about to dive for him when I see a spot of brown float toward the surface. Daxon shoots out of the water, his eyes bloodshot and his face as pale as the moon above. He runs toward me until his chest collides with mine and I'm pulled into the vice grip of his embrace. Muscled arms lock me in, and I struggle to breathe again. My shoulders shimmy and I press my palms into his chest, pushing ever so slightly to get his attention. "Are you all right?" I choke out.

"Me? Are you?" he counters.

His arms are still around me and it takes him a second to release. When he does, I see an emptiness flash across his face, but it's gone instantly. We both look me over, checking for an injury despite knowing there will be nothing to find. The river did not allow my death tonight, and I do not know why it chose to let me go when it could have as easily dragged me under. Quaking, I whisper a silent 'thank you' to whoever watched over me tonight and take a full breath in. My palm brushes against the soaked tendrils of hair at the base of his neck, and I battle the need to tangle them between my fingers. Behind us, Ally groans. "Let's get to shore," she says. "Bath time is over."

As she wades past us and runs back to the rocks, Daxon takes a few steps after her. His gait is lopsided and I wonder if it is difficult for him to hold me up despite the buoyancy the water offers. Since he doesn't complain, I let him carry me, my body aching to stay this close. Unlike before, I do not wish to untangle our bodies and the warmth of his skin against mine seeps into my bones. I welcome the touch.

Slower than is necessary, we reach the rocks and though our feet are on solid ground, I still feel out of balance. Remnants of the river linger in my lungs, and I lick my lips, tasting the bitterness of red water on my tongue. There will probably be a nasty rash covering my entire body tomorrow. I glance from Daxon to Ally; the cove will mark us all.

It is only when we are far from the edge that I notice the awkward slant of Daxon's stride. He is favoring his right leg and my cheeks sink as I roll my eyes over him. Right under his knee, his jeans are torn and I can see a dark stain forming on the fabric. Blood trickles down his leg, all the way to the rock, leaving behind a trail as he walks. "You're hurt," I yelp, dropping down to inspect the wound on his leg.

Peeling away the shredded fabric, I expose a deep gash and Daxon sucks in a breath through his teeth as I poke a finger at his leg. "What happened?"

"I think I cut myself on a rock while I was down there," he says.

My head traces the drips of blood leading to the water and I gasp. Blood in the cove. Red like poppies. Can this be what I saw when I touched Daxon?

"What are you thinking?" asks Daxon.

I was way off about the vision. "Nothing," I lie.

We tread toward Ally, no more words exchanged between us. As we reach her, she nods at my neck, then at Daxon's bloodied leg. "Help a boy out, Nastya," she says.

It takes me a second to understand she's means the silk scarf at my neck. Hesitantly, I untie it and hand it to Daxon, refusing to meet his gaze. My palm presses to the scar and I look toward the river while he wraps my only shield over his wound. At this point, there is no need for pretenses. Daxon knows what a freak I am, Ally too, and no amount of scarves or hoodies is going to change it. Despite everything, neither of them moves to leave and I don't know what to do with that. They should be running for the hills screaming bloody murder, not standing there and waiting for me to speak. Which is exactly what they're doing when I finally work up the courage to face them. Standing there. Watching me.

"So, you feel like explaining the suicide mission?" Ally asks, one foot tapping the rocks.

"Yeah, what gives, Nastya?" Daxon adds. He accidentally puts some weight on his hurt leg and cringes. I try not to let the guilt destroy me.

I check for the ghost of the shop owner even though she is long gone, then say, "I have something to tell you guys. You might want to sit down for this."

They do not move a muscle, so I continue, "You know the owner of the flower shop?" I ask. They nod in agreement. "She died. Heart attack according to the paperwork. Except it wasn't. I found a small incision on her body and then—" I weigh the words carefully until they are balanced on the mental scale in my head. "I saw her ghost, or whatever is left of her. And she led me here. To the cove. Please, don't ask me to explain how because I wouldn't even know where to begin, but I think she was trying to show me who killed her. I saw her again tonight, which is why I went into the water. I was following her."

"You followed a ghost into the river in the middle of the night?" Ally asks.

When she puts it this way, I hear how ridiculous I must sound. I try to smile, but it comes out crooked and lame. "It gets worse," I say. "I have to go back in."

"Absolutely no way in Hell," Daxon says before I even finish the sentence.

"I'm not asking," I say. Deep down, I realize how selfish I'm being, but there is nothing he can do to stop me. "Something is in the water she wants me to find. I have to do this."

"No. I'll go," he says.

"You won't find anything."

"How do you know that?"

He is frustrated, and it's in the sharpness of each word. I struggle to find a way to explain things to him, settling on the least crazy sounding explanation. "Because it isn't for you to find."

Daxon is about to argue when Ally skirts around him to stand between us. Her black eyes narrow and she plops her hands on her hips, letting out an exasperated sigh. "You two are acting like morons," she says. "We're all going in together, okay? No one is drowning on my watch tonight, so if you absolutely must go treasure diving, Daxon and I are standing guard. But so help me, Nastya, if you punch me again, I'm punching back."

I glance over her shoulder to Daxon. "Does that work for you?"

He mumbles words sounding an awful lot like curses and lowers his eyes.

"You guys ready?" I ask and turn to wade back into the river.

This time, the coolness of the water isn't as jarring, and I barely shiver as I walk until I am waist deep. My two friends at my side, I take determined steps to reach the same spot I saw the ghost before, boots scraping the river floor. My head keeps swiveling the entire time to look for signs of the shop owner's return, but we are on our own now. In the darkness, it's hard to tell we are in the right spot, but the water laps around my waist and I recognize it without doubt. The weight of the cove seems familiar here, like I had been shackled by it my entire life. Even the slippery surface of the riverbed steadies me somehow.

I pause, my friends a second too slow behind me, and let my palm brush the reflective surface of the water. "Here," I announce to neither of them in particular.

Somewhere near to me, I hear Daxon's disapproving moan, but he doesn't say anything to alter my decision. My mind is made up and we both know it. Giving myself little chance to back out, I fill my lungs with air and loosen my muscles. Legs sinking into the abyss, I drift into the depths of the river until I am surrounded by its emptiness once more. This time, I do battle against it. What the river wants, the river gets, I tell myself. It has always been this way.

Under this much water, it's easy to lose your way and for a moment, I forget myself as I drift. My eyes are shut and when I remember to open them, they snap wide and aware in an instant. A leg brushes against me, followed by a hand fishing for substance; Daxon trying to make sure I am still nearby. I sway my arm toward him, index finger brushing index finger; I am not lost yet. The same unbearable burning fills my chest and I count the seconds one by one, anchoring my mind to this moment. Beneath me, seaweed dances to the slow rhythm of steady current and if I were not looking, I never would have spotted it. The small metal box sitting on the floor of the river, hiding.

The box stands out amidst the blank canvas of the water like a clown at a funeral and I reach for it so fast, I accidentally let the air I cling to escape. My lips clamp shut and tension forms in the back of my eyes as the need to resurface takes over. I curl my fingers over the box and yank it to my chest, cradling it tightly as I push myself up. The cove doesn't fight me, and my head breaks through into the night with ease, slicing the buttery barrier of the water until I am next to Daxon and Ally. Their eyes widen. All three of us stare at the box in silence.

"What's this thing?" Daxon asks, shattering the silence.

I lift the box, noticing how uninviting it is for the first time. A simple metal container, like the ones used to store money in for a rainy day. There is nothing special about it and yet, I can sense its importance in every part in my body. I run my hands over the edges, searching for a keyhole, but all I find is a latch that isn't the least bit secure. If someone wanted this thing to keep their secrets, they sure didn't care enough to put a lock on it. Biting on my tongue, I flip the latch up and slowly lift the lid. My stomach muscles tense and my toes and fingers tingle as I flip it open and peer inside.

For some reason, I expected more.

The interior of the box is as uneventful as the rest; a crushed blue velvet lining which is surprisingly dry considering it has been underwater this entire time. In the center, a single capped vial rolls around as I try to keep the box from shaking in my hands with little success. Its contents are a mystery to me, as there is no label to indicate what it might hold, though I already have the answer to all the questions racing in my mind. *This is what killed you.* I flick the vial out of the way so I can get a clearer view of the only other object inside, one much easier to distinguish. The petals are wilted, and the stem looks like it had been pummeled by a strong hand, but I recognize the flower with certainty. "A poppy," I say to the others.

"What does it mean?" Ally asks. Her shoulders hike up and she rubs at opposite elbows as she struggles to make sense of what I found.

Daxon inches closer until his hip rests against mine and my heart skips a few beats in response. I slam the lid of the box shut, tucking it under my arm so the metal nestles close to my body. From deep inside, I hear the clinging of the vial as it hits the sides. "I was right," I say. "A heart attack didn't kill the shop owner, and whoever is responsible wanted to make sure no one found the evidence. Makes sense to dump this here, no one would think to search the river. No one even goes into it."

The two of them exchange uncomfortable glances then Daxon says, "So, what do we do with it now?"

"Take it to the police, obviously," Ally answers.

I speak before I have the chance to change my mind. "No," I say. "We have to find out what's in the vial before we tell anyone about it. She's counting on me, and I won't let her down."

Aggravation passes Daxon's blue eyes moments before he stalks away. I don't have the heart to tell him he's counting on me too, he simply doesn't know it yet.

You have served me well, she beckons, though she is not heard.

They do not need to hear her to obey.
And obey they will.
Sacrifices must be made and ties must severed;
Salvation does not come without its price.
Will they pay it? Will she?
The flower blossoms and she has her answer—
It has already been paid.
Her steps are light and calculated,
Conditioned by the shackles placed on her. She growls.
The serpents hiss. The dead recoil.
She is full enough for the time being, satiated.
The one she's tied to is nearly ready.
She waits.
And waits.
And waits.
Until she sees it.
A ray of light piercing the red.

Beyond the palace, the bridge rises and souls scatter to make room for what is to come.

She traces one nail across the flower, and says,

It is our time now.

She rests with one eye open.

Lolled by the whispers of the dead around her and the waters outside.

It has begun.

20

With the windows closed, my bedroom smells of a vile mixture of disinfectant and vinegar and I breathe through my mouth, refusing to let the stench of Mother's latest cleaning escapades fill me up. It's still there though, on the tip of my tongue, dangling like a curse word. My brain is foggy and I glare at the small box in my lap with unfocused eyes.

Why did you send me to find this? I ask the ghost.

She is not here to answer.

My skin pricks when I touch the rough etchings on the side of the box, the ones I couldn't quite make out in the darkness of the cove earlier this evening. Here, in my room, they are the only things I see. Four symbols, one on each wall of the box with an engraving of two snakes intertwining at the tails on the lid, a triangle between them. The symbols are exact replicas of the ones we found by the road, less rough but a close enough resemblance; lines arranged to form shapes that make no geometrical sense. Saliva pools in my mouth as I trace them one by one and memorize the spots where the lines meet to form crosses and triangles. I do not touch the snake carvings for fear of them coming to life in my hands and gobbling me up before I can fight back.

Four beady eyes poison my thoughts and when I snap the latch to open the lid, I can still feel the serpents' gaze on me even through the thick metal. The scar on my neck heats up and I grit my teeth, accidentally breathing in through my nose until my eyes water from the vinegar lingering in the air. I blink the tears away and bring the tiny vial to my face, shaking the glass bottle and making bubbles froth inside.

Whatever liquid is locked in here is clear as tap water, yet when I shake it, red speckles float around in a makeshift hurricane. It reminds me of the snow globes they sell during the holidays; the ones everyone buys, even though they are as useless as sunglasses in a cave. I watch the dust settle in the bottle and twist open the lid, sniffing the neck from a foot away. There is no discernible scent to the contents, though I get a whiff of perfume I'm not familiar with. I place the vial on my bedside table and pluck up the rotting poppy next, giving it a good sniff too. My eyes saucer. "Makes sense."

A flowery aroma fills my room, and I can tell without a doubt the liquid in the bottle is full of poppy juice; a cryptic perfume that drives me up the walls as it coats every inch of space around me. I shove the poppy back in the box, tossing the vial after it, and slam shut the lid. As I do so, the door to my room creaks open and I have seconds to throw a pillow over the box before Mother comes barreling in. She holds a small shoebox in one hand and a glass of water in the other. I notice the indents her glasses left behind on the ridge of her nose, wondering how many hours she spent tied up in paperwork today. Knowing her, way too many.

Mother sets the glass on my desk and places the shoebox beside me, not bothering to make herself comfortable. "How was the cove?" she asks.

"Same as usual," I answer. "Quiet."

"Good. I brought you something."

She nudges her head to the box, and I tip the lid up to look inside. My stomach knots as I register the strange gift she delivered. Old, crumpled photographs fill the shoebox and I catch a glimpse of a few, seeing my father's face staring back at me. Mother is not kidding around about this new obsessive cleaning she's taken on; everything got unearthed and I feel pricks of excitement to see the rest of the house. I wonder if she went room to room while I was gone and destroyed it the same way she did her own bedroom. I shudder at the thought of having to rearrange our life again after her.

"What's this?" I ask.

Her dark eyes flash between me and the box. "Just some pictures you might want," she says. "I put the rest in the shed, but I figured these might be better off with you. Do you know how much garbage there was in my room? I mean, honestly, why did you let me turn into such a hoarder?"

I shrug. "It's your room, Mom. I thought you liked it this way."

"I swear, one of these days, we're going to wake up to a television crew outside waiting to reorganize this damn house." She laughs under her breath. "What's that show called again?"

"Hoarders," I whisper.

"Fitting. Anyway, you can go check if there's anything else you want to keep before I toss it all this weekend. We need a fresh start, you and me."

My attention snaps to the box on the bed and I wince. At least this part of our past made the cut. I pull the lid over and glance up at her. "I'll take a look tomorrow. Thanks for bringing these over."

"Made sense for you to keep them," Mother says. "Your father may have been a bastard, but you should have some good memories of him."

"Mom."

"You know what I mean." She turns to the door.

Unfortunately, I do know what she means. At the time, my young brain was too stupid to see the tension between them, but as I grew older, I realized how awful their relationship was. How empty. The more I think of it, the more I realize I never saw them touch or exchange any of the pleasantries a married couple should share daily. It was as if they were only together for the sake of raising me, and while they did so wonderfully, I couldn't imagine being trapped in the same cycle with another person every day of my life. Waking up knowing they do not love you and you do not love them. Going to sleep with much the same understanding. Mother blames him for how things worked out between them, but I believe the fault is both of theirs. Neither of them fought to stay together; he left and she let him. There is no changing any of it now.

I am the by product of two people refusing to try.

"Dinner is almost ready," Mother says from the doorway.

"I'll be down soon."

When she leaves, I place the shoebox on the floor and slide it under the bed with my foot. There will be plenty of time to crawl down memory lane later; right now, another box demands my attention and unlike my mother, I will not turn the other way when someone needs me. I push the pillow to the side and pick up the metal container. My hands clasp over it and without thinking, I let my palm cover the two snakes on the lid.

The smell of burning rushes up my nose and my head spins as I bury my nails into the metal. Dizziness overtakes me and my hips roll on the soft bed, threatening to tip me over with each gasping breath. In my ears, low, whispered chanting echoes from somewhere behind me. I gaze around, but there is only darkness. Somewhere in the distance, the sound of water flushes out car honks and my spine cracks as

I uncurl it to sit up. A scream pierces the air. Daxon's. The same scream I heard before.

I whip my head around, spotting him for a second in the shadows of the trees surrounding the cove. My jaw unhinges to call for him, but he is gone before I could even move. I hear a rustle at my feet and drop my eyes to the ground, head tilted sideways, lips pursed. At the toe of my sneaker, a fluffy ball nuzzles in, its soft fur tickling my ankles. A white rabbit, I think. The snout is a little longer than the bunnies I used to play with in pet stores and its ears sit straight up as pointed arrows. The creature's fur ripples as it nuzzles a wet nose to my skin. I reach down slowly, afraid to scare it away.

Noticing me, the rabbit jumps backward, trembling as it hops away from me and disappears into the night. My gaze follows it all the way to the trees where Daxon is waiting for me to save him.

This vision is even more confusing now than before.

"What are you trying to tell me?" I scream.

The chanting I heard before engulfs me. My eyes spot a bright and orange light in the near distance, and I pump my arms and legs to run toward it. Warmth slaps my face and I skid to a stop, gravel flying in all directions under my feet. Before me, a massive fire erupts, smoke tendrils rise to the skies and light up the cove in a burning fury. My eyes water as the smoke fills my lids and I blink it away, trying to make out the figures surrounding the fire. Their hands are locked, and they sway from side to side as they chant in a language I do not understand. The figures are cast in shadows, and I see no faces from where I stand, not that I dare to move closer.

Suddenly, one figure breaks away from the rest and moves around the fire to walk toward me. A man. Everywhere he steps, poppies bloom and grow and I smell them as they crunch under his feet. The man towers tall in front of me, and I squint, leaning in to make out his features. He is limned in the light of the fire at his back. I trace my eyes over strands of wavy blonde hair grazing a defined jawline. My body screams and I claw at my cheeks, dragging my fingers down and leaving red streaks behind.

Only a few feet from me, the man reaches out a hand toward me. Pale skin illuminates from the glow of the flames and the shape of a slightly hooked nose catches my eyes. I know this nose. I know this skin. I know this person.

My breath cools in my mouth and I fight the rogue tears under my eyelids. "Dad?"

21

Mother hears me coming before I even hit the bottom stair, and when I tear into the kitchen—hair a mess and eyes puffy and red—she already has a cup of pitch black tea ready for me at the table. Steam billows at the top and fogs her reading glasses when she hands it to me. "What was all the commotion upstairs?"

The commotion she speaks of is me screaming when the vision finally departed, leaving the memory of Dad's face lingering in my mind. I don't bother filling her in. Instead, I take the hot mug from her hands and slam it on the table. Tea spills over the edge and stains the wood tabletop and Mother frowns at the sight. I slide a chair out, making sure to press hard on the backing so it screeches the entire time. "You need to tell me the truth about Dad," I say, steeling my voice. "Not the crap you've been telling me this whole time. The real truth."

"Language, Nastya," she scolds.

"I don't care about language right now, *Mom*." I sound like a spoiled brat, but I don't much care at the moment. "Tell. Me. Everything."

"You already know it all."

"I think we both know that's a lie."

Worry fills her face and I register it immediately. Unlike her daughter, Mother is not very good at hiding her emotions, though if I'm right, she might be a better liar than I thought. Looping a finger over the cup handle, I take a sip of tea; a white flag to show her I am capable of hearing her out without exploding. "Please, Mom," I beg. "Tell me."

"I don't know what happened up there, but there's nothing to tell. The bastard left us and it's time you grew up and accepted it." She shakes her head and rubs the ridge of her nose, sliding her glasses so high up, the frames tickle her eyebrows. "Why are you so bent up over it all of a sudden?"

I bit my tongue, wondering how much I should share with her. "I had another vision."

"What?" Mother screeches. "When? Why didn't you tell me?"

"A while back," I admit. "At first, I figured it was because Daxon was in danger, but now I'm not so sure."

"The boy who came here last week?"

I nod.

"I thought I told you to stay away from him." She is

disappointed, and it stings my heart to hear it in her voice. "I specifically said not to mess with the town or its people. What else are you hiding from me?"

I don't know how the tables turned to put me in the interrogation seat, but I will not let her play these games. Not now when so much is at stake; not with what I witnessed in my room. I put the cup down, carefully this time, and meet her gaze. "I need to know about Dad."

"You're being ridiculous," she says. I can see the perfect exterior of her act shatter as she shifts her weight, angling herself away from me as though the act would stop me from pressing. It doesn't and I am full of fire and hunger all the more. "Tell me about the vision," she demands.

"The first one was of Daxon screaming at the cove. There was blood, a lot of it," I say, noticing her expression sour when I reveal having more than one vision. "Then it was another girl, Ally Singh, a waitress from the diner. And this time, I saw Dad. I don't understand any of it. The visions are usually vague, but this time, they're a complete mess. It's like they're leading me in a circle and the more I follow, the more I realize the circle is really a maze with no end. I know you're keeping things from me about Dad though."

I suck in a breath and add, "And I find poppies everywhere. They were even on the body of the boy downstairs. Kye. The one who supposedly died in a car crash."

Mother waves her hand in the air like she is about to

dismiss me and stands up. "Wait here," she says, disappearing from the kitchen.

Stomping steps rise on the stairway and I hear a door open upstairs, then silence. It is good ten minutes before she returns, a rugged leather-bound notebook in her hands. She sets it down and grimaces. "What's this?" I ask.

"Your father's journal. He left it here, and I never bothered to ship it to him."

The tea gurgles in my stomach and heat warms my neck as I open the journal. It looks like a regular notebook, a diary of sorts, but it is what is inside that makes it special. Letters and notes, all in Dad's handwriting, and all a jumbled wreck leaving me even more confused. I stare at the pages, noticing a few symbols pop up which seem similar to the ones I've been researching. Somewhere in the midst of Dad's chaotic thoughts, I spot a drawing of two snakes, intertwined at the tails. I gasp. "I've seen this before," I say.

"I'm not surprised," Mother says. "If it's your father you're seeing in the visions, serpents are always close by."

For a second, I think she means to call him a snake for how he treated her. Something is here she doesn't want to talk about, and the serpents are important. She knows. She knows everything I don't. "What do the snakes mean?"

Mother stills, one palm pressing into my shoulder as she lowers to sit next to me. The warmth of her body slams into my side and chills run up my spine, my arms and legs turning to liquid. She closes her eyes, removing the glasses and tossing them on the table haphazardly. When she opens them again, I swear I see tears glisten in the corners. "I should have known this day would come," she says. "I tried so hard to keep you from this, from him, but you are too nosy, Nastya. Too stubborn for your own good. I wish you listened to me and kept to yourself. I understand this house feels like a prison, but it's the only place you're safe."

"Not anymore," I whisper.

"No, I guess not." She lets go of my shoulder and crossed her arms. "I'm sorry you have to deal with this. You got dealt a bad hand and I wish I could be strong enough to protect you from all of it."

"From all of what, Mom?" The riddles she weaves have to stop, and I'm tired of giving her the power she holds over me. She doesn't get to decide how I live my life and she doesn't get to barricade me from the truth, or from Dad. "What does Dad have to do with this? With the visions I'm having."

"Your father is not in his right mind. By the time I found out, it was too late. I was already six months pregnant with you. When we found out we were having a daughter, he was so happy, it was infectious. We talked baby names every night and I couldn't believe it was possible for a man to be this thrilled with being a father, especially since we had no idea how we would afford to raise you. But he stepped up, I'll give him that. Got a second job at the docks, helping out the fishermen. Then put enough money away to afford this place. A proper life, he called it."

"I didn't know Dad worked at the docks," I say.

"Oh, he did. Came home every night smelling like fish and I remember thinking, this man right here, he's going to be a great father."

"So, what happened?"

She scowls, lines deep and unforgiving around her mouth. "It turned out he wasn't excited to be a father. He was excited to be *your* father."

I don't understand the difference.

"At the time, I didn't know much about your dad's family. He was guarded and I chalked it off to having a bad childhood and not wanting to talk about it. I should have pushed more, maybe things would have turned out differently."

"What's wrong with his family?" I ask.

"Not much," Mother says. "Unless you count crazy as a flaw." She turns the journal toward her and flips to a random page, pointing to one word in particular.

I read it aloud. "Marzannite Order?"

"Your father and his family have some strange beliefs," Mother answers. "They were, I guess you could say religious, though not to any religion I've ever known before. He didn't tell me about it until well after you were born, I think you were two at the time. When I found out, I assumed it was a joke and let it go. I shouldn't have."

My eyes drift to the journal again and I deconstruct the name written on the page. Marzannite. Marzanna. No way. "As in Marzanna, the Goddess of Death?" I ask.

Mother's eyes narrow. "So, you've been sneaking around getting some reading done, I see."

Cheeks flushing, I look at her, quickly averting my gaze. There's no point keeping secrets from her anymore, and yet, I still feel ashamed I have done so in the first place. I shouldn't, considering how many secrets she'd kept herself. I shouldn't and yet, I do.

"According to your father, Marzanna is not the bringer of death as she is depicted," Mother explains without me asking. "Him and his twisted family think she is some sort of savior, sent to bring us all to salvation. You can see how I would have chalked it up to a joke, right? I mean, it sounds insane." She rubs at her leg as she speaks and I concentrate on her face, giving her little space to change the subject. "Anyway, when you were old enough to walk and talk, he started taking you around town. You remember that? Going out with him every day for your little adventures?"

I smile, though it never reaches my eyes. I do remember my days with Dad, and I remember them fondly. We walked around for hours, meeting new people every day. We often ended up in the diner where Dad made sure to have a crowd around us at all times. It was the highlight of my childhood, really; to get to know new people, to make new friends. Though it seems Mother does not quite recall this part as I do because when she sees me smiling, she rolls her eyes. "He made you shake their hands, right?" she asks. "Everyone you met?"

"Yes."

She scoffs. "Pridurok." Dark eyebrows lower down as Mother frowns, and she says, "He was testing you. Seeing if your gift would manifest."

"But I didn't have the gift back then," I say.

"That's what I told him, but he refused to listen. He kept saying it will come and when it does, you will fulfill your destiny."

"My what?"

"I told you," Mother says, shrugging. "Crazy. The man thought you were a messenger from this Marzanna, sent here for... I have no idea what. At that point, I had enough and told him if he can't keep his act together, he has to leave."

"Did he?"

"Clearly not," she answers. "At first."

Head pounding, I replay my childhood on a loop. All the fights and cold glares I witnessed weren't a sign of a dying marriage, they were so much darker. There was a war zone in my home, and I never saw it. "So, what happened to make him change his mind?"

Mother points to the scar on my neck. "You got sick and needed the damn surgery," she says. "When the doctor told us you died on the operating table and they managed to bring you back, I was destroyed. Your father, however, was happier than I've ever seen him. He was certain your death was fated, planned somehow, and that now, you were ready for whatever him and his family had in store for you. I couldn't take it anymore. I had to save you from him."

The mood shifts in the kitchen and melancholy numbs my bones as Mother continues to massage her bad leg. "What happened to your leg, mom?"

"I had to do what I could to get rid of him," she says. "The doctors wanted to keep you in the hospital for observation, so I took my chance. Your father disappeared a lot those days, so I was alone in this damn house with no witnesses. One morning, after he left, I took matters into my own hands. You remember how the stairs to the basement had to get redone?"

I blink. "Yes. You said they were a hazard."

"Only when you need them to be," Mother says.

Acid coats my mouth. Mother's eyes meet mine, determination swimming in their depths, not an ounce of regret to be found. "You made yourself fall?"

"I did," Mother says. "I had to make him leave you alone, and I couldn't do it on my own. I figured if I could make him seem like a violent man, someone would intervene. We would have a chance at a normal life, you and I."

"I guess it worked."

"It sure did. Right after I did it, I called the sheriff. He sent a few guys over to help me fill out a statement against your father. Renee helped a lot too. I didn't expect for it to get so out of hand that the mayor got involved, but she took the whole thing personally; threatened your father if he didn't get the hell out of dodge and never set foot in Cherry Cove again. Surprisingly, your father didn't object. He left the same day, didn't even pack a bag. Just disappeared."

"But no one talks about it," I say. "How come I've never heard anyone mention this?"

"We kept it pretty quiet. I told Renee I didn't want you growing up thinking your father is a monster, and she agreed to play along. It wasn't a lie, you know. I really didn't want you to have bad memories of him, so I buried the truth of who he was and made sure you never found it. I thought it was for the best." She adds, "Still do."

Reaching a hand for me, she runs a finger over my scar, and I am pummeled by her sadness. "Then your visions started and, well, you know the rest."

"You locked me up."

"I protected you. From his family. From him. From everyone, Nastya. I kept you safe and don't you forget it."

The chair legs teeter under me and I splay my arms out, resting my forehead on the cold mahogany tabletop. My eyes burn and my throat opens and closes as though it is struggling to figure out how to work. I gape at my mother through a curtain of silver hair. She watches me silently for a long while, dissecting my limp body with the scalpels of her eyes. I feel like a body on a slab. Cold. Sweaty. Dead.

Mother pats my back and walks to the counter, clinging dishes together. "Let's eat," she says. A plate scrapes the table and the smell of baked chicken wafts through my hair. A warm hand pushes the strands away while another lifts me until I am sitting rigid and straight in front of a plate of food. It looks tasteless and coarse. Mother cuts a piece off and waves it in my face, making airplane motions like I'm a child refusing to cooperate. "Eat," she instructs.

I open my mouth so she can shove the bite in and chew.

We continue like this until the plate is cleared, and she nods in satisfaction. "I'm going to bed," she says, pushing away from the table. "We can talk more in the morning."

When she leaves, she takes Dad's journal with her.

22

The night inhales and swallows the porch as I huddle on the front steps with my knees tucked under my chin. Deep in the house, Mother lies awake in her bed, her gaze burning into the crumbling plaster of the ceiling. I haven't spoken to her since dinner, but she is as sleepless as me. I can feel it. The earth under us shifted today, the foundation cracking down the middle and leaving us on opposite sides. Beneath, I can sense the darkness of her secrets as they reach for my toes and creep up my body.

I can't believe she kept the truth from me all this time.

Actually, the more time I have to process, the more I realize how fitting it is. Leave it to Mother to hide important information without a second thought as to how it would affect me. I want to believe she acted for my own good, has been all this time, but I cannot escape her betrayal. As much as she despises Dad, she is no different from him; constructing a web of lies and calling it a life.

I want to march upstairs and tell her exactly what I think. I want to punch things. Instead, I hug my knees tight and grit my teeth as I stare down the driveway into nothingness. No amount of yelling and arguing will change where we are now.

My eyes sting. I rub at them until they turn red and observe the space in front of the house through a bloodied lens. The entire world is red as far as I can see it and I lick my dry lips, thinking of the bomb Mother dropped in my lap earlier. Two words flash in my mind.

Marzannite Order.

Mother might think Dad and his family—the family she kept a secret—are lunatics, but I don't agree with her. The few details I saw in Dad's journal before she snatched it away ring too close to everything I've uncovered this past week. It's all linked and for the first time, I can feel the rough strings of the chaos surrounding Cherry Cove in my fingers; unraveling each time I pull. The snakes, the symbols, the elusive Goddess of Death. They are all a part of the mess I'm in and I cannot help but wish he was here to explain it further. Mother might not want to admit the truth, but she has not lived the life I lived; hasn't experienced the darkness I have. Unlike her, I can handle discomfort and tragedy. Besides, the visions wouldn't show my dad unless it was important. The strange group he belongs to knows what's happening in our sleepy town, and I have to find out more. It's clear what I must do and it's something mother would never approve of.

No matter, I tell myself. I don't approve of her right now much either.

I lengthen my legs, climb up, and head for the front door. The handle freezes in my palm and as I creep inside, my thoughts run circles in my skull. I have no way of contacting Dad, never have, but there has to be more of him in the house she kept. Mother might be afraid, but she isn't stupid. She doesn't burn bridges she might need to cross in the future.

The house is silent and every step I take rumbles down the hallway as I make my way to the basement door. My breath is ragged and worn, catching on invisible bumps in my throat and chest. I pull the door open, shutting it behind me until I am encased in the familiar aroma of formaldehyde and cleaner as it envelops me. Under my feet, steps creak and groan and I curse at them in my mind, skipping the last two to land at the bottom. Watching the morgue, I shake off the memory of the shop owner's ghost and Kye's cold stare and walk to the table in the corner.

My eyes scan it carefully.

She wouldn't hide information on Dad anywhere I can easily find it, so I resort to pulling open each of the three drawers on the side and rummaging through their contents. Files and notebooks pile atop each other and I push them aside, reaching for the dusty laptop beneath. It takes me a few minutes to power the stupid thing up and regret collects in my stomach when I recall Mother offering to buy us a new one and me urging her not to. Back then, I thought I was doing us a favor, saving money we needed. Now, I feel the full force of my poor decision. The beast in front of me barely runs, and the sound of the fan blowing to keep it alive is enough to wake the entire town up. It sounds like a rocket ship taking off.

When the laptop finally manages to awaken, I pull up the folders Mother organized, checking the ones with obscure names. All I find is medical records, police reports, and one batch of cat pictures she downloaded from the internet.

Useless.

A groan breaks free, and I slouch over the laptop, choking on my frustration. My legs stretch under the table and a hard surface hits the toe of my slipper. I wince, curling my toes to lessen the numbing pain running up foot and duck under the desk. Below, hidden in the shadow of the table's underbelly, is a brown accordion file folder. The edges are smooth and clean, not frayed like the other folders we use down here. I grip the top handle and bring the file up; it's lighter than I imagined. I unlock the knob holding the folders in place. My fingers dig into each slot, pulling out papers I haven't seen before. One is the deed to the funeral home with three signatures on the bottom; Mother's, the mayor's, and another name I don't recognize. Likely the previous owner of the place. I place the paper back inside, carefully positioning it so it doesn't look out of place, then move through the rest of the slots. For the most part, I find a tremendous amount of nothing. Paid bills, receipts to random things Mother bought for the funeral home, a few holiday cards to vendors in town she never sent. I'm at the point of giving up, yet my gut tells me to keep checking. I rummage through the papers, ignoring the tiny cuts on the tips of my fingers, and pull out another stack. The Cherry Cove hospital insignia is stamped on the top right corner of each page and the paper is old and yellowed, stained with lost time.

Reluctantly, I read the records of my hospital stay during the surgery. Every nasty detail of those weeks stabs at my heart and I reach for the scar on my neck, tapping the raised skin there. There is nothing here I haven't heard or lived through before, but seeing it all in one place takes me back to the sordid moment when my entire life changed. Or ended, if what Mother told me tonight was true.

I died. I really died.

Pressure builds in my head, and I fold the hospital records and shove them in the waistband of my leggings. I'm not sure why I want to keep them, but I do anyway. Something tells me Mother might sneak down here and destroy this memory as she had all the others. As painful as it is, I do not wish to erase this part of my past. It changed all of us and maybe, just maybe, it can change us again.

Flipping to the next page in the stack, I pause.

"Parental consent," I read aloud.

The form in my hands looks so formal, I almost don't recognize Mother's handwriting on the bottom. It is rigid and straight, not the standard chicken scratch she usually scribbles in a hurry. In the spot where a name and signature should go, I find two added, both written in her hand.

Mother's name, Elena Sokolov, stands out defiant and strong, but it is the other name I cannot stop staring at. Alexei. Dad. I read past the legal jargon all the way to the bottom of the page and swallow hard. 'In case of emergency, please, contact' then two phone numbers and two emails. One is Mother's and I recall it by heart; the other, a mystery. I pull out my phone and shakily dial the number. The line screeches in my ear and a recorded message says, "I'm sorry, the number you have dialed is not in service. Please, hang up and try your call again."

I follow the instructions only to be met with another screech and the same robotic female voice.

Heart leaping, I flatten the form out on the table and turn to the laptop. My wet fingers glide across the keys and in seconds, I am staring at the bright, colorful screen of the funeral home's email server. I pull up a new email message, and when I type the address I found on the form, I make two mistakes before getting it right. Nerves collect on my skin as I pound on the keys.

'Dad, it's Nastya.'

I delete the words.

'Hi Dad,

I don't know if this is your email. I hope it is. I'm sorry we haven't spoken all this time and I wish it was different, but I need your help. Mom told me everything. I need to see you.

If you get this, meet me at the cove tomorrow night at eight.

I can't wait to see you.

Love,

Nastya.

PS. Don't respond to this email, I will not get it.'

Clicking send, I wait until I get a notification telling me the email is on its way and proceed to delete it from existence. It takes the laptop longer to shut down than it did to start, and while I wait, I put the file folder back together and tuck it under the table. Around me, the morgue seems to whisper of my betrayal, and I close my eyes, concentrating on one mantra over and over.

You have to do this. She will understand.

Deep down, I know she won't.

"UM, HELLO? YOU STILL HERE?" ALLY ASKS. SHE WAVES her hand in front of my face and flutters her lashes. "Did you hear anything I said?"

I didn't and I tell her that much. When she goes on to repeat herself, I can't seem to follow the conversation. My eyes flitter across her room and I create a mental inventory of everything I see. The queen-sized bed we perch on is drowning in pillows, each one a brighter shade of yellow. Behind us, a tufted headrests stoically reaches for the ceiling and I trace my gaze over the dandelions painted on the gray wall behind it. They're so intricate, they look almost real enough to snatch up. To my left, a large window stretches from wall to wall with strings of outdoor lights draping over it. One of the strings is has come loose and hangs down haphazardly down the center and I wonder if it bothers Ally to have it undone. Judging by the state of her bedroom and the mountains of clothes scattered throughout, I doubt it does. One of my feet dangles off the bed and I run my toes over the white faux fur rug on the floor.

It's nice here.

Safe.

When Ally invited me over this morning, I had my reservations. What if it's a trap? What if her parents are home? Worse, what if they aren't? The questions bombarded me up until the moment I stepped through the threshold and followed her upstairs. They still bombard me now as I sit here, listening to Ally complain about a pointless incident that happened at the diner.

"Okay, I'm going to stop talking 'cause you're clearly somewhere else."

I shake myself awake. "Sorry. I'm here." I look around again. "Your room is nice."

"Are you kidding?" Ally exclaims. "It's so boring! I want

to change it up, but Dad says he's not spending any more money on decor. I mean, come on! This place could use a facelift!"

I can honestly say I have no idea what she means; the room is perfect. "I like it."

"You can have it." Ally laughs and picks up a frilly pillow, then proceeds to toss it to the floor. It lands on a pile of tank tops and shorts with a thud. "So, what's new in the land of the dead?"

"What?"

"The funeral home. Anything juicy happen lately?"

"If that's your way of asking if anyone else died, then no. Nothing juicy."

"Crap."

My lips purse. "Are you seriously upset no one died?"

"Not upset. Disappointed. With all the stuff we found in the library, I'm itching for some more excitement. It got my Sherlock nose twitching."

"About what we found..." I whisper and stop myself immediately. The point of coming over to Ally's house is not to spill all my deep dark secrets. It's to find some clues which might tell me why I saw her in the vision and why she was covered in blood. But Ally makes it impossible. She'd been glued to my side since we got here, chattering non-stop and giving me little chance to get away. She even followed me to the bathroom and spent the entire time talking on the other side of the door. Is this what teenage girls are like out there in the real world? It's exhausting.

Ally's ears perk up and she tosses another pillow off the bed and inches closer to me. "Tell me everything," she demands.

I sigh dramatically and hope it's enough to get her to stop prying. It is not. "I'm serious, girl. Spill it."

I try to think of an excuse to leave but nothing comes to mind, probably because I don't really want to leave at all. Can there be bodies buried in Ally's backyard? Maybe. Is she going to kill Daxon? Possibly. Do I still want to tell her everything I know?

Definitely.

I glower and lean back on my elbows. "Turns out my dad didn't leave on his own," I say. "Mom made him go."

"Bitch move," Ally says. "Sorry, go on."

"She thinks he's crazy and after hearing what she told me, I don't blame her. But there's something else," I say. "She said my dad was part of an organization that believes Marzanna is some savior. Oh, and he knew I was going to get the visions even before I had them. She said he was prepping me."

Ally's bottom teeth rest squarely in her lap. "No. Freaking. Way." She blinks twice and flips her long hair over her shoulder. "Why didn't she tell you all this crap before?"

"I have no idea," I admit. "I think she was scared of what he had planned for me. Or she really does think he's insane and wanted him out of our lives for good."

"It does sound a little unhinged."

"Not considering everything we found out so far. And I

do have the visions, so he wasn't wrong about that part. He left a journal behind, but Mom took it away before I had a chance to read through it."

Mischief glimmers behind Ally's eyes when she says, "Girl, you so need to find him."

"One step ahead of you. I already emailed him, but I don't even know if it's a current address."

"Holy crap!" She claps her hands together and pushes her face in mine. "Do you think you can like force a vision to happen? Tell you where he is and stuff."

A lump pushes against my tonsils. "It's not really how it works and even if it did, I'd rather not have any visions at all." I pause, rubbing my temples. "They're kind of horrifying."

"I could imagine."

She truly could not.

"Hey," Ally says. "Promise me if you ever see me die or whatever, you'll tell me?"

You dying is not the problem at hand. I avert my eyes and stare out the window. "There's more," I say. This is it. The moment of truth. I'm going to tell her about Daxon and see how she reacts, then I'll have my answer. Or I'll anger her enough to kill me first. Either way, I have to risk it. I rub my hands together and count the steps to the bedroom door, angling my body so I am ready to escape if needed. "I did see someone die. Not you."

Her eyebrows arch. "Who?"

"Daxon. I saw Daxon die."

"NO!" she yelps. "Who the hell would want to kill Daxon Thorn? He's too hot to die."

Wait, what? I tilt my chin and lean into her, breathing in the air around her. It tastes sweet and bitter at the same time, like licorice and vinegar. Or the diner coffee. She must have not had a chance to wash the smell off her before she called me over, though she doesn't seem the least bit bothered by it. I, on the other hand, am suffocating. I pull away from her and put a pillow between us. "You can't think of anyone who might want to hurt him?"

"Are you kidding? Everyone loves Daxon," she says. "What's not to love, right?"

"I guess."

"Have you told him yet?" Ally asks.

I wince. "No. I will, but I need more time."

"For what?"

"To stop it."

The pillow between us is thrown off the bed as Ally creeps in closer, eyes wild. "I'm in," she says. Seriously, what? Ally slaps her thighs and her long legs jiggle in response. "If you're going to defy death or whatever, I want to help. We're going to save that little bastard!"

My teeth start to show even though I'm trying hard not to laugh. Despite keeping my cool, my heart beats a tiny bit faster and my bones rattle in my skin. I wanted proof Ally was not a danger to Daxon and I think I might have found it. It isn't much to go on, but Ally's reaction to my vision is in direct opposition to what I expected.

But.

How do I explain what I saw?

I bury the thought down and cross my arms. "First thing's first," I say. "I have to find my dad. He has the answers we need, I know it."

"When did you ask him to meet you?" Ally asks.

"Tonight. At the cove."

Ally reaches over me to the bedside table and grabs a hair tie, scrunching up her hair into a messy top bun. "It always has to be the damn cove, doesn't it?" she notes. "Promise you won't try to drown yourself at least? I won't be around to save your ass this time."

She laughs and continues to finesse her hair into a wild creation resembling a lion's mane while I sit silent on the edge of the bed. I don't know how to explain to her the cove isn't the problem. Because it isn't always the damn cove, as she put it; it's always me. It has to be me.

23

The red spot on my stomach rubs against the waistband of my jeans and I fight the fingers reaching to scratch it. If I leave it alone, it should clear up in a few days; at least, it's what I heard from a kid in school once who boasted about his brother staying in the cove water for almost a half hour and returning with a fierce rash across his back. The boy—I don't remember his name now—said it was the color of salmon eggs, looked like them too. I pull up my sweater and inspect the dot. The description is spot on.

My skin is rippled with goosebumps, the evenings colder and less forgiving in this time of year. I think I feel a few snowflakes land on my cheeks, but it is only the wind nipping away at me. Near me, water laps the shore and I am relieved to be alone here. Gives me a moment to think before Dad shows up.

If he shows up.

All the ways in which I can be wrong run through my mind; it was the wrong email, an old email, or worse, the right one after all. Maybe Dad saw my message and decided not to come. I can picture him now, thick frames sliding down the bridge of his nose as he furrows his brow in disappointment at having been found after so many years of hiding. What if Mom is right, and he really is a bastard? I refuse to believe it. Dad didn't leave because he didn't want me, he left because she made him, and I will never forgive her for it. I don't care what reasoning she had for it. Mother took away a piece of me and lied about it. Parents are supposed to do what's best for their children, but nothing about what she did seems right to me. Despite what she thinks, I am not a child, not really. I don't know what I am anymore.

Someone who needs answers.

Talking with Ally this morning gave me a confidence I don't deserve to have and as I sit on the rocks, I feel it slowly draining away. In my head, visions replay on a deadly loop, and I choke them down, swallowing them like stale soup. They gargle on the way down, fighting to escape and scraping the inside of my throat until it is so sore, I dry heave in my mouth. Beyond the trees protecting the cove, the low hum of a car driving by echoes toward me and my shadow stretches in the darkness. A door slams, followed by footsteps. I narrow my eyes and watch the trees with anticipation and dread building in my stomach. Right where the rocky shoreline meets the trees, a figure emerges and as it grows in size, I get smaller and smaller. My heart beats loud and quick and I forget what to do with my hands, so I cross them, hoping to keep myself intact with the small gesture.

"Nastya?"

His voice is everything. Low and growly, like he was woken from a deep slumber. It is the same as I remember it.

I gawk at him, tears stinging the back of my eyes. "Hi, Dad," I say, burying my feet into the gravel to keep from running to him. He doesn't look much different from the photographs, aged, but not different. One side of his mouth is still crooked and raised in a permanent half-grin, and the unruly blonde hair I used to twist around my fingers hangs low on his brow, prominent cowlick parting it awkwardly to the side. I stare at the black frames of his glasses and fight the reflection to find his eyes, gasping when I find them. "Thanks for coming," I whisper.

He takes a step toward me, then stops. "I can't believe you're here."

"I could say the same to you," I bite back. I don't like the venom in my voice or the way it stings my tongue when I speak. Relaxing my jaw, I say, "I wasn't sure you'd make it."

It bothers me how formal we are with each other. Cold and hazy; strangers instead of family. Dad rolls his neck and dares another step forward. "Does she know you're here?"

I shake my head. We both understand who he's talking

about and while a part of me wants to change the subject and keep Mother out of this, I don't bother to say much more. I didn't ask him here to talk about her and I fear if we keep discussing Mother, I will waste the short time we have. I cannot risk it. "She told me everything," I say.

"Everything?" Dad cranes his neck, and his eyebrows rise in an arch over his glasses. "You're going to need to be more specific."

He is digging for information and for a second, I see so much of Mother in him. The same distrust and the same need to be one step ahead of a conversation. With the trees behind him and the river behind me, I am trapped. Rubbery legs strain to hold the weight of my body and I sink into the ground. I suck in crisp air and let it fill my lungs until they burn. "What am I?"

Dad stumbles back as though I hit him. His hand presses to his chest and I worry he's going to have a heart attack and drop dead in front of me. Tears moisten his eyes, and he rubs his fingers under his glasses before collecting himself. The man was always keen on theatrics, and when I was little, I found it amusing. Now, I want to slap him silly. I have no time to entertain his acts and even less patience. "Stop dancing around it," I say. "Mom told me what happened before you left, everything you tried to do when I was a kid. I need to know why. Who are you? What is the Marzannite Order?" Slouching, I add, "Why am I different?"

He doesn't answer right away, and when he does, I wish he didn't. "That is an awful lot of questions, Nastya," says my father. "Let me guess, Elena painted me as some monster. Or did she say I was insane? Brainwashed perhaps?"

"She didn't paint you at all," I respond.

"Ah. Yes, that does seem more her style."

"Look," I say. "All I have is what she told me and trust me, it doesn't make you come off great."

"And yet, you're here," Dad says.

I flick my eyes away and swirl the words in my mouth to taste them thoroughly, making sure each one is the correct flavor of truth. "She's right to be afraid."

"Hmm," he says, then pauses. "It's one way of looking at it."

"What's another?"

"Your mother will never understand me, us. She's too pragmatic and serious, especially when it comes to you. She couldn't see your full potential, Nastya; couldn't wrap her head around it. You needed me to guide you and she couldn't stand it. Wouldn't. I take it the visions finally came?"

I nod.

"Good, that's very good. When?"

My sight fails me, and I glimpse myself on the playground swings, rising higher and higher, the wind blowing through my soft hair. My fingers wrap around the chains, and I slam my teeth together moments before I let go. Then I am flying, soaring through the air with the determination of a hawk. My arms shoot out and crash into Christine's tiny chest as I tackle her to the ground. She falls backward, butt hitting the sand first. Head spinning, I roll off her and lie at her side, joy emanating through my body. Christine laughs and I laugh with her, our tiny hands clutched together as we try to contain ourselves before the teacher comes to break us apart. "My turn," Christine says, but I do not hear her. All I feel is pain, not mine, hers. I feel her heart stop. I see her die.

"Nastya?" Dad asks, pulling me from the memory.

"Soon after the surgery," I say. "They started soon after the surgery."

"What happens when they come?"

I suck in a breath. "Death."

"Wonderful, Nastya. Amazing, actually." He inches closer to me. "We were right about you. What you have, this gift, it's an honor. Your mother should never have pushed me away. She doesn't get it; you're special. Important."

The praise falls on deaf ears because he is so far from the truth, it is but a small dot in the rear view mirror. I am not special. I am cursed. "What would you know of it?" I ask. "You have no idea what it's like, you haven't been here. All I do is hide. I have no friends, no life, no future. Mom may have forced you to leave, but you're the one who stayed away. You could have reached out to me. If I'm so freaking special, why did you never come back for me?"

Rage coats my skin and it ricochets off him. My eyes flash red and the hands cradling my chest are now in tight fists at my side. I can't tell what I want more; to get answers or to pummel the man before me into the ground. Both, I think.

Dad's face pales, and his mouths twists into a bow. "I'm sure you didn't ask me here for this," he says. I am acutely aware of how unapologetic he sounds. "I may not have been around, but it doesn't change what you are. No amount of hiding will change it, and I wish Elena understood it."

"This isn't about her. It's about you."

"That is where you're wrong, bug," he says. "I am irrelevant."

"Convenient," I hiss out through clenched teeth.

As he draws in, I stand my ground.

"You're ready," Dad says.

My gaze catches his and I cock my head, struggling to make sense of him. Even this close, he remains a mystery. Not in the way mother is, but truly disguised. "Ready for what?"

"For the future."

The blood in my veins bubbles and tears through me. "I don't understand."

"You will." He reaches for me and pats my shoulder. "Come with me."

"No."

Dad chuckles and puts some distance between so I can breathe again.

"Do you want to find out why you are the way you are?" he asks.

I waver. "Why can't you tell me here?"

"You asked about the Marzannite Order, so I'll do you one better. I'll take you to them. It'll be easier to explain everything this way."

I should be afraid. I should really be afraid. Yet, I am not, and the way he smiles only reinforces it. Straightening, I glance back at the river and whisper a silent prayer to the water, then turn back to Dad. "I can't be gone long," I say. "Mother thinks I'm out for a walk."

"Understood," Dad says and walks into the trees.

I march after him, stomach in knots and hair loose. Branches slice my skin as I brush against them, and when we reach Dad's old beater of a car, I can't help but breathe a little faster. Rust coats the metal and the once shiny blue is washed out and dull now. It reminds me of Daxon's eyes. Dad jiggles the handle, the door screeching as he glides it open to let me in. The car is small, and yet when I climb in, it doubles in size. It might be a Coupe, but to me, it is an ocean on wheels; a tide carrying me off. The engine groans to start and as Dad shifts to reverse, I buckle in and keep my gaze out the window, watching the trees shrink into the distance until I cannot see them at all. Overhead, the moon lights up Cherry Cove and I hold on tight to the seatbelt, leaving the town behind. The road spans for miles before us and I glance at Dad, memorizing the way he looks in this moment. The way he feels on this night. Behind us, the town drops off and hills grow out of the earth on either side as we barrel toward uncertainty.

I sag in the ripped leather seat.

Answers. I am finally going to get some answers.

24

Dad pulls off the road and I check my phone to make sure Mother hasn't messaged me. Nervous energy runs through me as the car takes a sharp right and rolls into a motel parking lot that's empty except for a few scattered cars. I eye Dad suspiciously. When he notices me, his lips quiver and his cheeks flush. "Best thing I could get on short notice."

"Could be worse," I say, hoping to ease the awkward exchange between us.

Parking the rust bucket in one of the many empty spots, Dad climbs out and nods to the small staircase leading to the second floor of the motel. As we climb, I try not to touch the railing, or anything else for that matter. Everything in the motel looks to be covered in grime; from the dirty walls to the mud-covered cement balcony wrapping around the entire building. Shut doors greet us as we walk down the corridor. My eyes flutter to the parking lot below and I swallow the lump in my throat while Dad fumbles with the key. The door finally opens and light streams from inside and I shield my face with my hand. "This is her?" a sharp voice asks.

I peer around Dad's shoulders to see a scrawny woman perched on the only chair in the room. Her hair is light, brighter than Dad's and almost as silver as mine. They have the same hooked nose, but the woman's turns slightly to the right, making it look like it is attempting to escape her face. Her cheekbones are sharp enough to cut stone and the prominent length of her chin is unnatural to the rest of her face. She looks to be stretched out, made of soft clay and pulled to her limits. The woman rests her elbows on the round table in front of her and looks me up and down. "She's small."

Dad mumbles under this breath and steps aside to fully reveal me.

"This is Zasha," he says. "Your aunt."

My head spins and my thoughts lay in a jumbled pile in the corner of my brain. I inspect the woman, trying to find some similarity between us and come up empty. As far as I can tell, she is not a woman at all. Eyes devoid of any emotion burn into me and I battle the need to stumble back. The woman, Zasha, purses her thin lips and sneers. "Good to finally meet you, Nastya. We heard a lot about you."

I check the room. There is no one here but us so I'm not

sure who she could be referring to. "Um, you too," I croak out. "I think."

"I see she got Elena's mouth," Zasha says.

There is no venom in her voice, so she doesn't mean to offend me, yet I am hurt, nonetheless. Mother might have a mouth on her, but it's one feature I'm glad to have inherited. I grin, wondering if Zasha knows her attitude doesn't put her too far off from the same spectrum of rudeness she seems to place me in. At my side, Dad removes his glasses to polish them before waltzing across the room to sit on the double bed in the center. I watch him, grateful to have someone else to look at other than the viper on the chair.

Someone isn't great at first impressions.

"Where are the others?" Dad asks.

Zasha kisses her teeth, gaze never leaving my small frame in the doorway. "Went out for food. I wasn't sure when you'll be back, so I had them get you a sandwich to go." She looks past me. "Didn't get anything for you. Sorry."

"It's fine," I say. "I'm not staying long."

Dad and Zasha, his sister, exchange knowing glances, but no one utters a word. I turn to dad. "You said I'm going to meet the Marzannite Order."

"Not very patient either," Zasha mumbles. I shoot her a deadpan glare.

"If they're not here, I need to get back," I say.

"They'll be back soon," the viper hisses. "In the meantime, why don't you sit down and wait? And close the door behind you, the draft is giving me a headache."

Coming here was a mistake. Not only am I not getting the answers I wanted, but I'm starting to despise Dad's sister. I didn't come here to find heinous family members. Maybe Mom was right and I should stay away from the people Dad associates with. Before I have a chance to bolt out of the room, Dad straightens on the bed and fixes Zasha with a stare I am very familiar with. It is the same one he used when I misbehaved as a child; one which tells you trouble is coming. "Lay off her," he says. "Nastya is new to this world and we're here to guide her, not scold her like she's a child. I was hoping the others would be here to fill her in, but I guess the two of us will have to do for now." He gets up and walks to the coffee machine on the table. "Do you want something to drink?"

I shake my head, staying put in the open doorway to spite Zasha.

"What would you like to know?" Dad asks.

Everything.

I bite my lip and cross my arms. "You said I was special," I say. "Why? Why do I have the visions? Are there others like me? Have you met them?"

Firing the questions off relieves some of the pressure on my chest and my shoulders slump down as soon as I am done. I wait for Dad to answer but he turns to Zasha. "Elena kept her in the dark," he explains.

"Stupid woman," Zasha says. She looks to me. "Sorry."

I only just met her but I imagine this is the closest to

friendliness I will get from the woman, so I let it go. "It's fine."

The coffee maker sputters and spits out muddy liquid into Dad's cup and he recoils from it as he mixes in two spoons of powdered creamer and sniffs the rising steam. His face scrunched, he takes a gulp, cringing the entire time. "I really miss the diner coffee. Awful stuff," he says, winking at me. "Remember the time you tried it when you were little? I thought you were going to throw up all over the table."

"Probably why you're not supposed to give kids coffee," Zasha says with a scoff.

"Probably," Dad agrees.

They both laugh and I find myself taking a few small steps into the motel room. Dad mentions another memory, one I don't really remember, and Zasha nods in agreement as though she was there. I wonder how much of our lives he shared with her, with everyone else in his family. The idea makes me uneasy, and I tighten my arms over my chest to still my racing heart. The two of them seem so comfortable together, bickering and laughing as siblings should, and I can't help but imagine an alternate reality in which I fit into this mold of family they're a part of. A world where Dad never left and where Mother didn't become the cold and distant creature I now live with. Some non-existent world in which I am outside of myself and without the visions.

That's not your life, I remind myself. A chill runs down my back and as much as I'd like to keep Zasha uncomfortable, I walk into the room. The two watch as I stumble across the red carpet and lower to sit at the edge of the bed. My eyes find my shoelaces when I say, “I learned some things about Marzanna. I’m hoping you can tell me how much of it is true.”

“Hard to say without knowing what you discovered,” Zasha counters.

True enough. I flex the muscles in my lower back, using them to hold myself up like a rag doll. “All I learned is she’s the Goddess of Death and supposedly lives in some mirror palace underwater. Oh, and something about snakes guarding a bridge leading to the palace. It’s not much.”

“Not much, indeed,” Dad says.

At the table, Zasha crosses one long leg over the other and lets out an annoyed sigh. She turns to face me fully and I feel the mattress sink under me and wrap over my thighs so I cannot move. “Some of it isn’t too far off,” she says. “Marzanna is the Goddess of Death, but it isn’t quite as morbid as it sounds. We like to think of it more as rebirth, the beginning of a new cycle. The snakes are a common symbol in our circle, though no one truly knows their origin. No one has ever gotten close enough to the Goddess or her palace to confirm.”

She speaks of the myth as though it was a solid thing, and I hear Mother’s warnings in my mind telling me Dad and his family are delusional. I lock the thoughts away, determined to hear Zasha out no matter how crazy she sounds. Maybe if I wasn’t a walking predictor of death, I’d see things differently. For now, I reserve my judgment. Any explanation is better than none at this point. "And the order is what exactly? Like a religion?"

"Not quite," Dad answers. "Think of us as servants of the Goddess. We are here to facilitate her until she is ready to emerge again."

Mother was right, they are definitely not in their right mind. I try to keep my expression blank, but my doubts bubble to the surface. Zasha catches it, a frown spreading over her face. "This would all be much easier if Elena didn't poison you with her close-minded opinions."

"She did her best," I say.

"And I'm sure she raised you well," Dad interjects. "But if you really want to understand who you are, Nastya, you need to abandon everything your mother told you. Your gift is not a curse, and it is not to be hidden away from the world. As I said before, you are important. Not only to us, but to everyone."

"Why? Why me?"

It is Zasha's turn to make some sense of the crazy, and I see her battle the need to scold me again for asking questions she believes I should already have answers to. "Every fifth generation, Marzanna blesses a child with the gift to see those destined to join her ahead of their time. It is a great honor to receive such a gift, one I wish I had gotten myself."

"But you didn't?"

"No," she says. "It was not my time. It was yours."

My body recoils from her, bones swimming inside the

suit of my skin. "I fall into the fifth generation? That's why I have visions?"

"Correct."

"I don't understand what the point of them is if I can't do anything to stop them. Why would she give me a gift to see death coming but not a way to interfere?"

It's laughable how quickly I fall into their trap. As I speak, the words don't taste like my own. I scold myself for entertaining their delusions. Here I am, in a shifty motel room with a man I haven't seen in years and a woman who gives a whole new meaning to stranger danger. Yet instead of running, I'm fitting the pieces of the puzzle together and seeing which one fits. Surprisingly, what Zasha says makes sense to me and I wonder if it makes me as dangerous as she is.

"The visions are not there for you change them," Dad says. "They're a gift from the Goddess, so you can see the true power she possesses. She trusts you, Nastya. Enough to show you the ones she will take before she takes them. You should be proud."

"Of what?" I snap. "Of being surrounded by death all the time? I don't think that's something I want to be proud of."

"Then you are a fool like your mother," Zasha says.

"Zasha," Dad warns.

"I'm sorry, Alexei, but it has to be said. She needs to see how important this is if she's to do what is needed. The eclipse is almost here, and you need to get your daughter in check. We have worked too hard for it to get screwed up by Elena's meddling."

I spread my legs apart and cross my arms. Air catches in the base of my throat and I press my lips flat together, letting it escape slow as molasses. "What does the eclipse have to do with this? With me?"

Another silent gaze passes between them, and I am on the verge of losing it. "Tell me now," I demand.

Dad hunches, though I find no comfort in the gesture. "It is said on the day of a solar eclipse, Marzanna's soul leaves the mirror palace and drifts into the void between our worlds. She fills waters, red as blood, with her spirit until her power is in every wave. As the disappearing sun rises high above, she waits."

"For what?"

"To be welcomed in," Zasha whispers.

"Sorry, are you saying that during the eclipse, this freaking Sunday, this Goddess of yours is coming here? To earth?"

"Not without an invitation, but yes."

For a split second, my breathing suspends, and I fear I might suffocate in the retched motel room. I shake my hands out, battle my rigid ribs and force air inside. "But why? And did you say water red as blood? Like cove?"

"Why do the deities do anything?" dad asks. "We don't have this answer. We do know Cherry Cove is key to all of this and the center of where it will happen. In our years of research, it is the closest place resembling the myth we could find. With the water tainted red, it stands to reason it will be the center of Marzanna's ascension. This is our chance to bring the Goddess forth, and we need your help accomplishing our mission. She gave you the gift for a reason, Nastya. It's like a text message, a note telling you she will be there, and she will be waiting for you."

Spit gathers in my mouth, and I swallow it down as pressure builds at my temples. My fingers play with the string of my hoodie, and I try to find Dad's eyes. They are hidden behind the reflection of his glasses. "You're telling me I'm connected to her?"

"In every way."

Somehow, it makes sense. The visions, the strange pull I have to the cove; it all comes back to this story. A part of me searches for the lie, but I cannot find it. Dad and Zasha's story seems to fit, and, as strange as it sounds, it does explain the things happening to me. It definitely explains the visions. A thought pops into my mind and I choke on it. "What about Kye?" I ask. "And the flower shop owner?"

"I don't know who these people are," Dad responds.

"People from town," I explain. "I had visions about them, but long after they died. And I found poppies on both their bodies and in the place where Kye died. What do they mean?"

I didn't notice Zasha move, but when I look up, she is sitting beside me on the bed, her hands cradled in her lap. "If you saw poppies, I gather Marzanna is sending you a message. The poppy is her flower of choice."

"What kind of message?"

"Uncertain," Zasha says. "Perhaps a warning to be ready. When did you see these visions?"

"Recently. Last couple of weeks."

"It must be what I said, then. It would make sense for her to reach out to you so close to the eclipse. She must be eager."

At least someone is. "So, you don't think she had anything to do with what happened to them? With their deaths, I mean."

Zasha laughs in my face. "Impossible. The Goddess doesn't kill, she simply ushers the dead. Brings them from our world to hers to rest for all eternity. She watches over them, as any good mother would. If she sent you visions of these people, rest assured their souls are in good hands. You should be pleased."

My thoughts land on Daxon and Ally and I struggle to piece together how they are involved. If I am truly receiving messages from Marzanna, why would she warn me of Daxon's death? And why show me Ally? As usual, I am missing pieces.

The edges of my lips pull down when I remember what day it is. Thursday evening. Tomorrow is Kye's viewing and I'm sure Daxon will show up. How much do I tell him? I wish to share everything, but it's not the correct decision. After what happened to Mother when she found out about the Marzannite Order, I don't want Daxon following the same path. I'm being selfish. He deserves the truth, no matter how unrealistic it sounds. In the least, he deserves to know Kye's death was an accident after all. Perhaps he will find some peace in that and finally let his guilt go.

When he does, he will leave me.

I don't want that, but what I want is irrelevant. If Daxon is gone from my life, he might no longer be in danger. If I really have a connection to this Goddess of Death, perhaps I can bargain for his safety. Dad said I cannot interfere, but if the myths are true, the Goddess needs me. It's a long shot, but I still get some satisfaction from having the upper hand if I should ever need it.

The wind howls outside, and I shift my weight, pushing away from Zasha's cold glare. I don't trust her—Dad either—and I already saw how Mother can lie through her teeth without so much as batting an eyelash. Everyone around me spins webs of untruths, and I can't tell who I can believe anymore. The only one who remains solid and honest is Daxon, so if I have to raise a death Goddess to save him then that is exactly what I intend to do.

Rising on trembling legs, I peel my eyes off Zasha. "Take me home," I say.

Dad doesn't agree, but he doesn't disagree either.

"You will help us?" Zasha asks behind me.

I bloat my lungs with air and let it out slowly. "I'll think about it," I answer.

There is no need to think as my mind is already made up, but I don't show my cards yet. Time is slipping away from me, and I count the minutes I waste standing in the motel room. Tomorrow, I will tell Daxon everything. Until then, I must find out everything I can about Marzanna, so I can decide how to proceed.

"Mom has a journal of yours," I say to Dad. "Will it have more information on all of this?"

He nods, walking over to the bedside table and opening the top drawer. He pulls out a leather-bound notebook identical to the one Mother took from me and hands it over. "Elena will never give up my journal. Chances are she already destroyed it so you couldn't get to the truth." Dad nudges the book toward me, and I take it. "This contains everything about the Goddess. Everything I am is in this book."

I press the soft leather into my chest. Everything he is... Everything I am is in there with him.

25

Some pages in dad's journal are out of order and it takes Daxon and I the better half of the hour to piece it together. Scraps of notes and torn articles are shoved in random spots of the journal, most of which make very little sense to either of us. We've been in the woods behind the funeral home for quite some time now and I'm starting to wonder if Dad's journal is a gateway to more unanswered questions. Frustrated, I grab one article and unfold the ragged paper, spreading it over the tree trunk we sit on. "This one isn't in English either," I say.

Daxon takes out his phone and begins to input the words into a box on a translation website. It takes him a while to get through the title, his fingers clumsily hitting the keys of the Russian keyboard app he downloaded earlier.

"The body of a girl was discovered early this morning. Suspects remain at large," he reads out. Daxon checks the date of the article and frowns. "Twenty years ago, give or take."

I study the faded photograph in the body of the text, connecting it to some of the others we managed to translate. "Looks like it happened near the Volga River again. Why does my dad have these?"

"No clue," Daxon says, shrugging. He flips the journal to a handwritten page and turns it my way. "There's more on the Goddess here. Check out the date."

Hastily, I tear the book from his hands and read through Dad's neat entry. There is no title, only clumsy sentences carefully strewn together. The date on the top right corner reads October 22nd, 2001. The same day as the article. "It is beginning to occur earlier and earlier. Did we miscalculate the timing? Are we too late?" I read out loud. "Another body was discovered in the river today and the police are as blind as ever. If they could only open their eyes and see the truth around them. The Goddess taunts my waking dreams and I feel us running out of time. Winter is almost upon us, and we are yet to find the conduit. Perhaps this is not our year."

The entry ends there, signed with my dad's name and a rough sketch of the triangular symbol we've found all over the journal.

"You think the girl's death had something to do with the Goddess?" Daxon asks.

"Probably," I answer. My stomach tightens. "Dad seemed to think so."

"So he's been at this for a while. All over the world it looks like."

I glance to the photograph again, then back to Daxon. "I guess. I didn't even know he'd been to Russia, Mom never mentioned it."

"Maybe she didn't know."

"Maybe," I whisper.

Keeping my hands steady, I flip a few more pages. My eyes remain unfocused and even though I'm looking at the journal, I do not see it. If Dad thought this would provide me with some answers, he was way off. The entire book reads like the ramblings of a lunatic. Obscure passages on folklore, some of which resemble what we know of the Goddess, mixed with random pieces of broken thought. There is no rhyme or reason to anything in the journal.

It is as muddled as me.

I don't notice when Daxon takes the journal from me, staring into my lap through a lens of despair for what feels like hours. Dad's words replay in my mind on a loop. *Everything I am is in this book.* Who are you, Dad?

"Check this out," Daxon says, nudging my side. I turn to him, pupils dilated and skin crawling.

My fingers brush against the page in the journal he has opened and my spine steels as I begin to read.

'She craves to be free. Longing. Feeling. Waiting.

Beyond the bridge, they wait for her, and their light draws her in.

Water red as blood.

Sky dark as night.

She is everywhere and she is nowhere.

She is trapped.

But not for long.

The water ripples, dances before her as light streams from above.

She calls on them, her dutiful soldiers, those the earth forgot.

But she will not forget them.

She is theirs and they are hers.

And they are hungry. Starving.

Dead but not dead.

Reborn.

She will be reborn.

She will rise.'

I recite the words again in my head and close the journal, palm pressed to the indentations on the spine. My body quivers and my bones are liquid. I am liquid. Tightening my hold on the book, I bury my feet into the earth and straighten. The motion is harder than it should be, and it takes me a moment to regain enough strength to hold myself upright. "I don't like the sound of that."

"Me either. Dutiful soldiers doesn't sound good," Daxon agrees. "What do you he means by 'dead but not dead'?"

"I don't know," I admit. There's is so much I still don't understand, and it makes me want to scream and punch things. "Zasha said the Goddess ushers the dead, cares for them somehow. Maybe the soldiers are people who died?"

"It doesn't make sense. Why would my dad want to summon a Goddess guarding the dead?"

Daxon shrugs and leans back on the stump. "Beats me. Why does anyone do anything? People get obsessed and by the looks of it, your dad has been thinking about this for a long time. All his life maybe. It's a long time to convince yourself of a thing, even if it is impossible."

"What if it's not impossible?" I ask.

"You think he's right? The Goddess of Death is waiting to come out of hiding? To do what?"

I have no idea. Whatever she plans to do, whatever my dad plans to do, it can't be anything good. Even if I did believe he isn't delusional, and that's a massive 'if', I still wouldn't help him. I'd have to be as crazy as him to want to free a Goddess guarding the dead. Who knows what else will come through with her. I've had my fare share of dealing with death to know nothing good comes from intervening with what can't be changed. The Goddess, if she exists, is locked away for a reason. Sometimes, things hidden should remain so.

"Nastya?" Daxon says right as my phone vibrates on the stump. I pick it up and read the message from an unknown number, my blood freezing. Beneath me, the dead tree sinks into the earth, and I have to put more pressure on my legs to keep from sinking with it. My muscles throb and my skin is glued to the phone as I look at Daxon.

"Whatever Dad is up to, I'm about to find out," I say. "He wants me to meet him at the cove. Now. He said the rest of the Order will be there."

It's always colder by the river than it is in the rest of the town, and I zip up my jacket so heigh, my mouth is covered and only my nose and eyes jot out. As I walk through the trees and toward the cove, Dad's journal in my grasp, my pulse speeds up. In the near distance, I hear voices rise toward me and I pause, inspecting. Between tree branches, I spot my dad on the beach, Zasha beside him. Scattered across the rocks are people I don't recognize and their presence confuses me. They look normal and not the sinister group I expected. Though I'm not sure what it is I expected at all.

Robes and sacrificial lambs, perhaps.

Not this.

I part the branches and walk out. Strange eyes follow me as I cross the beach to Dad and Zasha. Whispered voices fill my ears and by the time I reach Dad, I'm sticky and covered in them. My legs shake and I try to keep a neutral expression despite the emotions rushing through me. Stopping a few feet from Dad and Zasha, I glance behind me, noticing a few people inching closer toward us. I fist my hands at my sides.

"Hi, bug," Dad says. His smile is wide and welcoming, but I don't feel welcomed at all. "Good to see you again."

"Why did you ask me here?"

Next to him, Zasha scowls and whispers something under her breath. Her sharp tone twists her features and elongates them, making her face look less human by the second. I make out my mother's name on her lips and my field of vision narrows to a pin. "Anything you'd like to say?"

"Welcome," Zasha bites out. She turns on her heel and walks away from me to join the others at my back.

"Don't mind her," Dad says. "Your aunt doesn't hide her emotions well. I'm sure you two will get along great once you spend some time with her."

I don't want to spend another minute with the woman, but I keep it myself. "So, why am I here?"

"I wanted you to meet the others," Dad says. "You're a big deal around here, Nastya. They're all excited to get to know you."

I look around, frowning.

"Come," Dad says. His hand brushes my lower back, never quite touching me yet leading me in the direction of the crowd all the same. Teeth chattering, I walk. I walk until I am surrounded by strangers. I walk until Dad stops.

I stop too.

At first, they are careful around me. They keep their distance and I'm grateful for it, relieved to have some personal space between myself and the crowd. Then it changes. Dad starts the introductions and I try to remember the names, but they all blend together. Hands reach out, unafraid of my touch. I shake them one by one, worry coursing through my veins for fear a vision might spur. When none come, I let my body relax. Dad continues marching us through the crowd and I continue to greet every new person I meet. Memories of my childhood parading around town flood my system. Is this what he's doing now? Checking for the visions?

I study Dad's expression, looking for a glimpse of malice, but find none there.

Calm down. He's only introducing you to his friends.

Family, I correct myself.

I check the crowd and search for familiar features, wondering how many of these people I am actually related to. Some have Dad's blonde hair, some have his nose. I even spot a few men with similar cowlicks. But none incite a familial connection in me. They wouldn't, of course. My parents are the only family I know. I glance to Zasha, standing off to the side and glowering, and disgust builds in the base of my belly. I still can't believe I'm related to her.

Perhaps Dad is right and she'll grow on me. Like a festering wound, I think.

Shaking the negativity off, I proceed to make my way through the crowd until I reach the last few. A young boy stretches his palm to me, and I almost don't take it. I don't think I can handle seeing another child's death. Dad watches me carefully and after an excruciating moment of silence, I give in and shake the boy's hand. His lips quiver and I worry I hurt him somehow simply by touching him. Then he does something I don't expect. The boy flips my palm and presses his small lips to my skin, then drops it and runs away giggling. His happiness is infectious and I find myself smiling from ear to ear. The boy runs up to an older woman, his grandmother I assume, and I see him whisper excitedly in her ear. They both turn to stare at me. The woman waves. I wave back.

I'm so entranced by the strange experience I almost forget Dad's journal in my hands. The leather scratches my skin and I push the journal in Dad's direction. "I almost forgot," I say. "I brought this back for you."

"Did you get the answers you needed?"

"Not by a long shot," I whisper.

Dad grins, pushing his thick-rimmed glasses further up his nose. "I'm sure it's all still very confusing. I had the journal for all my life and sometimes, I forget my thoughts might not transfer to paper quite as fluently as I want them to."

"What's with all the articles?" I ask.

"Ah, yes. Our family has been tracking instances of Marzanna's calls for some time now. Anything that might imply she is ready to come forward."

I grimace. "Girls dying is her way of telling you she's ready?"

"Yes and no," Dad says, answering nothing at all. "When I was younger, I spent a lot of time chasing deaths. I think I hoped one of them might lead me to the Goddess, or at least to the conduit. I was wrong, of course."

Of course. The conduit he seeks is me, or so he thinks.

"Thanks anyway," I say. I'm not sure what I'm thanking him for, but it seems appropriate. I dangle the journal between us. "You can have it back now."

"Keep it," Dad says. "It might help get you ready."

My eyebrows jump. "Ready?"

"For your destiny. If you choose to help us, of course."

"And if I don't?"

Dad takes a moment to think on it then says, "You'll do what's right in the end, bug. I know you will."

He is so sure of himself, it makes my mind waver. How can a thing so strange be black and white to him? How can he not see all the gray in between? I mean, sure, I can see death coming, but I don't believe some mystical Goddess is behind it. Maybe I'm simply an anomaly? Worse, maybe I'm crazy too, in a different way than Dad is. I look around the cove; different than all of them are.

I clutch the journal close to my heart and turn my head to see Dad clearer. "Tell me more about her."

He nods, leading us to a secluded spot on the beach away from the other members of the Order. When we settle on the rocks, Dad proceeds to tell me fables. Stories of a lonely Goddess forever cursed to guard the dead. Except the way he describes her, she doesn't sound cursed in the bit. She sounds blessed. Strong. Resolved. She sounds like the exact opposite of everything I am.

Dad tells me the story of how she came to be the Goddess of Death, how she was born of other deities and forever bound to a land hidden between the folds of our world. Marzanna was given the honor of caring for the souls which pass because of her intricate need to understand those lost. How she built a home in this land, Nav, a palace of mirrors to reflect not only herself but all those she protects. He tells me of her loneliness and all the ways in which the dead do not make for good company. This part I can relate to a little too seamlessly.

Then he speaks of Marzanna's first attempt at escape, which did not go according to plan. Despite her unnatural strength, the other deities, her parents, did not believe she belongs among the living. Some things must remain out of sight, as Dad puts it. It seems the Goddess did not agree and spent centuries trying to break free of the palace and come into our world.

"What of the dead she keeps?" I ask, wide-eyed.

Dad doesn't know and he says so. The dead will remain dead, but that doesn't seem to be of consequence to the Goddess. All she wants, all she hungers for, is to see the living. To be among them, if only for one day.

"So, what's stopping her?"

"The bridge," Dad answers. "While Marzanna can beckon the dead, she has no control over the entrance to Nav. Those were the conditions the deities agreed upon. If she truly wished to care for the souls long forgotten, she must sacrifice her own freedom and live among them for the rest of her days."

"Sounds lonely," I wager.

"I'm sure it is."

"Where do I come into this? You said she gave me visions as a way to communicate with me, to tell me she's waiting."

Dad's half-smile widens, his teeth gleaming in the sunlight. "When Marzanna realized she can never leave the palace on her own, she devised a new plan. Since the dead can pass the bridge unencumbered, she decided to use them to send a message. The legends are unclear, but it seems the message made its way here, to our world. Somehow, very long ago, a young girl on our side had the first vision. We're uncertain who gets them and why Marzanna chooses particular people to hear her call, but we do know it happens every fifth generation. Some muse it is because that is how long it takes for her strength to come back after sharing her gifts with a human. Some think it's the luck of the draw."

"What do you think?" I ask.

When he looks at me, I feel he is seeing me for the first time in years. Dad takes off his glasses, cleans them on his sweater, and puts them back on again. "I think it isn't luck at all," he says. "I think the Goddess selects only those strong enough to raise the bridge. Those who have seen it and did not feel its pull."

"People who died, you mean," I say. "People like me who died and didn't get stuck in this Nav place."

"Precisely. People like you."

The sun shifts its trajectory and harsh shadows fall across Dad's face. I glance at my watch, nervous of the time I've spent away from home. Mother must be going crazy not knowing where I am and though I don't much care what she thinks right now—I'm still furious with her for lying—I don't wish to keep her guessing any longer. Lies or not, she's still my mom and I shouldn't worry her this way. Dad sees me fidget and says, "You should get back home."

I'm pleased he understands.

"Will you come back tomorrow?" he asks. "I'll tell you more about the Goddess."

"Not tomorrow," I say. Tomorrow is Kye's viewing.

"But you'll be back?"

I smile and when I tell him 'yes', I mean it. Dad's stories may be just that, stories, but I want to hear more of them. Sitting here at the cove and listening to him speak reminds me of my childhood and I am not ready to say good bye to it yet. We missed so many years together, so many conversations, and the chance to have more of them—even if they are about things I don't quite believe in—draws me in. I need more time with Dad. More time to understand him.

More time not to be afraid like Mother.

I rise to stand, my shadow lengthening across the rocks. "Tell the others I enjoyed meeting them," I tell Dad.

With this, I tuck Dad's journal under my arm and walk into the trees and away from the river.

26

Melodies of ethereal bells and rain drops waft up the stairs, greeting me as I meticulously tie my hair up into a loose bun atop my head. As Mother's chosen soundtrack for Kye's viewing plays on repeat, I work to hide every unnatural thing about me. Today is not the day to stand out. My hands shake as I tie one of the silk scarves Mother gave me and pin it in place behind my ears. This one is red and orange, the color of burning, and the opposite of everything I fell right now. Icy blue would have been a more suitable choice. I step back from the bathroom mirror and inspect myself.

Black dress synched at the waist with thick, velvet fabric falling past my knees. The dress has a carnelian collar that itches like hell, and I have to bite down on my lip to keep from tearing it off. Mother bought it a few months ago in hopes of replacing my standard uniform of hoodies and leggings. I bet she didn't know I'd be wearing it to defy her today. It seems fitting enough and appropriate for a viewing, so despite the discomfort I feel, I straighten the folds of the skirt and walk out.

My shoulders beg to relax, but I flex them straight as I make my way down the stairs. Instead of turning left as I usually do, I face the other way, toward the back of the house and where the viewing room is set up; ready for this morning. From here, I can already smell the incense burning and the scent of sandalwood bombards me with every step. The melody gets louder, so loud in fact, I can barely make out the hushed whispers of the people inside.

People from town.

I wonder if Daxon is here yet.

A sudden need to flee twines through me when I face the wide French doors hiding the viewing room. The glass shimmers before me and I make out shapes within. All sitting. All quiet. All sad.

I take a deep breath, hold it, then swing the doors open to walk in.

As soon as I enter, the whispers stop. I am met with faces I don't recognize, and they all watch me so intently, I want to scream. White wooden chairs line me on either side, and I'm surprised to find most of them filled. Ally wasn't kidding when she said Kye was a popular kid because it seems half the town is here. On my right, I spot a familiar head of brown hair and my teeth split open when Daxon's eyes meet mine. He nods a curt hello, one corner of a quivering lip rising. Behind him, Ally waves and though she tries to appear nonchalant, I can see the darkness behind her eyes. They are red as blood; as though she had been crying for hours.

Strange, I think. It seemed like she didn't know Kye well enough to mourn him. Then again, I doubt any of the people here knew Kye. None of them except Daxon, who looks to be crumbling by the second. My eyes flick to the two people sitting beside him and nausea rips at my gut at the sight of his father. Mr. Thorn's expression is vague and hard to read but I can see right through him, straight to the nightmare beneath. He doesn't look at me when I enter, doesn't look at anyone. Not even his wife. I'm certain Daxon prefers it this way and a small sense of victory thrums in my chest as I walk.

I pass the Thorns, heading down the isle to the front where Mother is busy checking items off a list before starting the service. When I near her, it is as though she can sense my presence. Her eyes dart my way, a crestfallen expression on her face. Her nose wrinkles and I can all but hear her cursing me out under her breath. Or cursing herself out for not making it clearer that I am not to set foot down here today. Prior to today, Mother never had to instruct me to stay away from viewings. It was an unspoken rule and one I obeyed without question; hide from the world and never come in contact with anyone in town. She says it so often, it's become a commandment in our house; words etched in stone.

Mother's fingers are white around the clipboard, and she turns away from the mayor standing beside her to face me head on. My blood runs cold.

I watch her the entire way down the aisle as the people in the room come alive again. The silence is broken, floodgates bursting wide open. Whispers of disapproval rise around me, and I wince with every hushed word. They sound like snakes hissing.

"Is that her?"

"I can't believe they let her come here."

"Hasn't the poor boy suffered enough? Someone lock this monster up already."

My chest aches and I flinch, walking through the seated crowd like I am being shot with bullets. Legs numb, I reach Mother and stand beside her. She looks over my head to scan the room. "You should not have come here, Nastya," she says low enough for only me to hear.

"I had to," I respond. "For Daxon."

His name makes her skin pale, and I hate knowing that the simple act of me speaking of Daxon hurts her this much. I do not take it back, I will not. Kye was a stranger to me, but I am more connected to him than most of the people here. My eyes catch a middle-aged woman sobbing into the shoulder of a dark-haired man. I am immediately ashamed of my own thoughts. These must be Kye's parents. Neither of them looks my way and I am thankful for it.

Clearing her throat, Mother shakes her head then proceeds to raise the clipboard to her face. With one hand, she reaches for her phone, tapping a button to make the music lower in volume. A throat clears somewhere in the crowd, and I seek to spot the person it belongs to. I cannot see over the sea of eyes rolling over me.

"The Mitchells would like to say a few words," Mother begins. She doesn't have time to continue when chaos erupts in the room.

"Get her out of here!" someone yells.

"This is a disgrace!" another voice echoes.

I stand my ground, but it is quicksand under my feet.

A few people in the back stand and scurry out of the room, and my heart sinks to the floor. Not meaning to, my gaze flickers to Kye's parents, and this time, they look back. Tears flood Mrs Mitchell's eyes and Mr Mitchell hugs her closer to him. She opens her mouth to speak, but only a gasp escapes, followed by agonizing wails.

I am torn into pieces.

Beside me, Mother stiffens. "Go upstairs, Nastya," she instructs. "We'll talk about this later."

"But—"

"Out! Now!"

Her bark is equal to her bite, and I stumble back from the attack. My heart beats violently and my face burns as I run down the aisle and flee from the room. Shouts rise behind me, and I don't turn around, I don't stop running until I'm at the back door and pushing it open to let the cold wind inside. It hits my face, tying me in its fury as I rush out of the house and into the backyard. My body shakes violently, and my legs give out. I drop to my knees, skin scraping the dirt. The black velvet of my dress is muddy now, covered in every piece of filth it can swallow up as I dig my fingers into the ground. Heaving breaths burst from my mouth and I try to count to ten in my mind to collect myself, but I'm dizzy and undone before I can finish.

"Nastya?" a heady voice sounds behind me. I spin around and look up at Daxon. Sadness fills his face, but there is more there, beneath the surface. Anger, I realize. He crouches next to me, so close, I can taste the mint of his breath. "Are you okay?"

"No," I say truthfully. "Not really."

"They're assholes. All of them."

"They're not wrong," I say. "I shouldn't have come."

"Why did you?"

Our eyes meet and I sink further down. Daxon is closer than ever, and I do not wish to back away. His hand reaches for me, index finger tucking a strand of hair which refuses to stay hidden under my scarf. I choke on rising nausea. "For you," I whisper. "I had to come for you. Because he was important to you."

Daxon's mouth opens and closes like he is trying to find the right words. I feel foolish and exposed and when I move to stand, he stops me. The hand still lingering near my ear loops behind my head and Daxon weaves his fingers through the small hairs at the base of my neck. He pulls me into him, and I don't stop him. My eyes snap open and when his lips brush against mine, my entire body convulses. Daxon's kiss is feral, full of need and confusion. Full of hunger. It's nothing like what I see in movies or read about in books late at night after mother has gone to bed. This is... more.

A low moan stifles me and I exhale it into his mouth seconds before Daxon pulls away. There is a look of astonishment behind his eyes and though I cannot see myself, I am certain mine have the same. His lips quirk into a grin and the hand pressing into my neck stays solid and warm.

I don't want to interrupt this moment, but I must. "Daxon," I whisper.

"What is it?" he asks.

I swallow hard, mouth filling with saliva immediately after. My headache careens from temple to temple as I say, "I had a vision."

Daxon's hand drops away from me and he tilts his head to the side. "Now? In there?"

"No," I answer. "Before. Long before."

"I don't understand."

You're about to. I straighten, rubbing the grime on my hands on the skirt of my dress. "When we first met, back at the cove, I had a vision. It was about you," I explain. "I think you're in danger. I tried to figure it out, but I don't know what it means. Whatever it is, my visions are never wrong. I'm sorry."

I wait for him to respond. He only stares blankly. "Daxon, say something. Anything, please."

"You lied to me," he says in a hushed tone. His voice trembles, then steels. "You've been lying to me this whole time. I thought you were different, Nastya. You said you were different."

"I am," I object. "I didn't tell you because I didn't want it to be true. I wanted to stop it before anything happened to you. Then this whole thing with the Marzannite Order happened and my dad—"

"Your dad?"

I sigh. "There is so much I need to tell you. This thing, it's bigger than what we thought. But there's good news too," I add. "Kye's death, it was an accident. I'm sure of it."

I say this to offer a semblance of shelter from the brutal secret I've been keeping; some form of defense against the girl he should have stayed away from but didn't. I hope it is enough. I hope... I'm not sure what exactly.

Anything.

I watch as Daxon climbs to his feet and looks down at me. "You lied," is all he says.

Then he turns and walks back into the house, slamming the door shut behind him.

WITH DAXON GONE, I STAY ON THE GROUND AND LET the earth seep into my skin. My eyes are red and dry and though I attempt to cry, no tears come. Inside, sand swirls in my blood and I can taste the grain on my tongue. My body craves moisture, craves weeping, but I cannot provide it with relief. I do not know how.

Fingers digging into dirt, I stop dead when a door creaks open behind me.

"I ushered everyone out the front," Mother says to my hunched back. "You can go in now."

I don't.

She walks around me and leans in, towering over my shape and obscuring the sun like a stormy cloud. Mother tucks an index finger under my chin and pulls me up to look at her. "Do you want to explain why you decided to make that poor boy's final moment a circus act?"

My skin prickles and balls of frustration build up in my belly; Mother doesn't understand me at all, and I'm starting to realize she never did. She is as afraid of me as the rest of them. I think I might hate her. Pulling away from her, I wipe the spot her skin touched mine in disgust. "All I did was show up to a viewing," I say. "Didn't know it was a crime."

"Give me a break. We both know what this was," she

says coldly. "I understand you have a need to rebel against me, but, please, don't play me for a fool. You've been hiding things from me and I'm not so blind I can't see it."

"I guess it runs in the family then."

Mother scoffs, her chin butting out into a sharp point. Her nose follows. "What happened with the boy?" she asks. She still refuses to use Daxon's name. "I saw him follow you out here."

"Nothing happened. You don't have to worry about him anymore."

Digging the dirt from under my nails, I study her expression and patiently wait for the next attack. She must be proud of herself, pleased with the wedge between Daxon and I; ecstatic over owning all of me again. My knuckles are white and cold as I fist my hands at my side. The seconds of silence between us stretch to years, and I have to touch my brow to check for wrinkles by the time she speaks again. "I'm sorry," Mother says, so quietly I almost don't hear her.

"Are you?"

"I am. I know you're upset with me, but it doesn't change anything. Everything I've done is to keep you safe, to keep *us* safe. Tell me you understand that."

I don't tell her anything at all.

When she realizes I am not in the mood to converse, she purses her lips and looks down at my stained dress. "Toss it in the laundry," she says. "I'll wash it later."

Then she is gone, and I am alone in the backyard once more. I'd been out here so long, I think I see the trees lining the tilted fence containing our property line wilt before my eyes. Even with Mother gone, the sun refuses to brighten up this horrid day and I frown as I pick the last bit of earth from my fingers. Despite wanting to stay here forever, I walk back into the house and stand in the doorway, legs unsure of what they want to do next. From inside the viewing room, I hear the scraping of chairs across the wood floor as Mother tidies up after the service. Tendrils of smoke from blown out incense sticks tickle my nose and I gag, rushing past the French doors to my room. I shut the door behind me, turning the lock with more anger than is necessary, and head for the bed.

I want to sleep the day and my entire life away.

Not bothering to change out of the filthy dress, I hop onto the covers and rub my sneakers over them. Muddy footprints stain the swirling blue pattern until it looks like a puddle on a rainy day.

The covers are warm and welcoming, and my eyes are half closed as I climb into the bed and relax my head on the pillow. The pins holding the scarf in place dig into my scalp, though I don't take it off. My limbs are too tired and resemble the consistency of day-old pudding.

Under the pillow, a hard edge pricks my palm and I pause. My fingers claw under the pillow and in seconds, the fluffy mount is catapulted off the bed. I stare, dazed, and pull out the small envelope tucked under there and bring it up to my face. It is no different from the ones Mother sends out in the mail every week. A bill, perhaps?

I turn the envelope around, tongue glued to the top of my mouth as I inspect the wax stamp sealing it shut. A poppy red wax circle with a symbol in its center. My hand presses to my neck and I gasp. Though much clearer, the symbol is a replica of my scar. A single snake-like shape curving and slithering inside a cage of melted red.

My palm is grimy and wet and the paper wrinkles at the edges as I rip into the envelope to pull out the letter inside and read.

"Sunday, three o'clock. The cove."

My thoughts muddy up my brain and I glance to the wall-calendar above the small table in my room. "The day of the eclipse," I say in a hushed tone. "The exact time."

Blood runs cold within me as my gaze drifts down the letter to the bottom right corner where a single signature is etched in black ink.

The Marzannite Order.

I crumple up the letter and shove it back under my pillow. Absolutely no way in Hell. My fingers itch to reach for it again and I oblige, pulling out the rough ball and unfolding it in my lap. My pinkie taps against it as I settle my head, palm flat across the invitation from the people I should want nothing to do with. Dad's face flashes in my periphery and I shake my head, closing my eyes to shut him out. When I finally regain my senses, I toss the letter to the side and reach for Dad's journal tucked under one side of the mattress. It's warm and my nose is bombarded by the deep smell of worn-out leather as I flip it open to a random entry.

'Rivers red as blood welcome her home.
She is restless, eager, and ready for what lies ahead.
All around, there is only darkness and death.
But in the distance,
Too far to see clearly,
Is the one she chose.
Settled.
Strong.
Determined.
The rivers too will part and she will lead them forth
Into salvation.'

I slam the book shut with a groan.

Dad's journal is nothing but more riddles and wasteful words offering little solace or companionship. My eyes dart to the letter and I pick it up, hesitating. "The one she chose," I recite to the empty room. Me. I do not feel like a chosen savior, not even in the slightest. What I believe myself to be now, more than ever, is a beacon for death and for the Goddess who commands it. More than that, though. If I am truly picked for one impossible act, I get to decide what the act will be, and it is not what my dad or Marzanna had in mind. Yes, I will meet her as Dad expects. And yes, I will welcome her to our world, but I will not do so without getting what's mine. There is a deal to be made here.

A bargain for Daxon's life.

If the Goddess of Death wants to be free, she will give me something in return. She will give me Daxon.

Pressure builds behind my eyelids, and I part my lips to breathe until I sleep comes for me. It is slow at first, gnawing and aching and dragging me away from reality. When it finally takes me, the letter is still clutched in my hands.

I dream only of water.

27

How many times must I tread the same path before I finally learn my lesson?

It seems no matter what I do, I end up in the same spot. Back at the cove with my hands soaked in sweat while my feet shuffle across the stones. High above, the sky is already darkening and I can feel the air cool down as the moon spins around us to block the sunlight. The trees are quiet now; birds and animals hiding from the gloom about to overtake them. I wish I could hide with them.

My legs follow a familiar path and I swat branches out of the way as I make my way to the small beach waiting for me. My soul aches for an alternate reality; one in which I am walking to meet Daxon as I used to. I stop and look at my phone, grimacing at the lack of messages in my inbox. Ever since the viewing, I haven't heard a peep from him.

Ally has been quiet too, and I wonder if she decided I wasn't worth the bother after she saw how the town reacted to my presence. Mother has been quiet too, but it doesn't strike me as odd behavior. She tends to shut off any time we disagree, so I'm certain it will be some time until she's back to her usual self and trying to control my every move. A part of me understands, but a bigger part of me, the part which longs for more, is angry. With her, with Daxon, with Ally. With everyone.

Everyone but Dad.

He might be crazy, or he might be telling the truth, and I realize I don't care one way or another. What matters is he is the only parent that has been honest with me so far. I see the flaw in my logic as soon as I think it. I was as dishonest with Daxon as Mom was with me. We are alike, Mother and I, and it makes my skin crawl. Both of us choose the wrong actions to justify what we believe is best. Though I don't think Daxon will ever forgive me, there is one thing I know now I didn't before—lies are never the answer. Even if they're meant to save someone's life.

My stomach turns when I remember the fate awaiting Daxon and the reasoning for my presence here today. Let the Order guide you, find the Goddess, demand Daxon's safety.

She can't have you. You will live.

I pocket the phone and take a sharp right to burst through the trees to the other side. As I emerge, I am surprised to find the cove is not as lonely as I left it. People crowd the rocky plane of the shore; strangers, at least some of them. Even though I'd met member of the Order before, they still feel like blank faces to me now. They are not people, not *my* people. The Marzannite Order is only a means to an end; my way of securing Daxon's life in exchange for them welcoming their pathetic Goddess. I look around, spotting a face I can never forget in their midst, and wave to Dad. My smile falters when I spot Zasha next to him, her serpentine gaze glued to me. Shoulders tight, I walk toward them. "Got the invite," I say. "You could have called."

Zasha bristles. "At least she came alone," she mutters under her breath.

"Good to see you again, bug," Dad says, ignoring her. He clasps my waist and spins me around to face the others. "Everyone, if you haven't met her already, this is Nastya."

As I take in the group before me, I try to hate them, but in truth, I feel nothing at all. I don't get these people or why they're here and whatever stories Mother told me of Dad's strange crew, I have to give them the benefit of the doubt. Misguided or not, they believe me to be some twisted savior, and if I'm to save Daxon, I have to keep an open mind. The Goddess is the only way to break him free of the curse cast upon him, and if trusting the fools gathered here today is the answer, then it's what I must do.

Blood rushes from my face when I notice the rocks on the shore had been rearranged. No longer are the large boulders strewn casually across the ground, instead, they are stacked one atop the other in a circle behind the group. In their center, twigs and branches are piled so high, they nearly block the trees from my view. A fire pit. My head spins as images from the last vision I had drown out my thoughts and I glance at Dad briefly before turning back to the others. I count at least twenty people between me and the pit, each one looking as normal as ever and not the lunatics Mother described them as. My attention catches on a young girl no older than me, and as she huddles close to a woman Mother's age, I realize they must be related. The same mousy-brown hair frames their heart-shaped faces, and their green eyes watch me carefully. The girl whispers something to the woman and they both nod in my direction.

"This is the rest of the Order?" I ask Dad, not breaking eye-contact with the girl.

"Some of them," he answers. "There are more, of course, all over the world, but these are the people I grew up with. My family." He places a hand on my shoulder and adds, "Our family."

I very much doubt that's true.

Whoever these people are, they are no family of mine.

The group, the Order, seem to grow tired of inspecting me and their backs turn one by one as they continue piling branches into the pit. A few break off and dash into the trees, not returning. Some cast ominous gazes in my direction as they work, and I bite the inside of my cheek each time. They make me uneasy, and I wish I had brought someone else along. Backup. I'm stupid to think it since no matter how much I pray I was not alone in this, I have no one else to turn to. Mother would pack our bags and race into the night with me in tow if she knew I had any contact with Dad. That only leaves Daxon and Ally; so no one at all.

"Walk with me," Dad says. As he leads me to the water, I notice Zasha hangs back for a moment before joining the others at the pit. I am glad not to have her nearby. The woman unnerves me, and I doubt there will ever come a day when her and me get along.

We reach the edge and I stand close enough for the water to splash against the toe of my boots as it laps the shore, leaving red streaks behind. I roll my gaze over the cove, eyes tracing the shiny surface growing darker each minute. My head swivels up and I shield my eyes with my palm to watch the last glimmer of sunlight above. "So, what happens now?" I ask Dad.

"Now, we wait," he responds. "This must come as a shock to you, bug, but I want you to be prepared for what's coming. You might think the visions have prepared you for this, but it's best you know what to expect. It will make everything go smoother."

There is a lot to digest, but I focus only on one word; bug. Dad hasn't used the nickname since I was a child—hasn't called me anything—and to hear him use the word so freely after all this time floods me with memories of better days. It's not the first time he said it, but somehow, I latch on to it now, my mind gripping it in a vice. My eyes sting as though they beg for tears, but I refuse to cry. I twist a lock of hair around my finger and pull it taut. "Why the fire?" I ask.

Dad shakes his head in disappointment. "Damn Elena," he mumbles. "The fire is for the ritual. Once the sun is hidden, we will burn a new light to guide Marzanna to the surface. You will see and hear things that might sound strange, but do not be alarmed. It is all part of the plan."

"What kinds of things?"

He sneers and dread ices my skin. "When the fire reaches high enough to reflect in the water, we must call to her so she knows she is welcome to come up. During this time, we must take a leap of faith."

My forehead creases and I peel my gaze off the water to look at dad. "A leap?"

"Into the fire. Or through it," he clarifies.

"Um, what? No, thanks," I say.

He laughs again. "It won't hurt you," Dad says. "We must warm our bones and flesh so the Goddess doesn't confuse us for the dead."

The explanation doesn't help one bit, but I let it go. If the freaks want to jump through fire, they can do whatever they want. I will not have any part of it. "Then what?"

"Then it's time for the main event." Dad claps my back. "You, Nastya. Once the ritual starts, it is your turn to play."

I frown. "I don't even know the game."

"No matter," Dad says. "I will be with you the entire time, so you don't need to worry. All you'll have to do is follow my instructions exactly and all will be well.

Marzanna knows you are here, I'm sure of it. You will feel her when the time comes."

"I still don't understand why it has to be me," I say.

"It simply does," Dad responds. "You are a conduit for the Goddess, and she needs you to cross over. Only you can help her pass the serpents guarding the bridge."

"Wait, actual serpents?" I ask.

Dad's lips tighten until I almost cannot see them. "That, I cannot answer. As I said before, there has not been anyone fit to bring forth the Goddess in generations. What happens after the ritual begins will be a surprise to both of us."

He's trying to ease my nerves, but I feel flustered and trapped. Suddenly, the cove is smaller and the trees inch toward me on either side. "Hey, Dad?" I ask. "Am I going to be able to talk to her? When she's here, I mean."

"I certainly hope so."

I crouch down and test the water with my finger. Red stains my skin and I shiver at the frigid sensation it leaves behind. Daxon's reflection catches my eye and when I blink, he is gone and all I see is the river. "I hope so, too," I whisper.

Cheers erupt behind us, and I startle, jumping up to my feet and spinning around. The order is no longer by the pit and sticks and branches lay abandoned on the shore from where they dropped them. I follow the crowd as they rush toward an opening in the trees, noticing the few who left before returning. Their faces are bright and eager, and my mouth opens wide when I make out the creature galloping behind them.

"Is that a—" the words thicken in my mouth.

"A horse," dad says. "A palomino, to be exact. Her favorite and our gift to you."

I run my eyes over the animal, counting the beige spots on her hind. "You got me a horse?"

Dad wraps an arm around me, tugging me after him. "Want to ride her?"

28

The mare is sturdy, a tree trunk under me with thick legs that don't budge as I wiggle around to find a comfortable position. She doesn't seem bothered by the crowd of people around us and stands patiently still while hands reach out to graze her hide. I tangle my hand in her mane then thread them through, letting the hairs slip through my fingers. Dad looks up at me and winks. "Do you like her?"

I nod. "She's pretty."

Someone slips by my father, a woman with long red hair braided to one side. She reaches up and when I find her, I realize she's handing me something. My thighs press into the mare's sides, and I seal my lips shut, staring wide-eyed at the small rabbit in her hands. White as snow and trembling. Like in the vision.

My head shakes and I glance from the rabbit to dad. "Um, why?"

"Another of Marzanna's favorites. These two were the easiest to come by," he answers.

I try not to think about what other creatures the Goddess favors if a horse and rabbit are the obvious choice. At least they don't expect me to ride a freaking lion. My arms stretch to the hare and I lift it up, cradling it to my chest. It relaxes immediately and nuzzles its wet snout into my neck, tiny paws pressed to my wild heart. My hold stays strong on the rabbit while I use my free hand to grip the horse's mane.

Not far from me, someone lights a match and tosses it into the pit. Fire erupts, climbing higher and higher, smoke drifting toward me. The way the fire burns, bright and furious, makes me realize there's enough fire starer in the pit to last for days. Someone is bound to see the smoke and come checking, and I wonder how much time we have for whatever Dad and the Order have planned. On any other day, I would be happy to be saved, but not today. Today, I need Dad's story to be true. I need the Goddess to be real. The mare shifts her weight beneath me, and I slide to the side, legs locking to keep from falling over. My nose tickles as black smoke pushes its way into my system and I wiggle it back and forth, having no hands left to scratch the itch.

The cove smells of bonfire and sweat, an uncomfortable opposition to the sour smell of water I am used to.

Dad pats the mare's side and then we are moving,

galloping toward the fire and the crowd gathered there. They part like waves, allowing us to pass. In my arms, the rabbit must sense the flames and buries its face deeper into my chest, the tremor it had before returning. I ran my thumb over its soft fur and whisper, "Don't be scared."

I'm not sure if I'm talking to the hare or myself.

As we pass the members of the order, their eyes glaze over and they begin to chant in a language I don't speak. It is familiar and I quickly place it to the vision I had of a night quite similar to this one; the vision that brought me to Dad in the first place. I crane my neck and search for him in the crowd, relieved when I see him keep up pace to walk beside the horse.

"Someone is going to catch on," I say.

Dad points to the sky and I follow his finger. Night surrounds me. "They're all too busy watching the eclipse," he says.

"I don't think you're supposed to actually watch it," I say. "Bad for your eyesight."

"Since when does Cherry Cove follow the rules?" He smirks.

Light glistens in the distance and I turn away from Dad to see one of the members unsheathe a large knife from a blue velvet bag. My throat closes up and my grip on the rabbit deepens, fear soaking its fur. I peer down at my father and ask, "What's *that* for?"

He doesn't answer.

"Dad, what is the knife for?" I repeat.

"Is she ready?" Zasha asks. She appears as an apparition, ghostly and sheer. Her eyes never meet mine and when she snaps her teeth loud enough for me to hear, I realize she is looking at the man holding the knife. "We are about to begin."

"What's happening?" I ask.

No one bothers to answer me.

My hands fidget and I struggle to balance the rabbit in my arms as I scramble to jump off the horse. Fingers clutch my boots and hands reach around to keep me steady, to keep me locked in place. I kick out and a low yelp sounds behind me as whoever is holding me down meets the heel of my shoe. The hands loosen on my ankles, though they are quickly replaced with another pair. Then another.

I find Dad again, but he is no longer next to me, standing a few paces away with his eyes locked on the ground. "Dad?" I plead with him. "What's happening? What are they doing?"

It is Zasha who replies. "You are a conduit, Nastya. A direct link to the Goddess."

"I already know that," I spit out. "Why do you need the knife?"

She shrugs. "Marzanna is the Goddess of Death, the holder of it. You need to speak her language."

The surrounding chanting intensifies and I see one person leap into the fire, bursting to the other side unharmed. More follow, and soon, the entire order has taken a turn through. All but Dad and Zasha. The flames nick the sky and the entire cove lights up in red. My skin is raw, back so tense I feel every bone under my skin. Someone shouts and I swerve around, losing balance and sliding off the horse's back. The rabbit's red eyes bulge in fear and I grip its fur, cradling it close as I tumble to the ground. Falling off a horse is without a doubt the least fun activity I can think of.

My shoulder slams on a rock and a crack rips through the air. Pain shoots up my arm and chest, and I bite down on my tongue to stop the scream about to burst from my lips. Boots kicking, I fight to sit up and the pain in my arm intensifies. I am on fire.

Speak her language... The bastards want me to die!

The fall I took makes Dad snap into attention and in seconds, he is at my side. His eyes are red, like the rabbit's, like a poppy. I set my jaw and watch him as I lower the rabbit to the ground and let it hop away. "I'm out," I announce. "Mom's right, you lost it. All of you!"

For a moment, I think dad will let me leave, but I am very much mistaken. His features darken and he rips his glasses off, shoving his face in mine. "You will do as you're told," he hisses. "Today, we set Marzanna free, for good."

"What are you talking about? You said she only wants to see the living. For one day! You said one day, dad."

My eyes fog as he draws closer and closer, his breath warming my cheeks. "Death is eternal," he says. "And it cannot be contained. She must be set free, Nastya. She must walk among us and show us the true path of salvation.

The rest of the world might be blind to the truth but we are not. I am not. Don't you understand? If we allow Marzanna to pass through, she can do so much good; help so many. Dispose the world of the monsters we send her way and make it safer."

"You want to raise an ancient Goddess so you can what? Throw people you think should die her way?" I scoff. "You're insane. No one should have the power to decide who lives or dies, definitely not you, dad."

He smirks. "That is where you're wrong. We are the only ones strong enough to do what is right."

"I thought Zasha said the Goddess doesn't kill."

"Not kill," he clarifies. "Balance. She will create balance in our world."

Stomach clenching, I widdle my teeth down into sharp points and swallow my tongue. My flesh is goose-like and anger bubbles inside me that I cannot contain. I growl and stare him down. "I will not help you."

"I have worked too hard to get you ready for it to go to waste."

My brain stops working. "What the hell are you talking about? You weren't even around!"

"Oh, really?" Dad sneers. "How do you think you got this far? With Elena? If it wasn't for me, you'd never even know how important you are. You wouldn't be here tonight to fulfill your duties."

It happens in a flash and I finally understand. Everything starts to come together. The poppies, the symbols, the visions; they all lead to Dad. To tonight.

I square my shoulders, wincing at the sting it leaves behind. "You lied," I tell him. "You knew Kye and the shop owner. You killed them."

"I had to steer you to the right path."

He says it so calmly, without so much as a sliver of regret in his voice. Bile burns my throat and I gag in my mouth. The acid swirls around my tongue and my chest heaves as warmth spreads through me. I turn from Dad to spit the pooling saliva on the ground then push myself up until I'm level with him. "Skatina," I mutter. The word Mother uses to describe him seems quite fitting right now, and I don't even feel bad saying it. He is a bastard. They all are.

Pressing a hand to my hurt shoulder, I whip around and start for the trees, but I am yanked back immediately. Long fingers rip into my hair and pull me back so sharply, a few strands come off in the process. My scalp stings and I yelp as my butt hits the ground, hips almost shattering from the impact. Above me, Zasha's snarl comes into view, and I swallow hard when another face joins her. The man with the knife. He glares at me over her shoulder, laughs as she stomps her foot into my stomach. I cry out in pain and roll to the side, arms covering my midsection to avoid another blow. Somewhere close, dad lowers his head. Coward.

"Enough!" Dad yells out somewhere behind them. "Get her into the water, it's about to begin."

29

They drag me to the water and no matter how much I kick and scream, I cannot escape the shackles of their hands. At some point, Dad curses and grabs hold of my ankles, yanking me up like a hammock while Zasha holds my arms. I swing and thrash, hoping to get enough momentum to break free, but they are too strong. Water splashes over my stomach and thighs as they tread into the cove with me in tow. On the shore, I see the fire rise higher. My eyes sting.

The order stands in a semi-circle behind us, inching close to the shoreline to form a barrier of bodies, all chanting without pause. Even if I managed to get away from Dad and Zasha, there is no way they are letting me leave. My head rolls skyward, begging the sun to return. The words fall on deaf ears. There is no one here to save me; no one to stop the monsters under the bed. It is my fault. I am the one who invited the monsters in.

Suddenly, my body is flipped to the side and half my face is drenched as water rushes over me. Something is tied over my legs, and I struggle to look down. Dad holds me still, one hand balancing under my thigh to keep me straight while two women from the Order weave straw over my lower body. The knots they form are solid and strong, impossible to tear through. I scream and try to thrash but Zasha's hold on my shoulders strengthens, and I'm instantly flattened out atop the water and unable to move. The women move up my body, tying me up in straw ropes all the way to my chest. They tuck my arms in and I cry out. My scream echoes down the shore.

No one bothers to help me.

"Dad, stop!" I beg. "There has to be another way to call the Goddess. This can't be what you want." I think both him and I know it, but it doesn't stop me from trying to reason with the man willing to sacrifice me for the Goddess. Because that is exactly what this is, what I am. A sacrifice.

The man with the knife wades inward and I kick my legs, nicking Dad in the gut. He stumbles back, regaining his balance quickly to grasp my tied legs and ankles. I start to scream again, but stop. The man standing beside me tucks the knife into his belt and digs into a pocket to pull out a small vial. I recognize it without doubt. "What are you doing?" I ask, inspecting the bottle. Clear liquid splashes against the glass as the man uncaps the top and brings it to my mouth. The scent of poppies overtakes me. "No! Stop!"

I am flipped around again, eyes to the sky and back in the water. At my head, Zasha lets go of one shoulder and pinches my nose, forcing me to open my mouth to breathe. As I do, the man tips the vial and pours the liquid into my mouth. It slinks down my throat and I choke, trying to cough it up. Zasha clamps my mouth shut and grins. "Drink up, kid."

I want to rip her face off.

The liquid—the poison—slithers into my body, and I am wobbly and weak. My vision swims, my mind swimming with it. My body does the exact opposite and I sink like a rock. Everything shows up in doubles. I clench my jaw and try to use my tongue to block the poison from making its way into my system, but it is a futile task. You cannot stop the unstoppable. My heart races in my chest and my pulse pounds against my temples. As I look skyward, I am paralyzed with fear.

Frigid air whips around me and white flakes fall from the blackness and land on my cheeks and neck. It is so cold, unnaturally freezing for this time of year, and I gasp as my body is covered in white, fluffy particles.

Snow.

It coats my cheeks and lids and goosebumps spread over my skin as it continues to bury me in whiteness. The dullness in my chest intensifies and I try to take a ragged breath in, lungs refusing to expand. The snow pushes into my nostrils and ears, and I am frozen solid. No longer a girl but a block of ice and emptiness.

The pressure on my ankles disappears, and someone spins me around to stand in the river. The water splashes over the straw bindings covering my body and ices every part it touches. My gaze runs over the cove, past the line of people at the shoreline, past the fire, and straight for the trees. Boots digging the rocky bed of the cove, I try to walk but lose balance in seconds. My chest plummets down into the water and I am inches away from it when Zasha grips my hair and tugs me back. "Not yet," she whispers, her vile breath warming the top of my ear.

Around us, the trees rustle in the wind and shed leaves in buckets. Even in the dark, the colors of the woods change from green and yellow to a sickly gray. Death and winter surround the cove. They surround all of us.

I part my lips and nausea mixes with the remnants of poppy poison on my tongue. "Please—"

My begging is cut short, and a flash of movement catches my attention in my periphery. A silver glisten followed by a sharp pain in my side. The sound of my heartbeat thrashes in my ears and I gaze down to the hilt of a knife being yanked out of my stomach. Red liquid pours from the wound and stains the straw which holds me.

My legs grow weak.

A short moment later, Zasha's hold on me lessens, and she steps away, joining Dad and the other members of the Order. They stand united, hands clasped, and watch as I go under. Blood pours and mixes with the water, staining it a deeper red than it already is. My body sinks into the depths of the river, and I point my nose to the sky, trying to gulp air as long as possible. Soon, the water is at my eyes, and I keep them wide open and trained on Dad.

I want my lifeless eyes to be the last thing he sees.

For a second, I think I notice him flinch, but he squares his shoulders and stays quiet as I slink down into the river's void.

Then he is gone.

Muscles flex in my stomach and numbness overtakes my limbs. I whip around in the water, but every movement causes the deep gash in my stomach to open and more blood pours out. There is red everywhere. Head spinning, I recall the vision and the depth of my stupidity hits me like a brick wall. Daxon was never the one in danger. It was not his death I foresaw; it was my own. Our fate is so intertwined, even death can't tell the difference. Tears sting the back of my eyes and I let the river wash them away as my butt hits the bottom. Not far from me, a shadow rises from the depths and spreads through the water, and I tighten my lips to keep from screaming. The ground beneath me rumbles and the scurry of feet sounds behind me; Dad and his minions rushing back to shore. I swallow hard, my attention on the darkness in the distance.

On the floor of the river, rocks tremor, rolling away as massive columns spawn from the ground and shoot up toward the surface. Waves loll me from side to side and I'm propelled backward with the current as a gargantuan bridge takes form before me. I push my elbows out, managing to tear through some of the straw to free my arms, but I am much too late. The bridge continues to rise, higher and higher, until I cannot discern anything past it. Wide as a highway with thick, gargantuan columns on either side spurring toward the top of the water. It is beautiful, really.

Get out of here, I tell myself, and squirm to free my body from the straw. As I struggle, a light glimmers past the bridge and I come to a dead stop. Pointed turrets of reflective glass shoot out from the ground and in a flash, a brilliant palace sprouts before me. It is as wide as it is tall, and the way the water flows around it makes it seem like it is clear as glass. So damn stunning. Small openings line the outskirts of the palace, and I follow them down to a set of mirrored doors at the center. A cry bursts from me as the doors swing wide open and ghostly figures swarm the bridge. They run toward me, or float, I am not sure how to describe them better. Hundreds of them pour onto the bridge and as they get closer, I understand what they are.

Souls of those passed.

Is this Nav? Am I in the underworld?

Am I dead?

There are so many souls, they start not to look like people at all. Sheer bodies twist together to create a new being, one that is long and unnaturally fast. The body of a snake made up of so many lost. It slithers over the bridge and two, glowing beady eyes meet mine as it comes closer. I blink, only for a second, but that's all it takes. The snake's head rises over me, its long body twisting at the base. My lungs burn with the need to breathe, but I cannot move a muscle. I am paralyzed and woozy, with my sight failing by the minute. The beat of my heart slows, and I no longer have the power to fight. As the poppy poison overpowers my will to live, all I can do is watch the snake creep down the bridge.

Souls sprout from its round belly. The snake's mouth opens wide and hands reach for me from within. From down below, they look like a forked tongue; licking, tasting, claiming. A hard surface balances my broken body and rises me higher in the water. I glance down, feeling the base of the bridge under my legs. It is not made of the stone I expected, but rather a smooth, shiny surface that glides against my fingers as it rattles. Mirrors, I think. Everything is made of mirrors.

My teeth clench and my feet jerk out as a new sensation fills me and I cannot stop myself from falling back. The flowery scent of poppies fills my nostrils and my vision clouds enough for me not to see the snake hover over me. I blink again and loosen the last breath left inside, then close my eyes. I cannot bear to watch the snake unhinge its jaw and swallow me whole, though even without me witnessing, it does so anyway.

Head spinning, I wonder what Mother is doing right now and if she's discovered I'm missing yet. Is she scouring the town looking for me, or is she relieved to finally be free of the burden I imposed on her all these years? I often wondered what her life would have been like without me in it. Happy, I reckon. So very happy. With eyes closed, I try to remember every freckle on her nose and the way her lips quiver when she laughs. Perhaps with me gone, she will have more occasions to do so. Pain wraps over my heart as Mother's face is replaced by Daxon's and guilt thrums through my veins when I think of him.

Dad lied; speaking to Marzanna was never an option. I was never going to get a chance to save Daxon. I'm going to die before I even get the chance.

There is no bargaining with the Goddess of Death.

My chest heaves and red water rushes into my lungs as I wriggle on the shiny floor of the bridge and finally let go. Eyes parting to slits, I dare to look around. I am in the belly of the beast, inhaled like an early supper. Around me, ghostly faces come into view and I recognize some of them from the morgue. They swarm my vision and I notice their grayish lips moving as they try to speak, but I can't understand what they're saying. There are too many words, I realize. Too many stories.

My pulse slows and my muscles relax as I flatted inside the beast. I shut my eyes and press my back against the glass, thinking only one thing as I die—who will hear my story when I'm gone?

30

Garbled screams surround me. My lids flutter open, and I whip my head around as the pressure of river blasts into my eardrums. I bite down a scream. Air bubbles swarm the darkness before and hands grip my arms.

My body pierces the water like a bullet and my legs drag behind me as someone pulls me to the surface. Bright lights shine in my eyes, and I clamp them shut, head breaking the rim of the river to emerge on the other side. My lungs ache and my body convulses. I open my mouth to draw air, but it is as though I don't know how to breathe. The air tastes like seaweed and dirt, and I choke, coughing to expel it from my body. My chest meets a hard surface and a palm lands on my back, hitting it repeatedly. I bend over, blue lips grazing the water, and continue to cough.

Peeling my eyelashes apart, I notice the arms clutching me for the first time and panic sets in. I jerk my body and kick my legs to get free.

"It's me, Nastya," a voice whispers.

I stop fighting. "Daxon?"

My legs slow their pacing and I raise my head, twisting to face him. His hair is soaking wet and hangs over his eyes which shine so brightly, I confuse them for the light I saw before. Even as I squirm to turn around, he keeps his arms locked on my waist, pressing me so close my rib cage strains under the pressure. Daxon unhooks one arm and brushes a wet clump of hair from my face. "You're okay," he says. "You're okay."

I want to tell him I'm really not, but my voice shakes as more water rushes up my throat. I bend over him, retching. As I do, he rubs a hand over my back and sucks in a breath. His chest presses against mine and warmth spreads through my body. I am all too aware of how cold it is without him near.

Pressing a finger to my wrist, I check for a pulse and a relieved laughs bubbles out when I find it. Somehow, I feel I've been here before; shivering and wet inside the river with Daxon holding me up. It's a vicious game we seem to play. Cat and mouse. Life and death. Who will break the cycle first? I press my nose into his neck and breathe him in. "What are you doing here?" I ask, voice hoarse.

"Your mom called me."

I pull back to meet his eyes. "My mom?"

He nods to the shore and my stomach rings itself out when I spot Mother's face in the distance. She is still wearing the morgue's staple apron and her wild hair whips from side to side as she buries a finger into Dad's chest. Shouts drift over the cove as the two argue and my heart aches thinking how similar this is to the memories of my childhood. Mom and Dad tearing into each other while I watch from the sidelines.

"We have to get you out of here," Daxon says.

I fidget with a slimy strand of hair. "I can't leave," I say. "They did something to me. Started something. I think... I think I died, Daxon. Again."

"I know." His heady voice is filled with knowledge, and I want to ask him what exactly he understands, but before I can, Daxon says, "We have to leave now. We don't have much time."

For a moment, he glances to the water as if he sees the chaos I know lurks within it. Daxon pulls me with him and begins treading back to shore. A sharp pain in my side makes me wince and my teeth chatter as I press a palm to the wound in my side. Daxon pauses to look down. "What the hell did they do to you?"

I fight against the pain and press harder on the wound. "I'm fine," I say. "The vision, it wasn't your death I was seeing. It was mine. We can't leave. Daxon, we have to stop them. Whatever Dad did, he opened a wound and it's not over yet."

An ear-piercing scream tugs my attention and I turn

back to the shore, blood rushing from my face. At the edge of the water, Dad holds Mother by the neck, her back to his chest. He brings a knife to her throat and his gaze meets mine, narrowing. Mother shouts, but I cannot make out her warnings. I am glued to the knife at her neck and the blood welling around it. The order crowds the shoreline, inching toward my parents with feral eyes. They move like predators and fear laces through me when I hear the chanting resume. It gets louder and louder, a symphony of words I do not understand. Mother jabs an elbow into Dad's side, but he rips at her hair, tightening his hold on her and pushes the knife deeper into her skin.

I scream.

Legs pumping, I push through the water to get to her. My muscles ache and my chest is still burning from the time I spent underwater, but I do not stop. I have to help her. I have to save her from him.

"Nastya! No!" Daxon yells at my retreating back and I hear water splashing as he races to catch up with me. I do not break.

Before I can reach the shore, another face appears behind Dad and I stumble as Ally lifts a massive branch over her head and brings it down on my father's shoulder. The knife at Mother's throat falls away, and Dad clambers backward, swaying like a disoriented raccoon in the light of day. He falls to his knees, and I watch Mother tower over him, bringing her foot down on his face as she kicks him to the ground. A few members of the order break free from their chanting and run to help him but Ally jumps in the way, Dad's knife in her hands. Blood covers her hands, and her hair falls over her face and chest, slick with sweat. My gaze runs over her, landing on the diner uniform she wears and the small logo on her chest.

This is her vision.

I don't know what rattles me more; the fact I saw it all happen before or that the visions I had about my friends were this intertwined. Ally was never meant to kill Daxon. He was never meant to die. This is the vision. This night. This moment.

On the shore, Zasha pushes through the crowd to get to my father, but I don't stay long enough to watch what happens next. My body twists away from the madness on the beach and back to the water. Above me, glimmers of light break the darkened sky and my chest heaves with rapid breaths. A shadow moves beneath the surface, and I look down, seeing only red. The blood dripping from my side coils over the waves and pressure forms around my ankles. It pulls on me, beckoning me down. Fingers clawing up my thighs to drag me under. Flashes of red form in the water and I watch in awe as poppies burst from the ground. They swarm around me, swaying with the movement of the water, and I find myself swaying with them. A darkened shadow crawls toward me from the depths, and this time, I do not shut my eyes. Keeping them trained on the shadow, I follow its murky path all the way to where the bridge continues to rise, then past it to the mirrored palace in the far distance.

My head pounds when I turn to Daxon's ashen face. "I have to finish this," I say.

I don't know if he understands or how much he knows of what is happening here tonight. Deep down, I only hope he trusts me enough to let me go. Dad was right about one thing, Marzanna did choose me—called for me—and I cannot let her call go unanswered. All this time, this dreadful life I've been handed, it cannot be for nothing. If I don't go, she will never stop coming for me and I will never stop communing with the dead. Whatever Dad and the Order thought they were doing, they were so very wrong. I was not born to bring the Goddess into our world. I was born to stop her.

A pair of ghostly eyes appear behind Daxon, and I nod to the shop owner's spirit as she stretches out her hand toward me. Taking a deep breath in, I flash a weakened smile Daxon's way and set my shoulders. Then I dive into the water and swim.

31

The shop owner's hand in mine is cold and slick like oil. I look around, feet planted firmly on the bridge underwater, blink rapidly. Glacial fingers tap against my skin, and I whirl to the shop owner to see why she's so desperate to get my attention. She points to her blue lips before opening them wide like she is about to scream. I shake my head, not understanding. When she does it again, it starts to sink in; she isn't screaming, she's breathing.

I tighten my stomach muscles and slowly, so slowly, pry my lips open. Despite being surrounded by water, none of it makes its way into my lungs and I am able to breathe freely. Almost like I am back on shore. My lungs strain as they get used to this new state of existing and I crumble as I step forward on the bridge. Next to me, the shop owner grins in delight and leads me onward.

"Valentina," I whisper. The word pops into my head and I quickly realize it is not mine. I peer up at the shop owner, and ask, "Is that your name?"

She nods, short, translucent hair sticking out in all directions.

I am embarrassed I never learned her name when I still had the chance. "It's nice to meet you," I say.

We walk the bridge to inch closer to the mirrored palace ahead and I feel the energy of the souls behind us pull on my shoulder blades. More names tangle in my mind, and I try to match them to the faces when I turn to look behind me. Some make sense, modern names to match modern clothing, while others are beyond my time. Long gowns trail the smooth surface of the bridge as women with tight curls piled high above their heads float behind me. Next to them, men in petticoats adjust their monocles. Strangely enough, underwater, I can make out the faces of the ghosts clearly and unlike the interaction I had with Valentina at the morgue, I am not afraid.

I swallow hard and train my hot and blurry eyes on the palace as it grows larger on our approach. The mirrors jut out in perfect symmetry before me, framing the gaping mouth of the entrance. I come to a dead stop a few feet from the tall, arched doorway.

Gaze meeting Valentina's, I crook an eyebrow. "Is she inside?"

The shop owner lowers her chin and drops her hand from mine, pointing it to the doors.

"Why did you bring me here?" I ask. "Why does she want me?"

I receive no response, at least not in the way I expect. Instead, images flash through my mind, souls with ghostly faces clutching hands to stand in a protective line around the palace. Their chests rise and fall as though they are breathing, alive. I scour the formation and my heart pounds in my ears from the fearful expressions darkening their features. Their heads loll back in unison, and I follow their eyes to the top of the water, all the way to the darkened sky above. Over the highest turret of the palace, a beam of light pierces the red water. Its laser hits the mirrors, reflecting in rainbow shades of blue and green and purple. I shield my eyes, squinting to fight the blindness setting in.

The ghosts stretch their arms up to the sky and reach for the light. Agony laces through my chest and body; their desperation filling me like gas in a tank. They want to be free of this place, I realize. Whatever the light is, it's the answer.

"Go!" I shout, but they don't move an inch. "What are you waiting for? GO!"

My eyes roll over their arms, then down their faces and chests, to their lifeless feet. I gasp.

Sprouting from the bridge and winding tightly around each of the souls' legs are serpents. Some small and thin, others massive and destructive. They hold on to them, anchoring them in place so they cannot budge. My chest heaves with sobs and my knees buckle. The souls are trapped here, imprisoned on the bridge and unable to move on. I know the feeling all too well, understand it in the core of my being. I am as trapped in my living life as they are in their death. We are the same if not for one small difference —I am still alive.

At least, I think I am.

I push back on my heels and run for the doors of the palace. Snakes slither as I run, crawling toward me, but they do not block my passage. They part for me one by one, dragging the souls along with them to create a path straight to the entrance. A rogue ghost hand passes through my arm and chills run down spine as it slices to the other side. I shiver and pump my legs harder.

When I reach the entrance, I skid to a halt.

My fingers drum against the smooth mirror as I search for a handle, yet there is none to be found. My palm presses to the glass and I pale as the doors rattle under my touch. Water slashes at my ankles, flushing the bridge with the widening of the doors. I jump out of the way, giving the entrance a wide berth to split its mouth open. Inside, the palace is no palace at all.

A sprawling open space greets me, and I take a step inward, glancing back to the ghosts and serpents before making my way inside. More mirrors line the palace interior in an odd pattern of sharp points. I suck in a breath and walk further in, searching for the beam of light.

Not far from where I stand, I find it.

A beacon calling me home.

Legs trembling, I slow my pace and head to where the light hits the reflective floor and kneel down. My hand reaches for the light and when I touch it, the floor beneath rumbles and cracks. A burst of red blooms in the small opening and I fall back, my butt hitting the floor. In the center of the cracked mirror, a poppy shoots up. Its petals unfurl, the beam of light glistening over the soft skins.

I reach for it, plucking it out in one swoop motion and hold it up before me. As soon as the poppy is in my hands, the palace walls begin to move. They scrape against each other—like nails on glass—as they rearrange themselves around me until I am encased in a mirrored circle. My eyes bulge and my heart rams into my chest as I scan a million of my reflections stare back at me.

Though I am not me.

My features are still the same; a sharp nose, a set jaw, the look of constant disdain hiding behind my eyes. I am me, but I am also someone else—someone stronger. In one of the mirrors, I see myself atop a horse with beige spots on its hide. In another, a white hare nuzzles into my chest as I stand with shoulders straight and chin pointed. Another mirror shows me in a field of poppies, twirling over and over until I am too disoriented to stop. I look around, scanning the images and trying to put them together and back into a shape resembling the girl I know. The walls shift again, and

I press my knees into my chest, holding the poppy tight in my curled fingers.

Every version of me swirls in circles and intertwines until another image forms.

I am on the bridge, the palace at my back and the souls gathered around me. My arms are stretched wide, light from above beaming down on my face. Snow covers my feet and flakes of it fall on my gaunt cheeks as I throw my head back and open my mouth. The light blasts into my body and my skin, the mirror me's skin, changes colors. A kaleidoscope of a human; a bomb ready to explode.

My belly grows and I close my eyes as the light buries itself deep within me.

When I open them, I am staring back at my own reflection.

Bones rattling, I stand, leg muscles tense as I glare at the image in the mirror. It is as though time stops in that moment. I watch the reflection, seeing myself for the first time as who I truly am. A mane of silver hair floats around me, and my colorless eyes shine brightly with the light filling them. On my neck, a serpent winds itself like a noose and I smile seeing the scar I spent most of my life hating in a new way.

It isn't a scar, I think. It is a birthright.

A low laugh escapes me, and I tilt my head to the reflection. Dad was a fool to think he understood what Marzanna wants. The Goddess of Death didn't choose me, and she was never waiting for an invitation to leave the palace. She doesn't need some lonely child to call for her. She doesn't need a ritual to bring her forth. Marzanna wasn't waiting for this night and for my presence here. She was waiting for me to wake up.

I was waiting for me to wake up. *I am Marzanna.*

The river does hide treasures after all. Not the kind most people dive for; nothing quite so valuable. There are no chests filled with gold coins in the palace, no diamonds or precious stones one might hope to discover in a long-lost shipwreck. Instead, the river cradles something else in its depths. Secrets and things long forgotten. Pieces of people left behind. Pieces of me.

My laugh grows louder as I press the poppy into my chest and walk toward the doors leading me back to the bridge and to the souls upon it. The Marzannite Order wanted to greet their Goddess and I will give them what they want. Bursting through the doors, I kick at the snakes gliding at my feet and stand amidst the ghosts. My eyes rake over them, finding Valentina in the midst of the ghosts. Her feet are bound by snakes, but I can see the resolve harden her face as our eyes meet. Next to her, another face appears. Kye's. I sneer and they both return it, all of us knowing what is coming next.

I am leaving the palace and I'm not leaving it alone.

32

I slow march down the bridge with an army of the dead trailing behind me. Their excitement to leave the confinement of the palace is contagious, and I find myself hopping every second step as we near the end of the bridge. Light pulses around me and swallows me and the ghosts entirely, its bright essence creating a barrier through which the serpents below cannot pass through. My eyes stay trained on the watery distance, the grays almost wholly white and shining like two flashlights in the river's depths.

Determination fuels my every step.

Up ahead, the water changes to a lighter shade of pink as I dredge toward the shoreline. My feet glide smoothly and though only my toes touch the rocky bottom, I feel stable and connected to the floor. The pressure on my lungs lessens with each creeping step in and my body aches to resurface. Even this deep down in the cove, I see the light show I'm putting on. My throat tightens and I look up, parting my hair to bring the edge of the water into focus. It glistens from the light of my eyes, so beautiful I can almost cry.

I glance behind me to find Valentina's tight-lipped expression and nod.

Under my feet, the bridge rumbles and rises higher and higher, bringing me up as I walk. The top of my head grazes fresh air and my hair falls in wet clumps over my face. I do not rush to surface, taking my time to make sure the souls I'm guiding have a chance to keep up. They have no trouble staying close to me, bound to the lifeline I am providing. A few brush up against me and my teeth split open. I clench my jaw shut and keep on. My clothes suction to my skin and soon, my entire upper body is out of the water and I'm suck in cold air, scrutinizing the shoreline.

The madness I left behind has erupted into pure chaos, and my heart lunges into my mouth when I spot my mother's thin body near the fire. Her hands are bound behind her back and two members of the Order work in concert to push her closer to the flames. She curses and spits in one of their faces, though they do not flinch. They keep pushing her. Further. Further. Further. Sweat beads down her cheeks and neck as the fire nips at her skin. The bastards laugh and push some more.

Close to them, my father holds a book open and his eyes

are trained on the page he reads from. Words muddle together, but this time, I understand the language I was never taught. Every syllable makes sense. It's surprising I had so much trouble deciphering father's journal before. I should have known the incantations by heart; it was me who wrote them.

Or a version of me. One long drowned and forgotten. The version burning in my heart right now and begging to be set free.

As I move in closer, the light emanating from me spreads and it surprises me that no one seems to notice me arrive. Either they truly have no idea what to expect, or they assumed I had drowned when I dove to the palace. Either way, their oblivion is welcome. If they don't see me coming, don't see *us* coming, I can get this over with quicker.

I stretch my neck and peer through the crowd of people gathered around the pit to find Daxon and Ally. Both are bound like Mother and held in place by angry, vile people all waiting for their turn to force them into the flames. Ally's body jerks violently as she tries to break away, but it is Daxon I cannot stop watching. He is calm and collected, eyes vacant and mouth down-turned. The usual resolve of his hard features is gone, replaced by an expression I am much too familiar with. He's given up.

Wet stone slides beneath me as I pad the shoreline, red water dripping off me and pooling at my feet. The wound on my side cries and oozes, and I don't bother stopping the blood flowing from it. I let my blood stain this place just as my father wanted.

My arms rise and I look at Valentina and the others, pleased when they follow my movement. Limned in the bright light around us, we must look like angels rising from the darkness. The souls shuffle closer together and their sheer bodies float from the water and into the air. There are hundreds of them now, thousands even, and they all float behind me, tied by invisible strings like balloons in a child's hand. Though I am no child and I know it.

I am ancient. I am never-ending.

I am time itself.

"It can't be," a voice calls out from the crowd. I recognize it instantly, and my heart drops when my eyes land on Zasha. She no longer seems as threatening as I remember, even though I have only been gone a short while. Right now, she looks small and broken, ready for me to snap her in two. Our gazes stay locked together and others turn from their posts to see what Zasha is so concerned with. Their mouths gape when I inch toward them, then they look behind me at the company I brought.

Screams fill the cove.

No, I think. How can they see the dead?

Turning on my heel, I search for Valentina and she points a finger to the sky where my light hovers over the cove in a bubble. She tilts her head, fog swirling over her as she moves. I spin back to the Order, yanking my head back and forth between the ghosts and the foul people on the shore. "They see you because you're part of me," I guess. Valentina grins to acknowledge my discovery, but it quickly turns into a snarl.

I inwardly cower from the force of the energy dripping off her. As her eyes lock on my father, I feel only hatred. This is the man who ended her life, and I cannot blame her for wanting to return the favor. My wet hair is sticky against my neck, and I flick it away, sending splashes of river water in all directions. If the living can see the ghosts, does that mean they can interact with them? The predatory way Valentina watches my father makes me think the dead can do whatever they want now they're no longer bound to the palace.

I realize a little too late I did not think this through.

The ghosts vibrate faster, their bodies blurring, and I position myself between them and the people on land as if I am a shield. My head shakes from side to side, and I bring one hand up. The ghosts stop their rustling, turning to face me.

"You are not to hurt anyone," I say, praying they listen. "Not tonight and not ever."

They are confused; blank eyes growing and stretching. "Do you understand what I'm saying? No one gets hurt," I repeat. "This is not why I brought you here."

"Why did you bring them then?"

I loop around to Dad halfway up the shore and moving closer to me. On instinct, I buckle back and square my shoulders. "Don't come closer," I warn. "Trust me."

Luckily, my stubborn father listens and halts. "How is this possible?" he asks. "You're supposed to be dead."

My belly clenches. "Guess your plan didn't work."

"But the sacrifice, the blood. I don't understand," Dad mumbles. "Did she save you? Did she even come?"

This is the part where I should be telling him where to shove it, but all I can do is scoff and squeeze my mouth shut. Whatever anger I held for him before evaporates and is replaced by only pity. I am sorry for the lost man standing before me. He had so many chances to make things right, too many, and he chose the wrong path every single time. The way he treated mother all those years and what he tried to do with me should be unforgivable, and yet, I forgive him all the same. Misguided as my father is, it doesn't change who I am in the end. Hell, without him, I never would have found out what my visions mean or the true purpose behind my existence. I would have never found me. "You messed up, Dad," I say. "The Goddess was never coming. She was already here."

Face ashen, Dad opens his mouth; a fish gasping for air. I wait patiently until he starts to understand my meaning and when his eyes twinkle with fear, I solidify. Dad runs his tongue over his front teeth and says, "You don't mean..."

"I should thank you," I say. Glancing to the souls behind me, I add, "We should all thank you. Without you and your damn Order, I could never have saved them. The Goddess wasn't waiting to come up. Dad, I am her. I am Marzanna and all you did tonight was make me whole."

"Nastya, whatever you did, you need to undo it."

"Excuse me?" My eyebrows touch the edge of my hairline as I try to comprehend what he's saying.

"They are not supposed to be here," Dad croaks out. "If you really are her, you would understand. Your job is to guard the dead, Nastya. Not let them run amuck!" His reaction stifles me and I shake my head, disgusted. He was so eager to bring forth the Goddess, to give himself a weapon of destruction, he didn't once consider that some weapons cannot be controlled. Death cannot be wielded like a knife. *I* cannot be wielded.

"My job is to make sure you never hurt another kid!" I roar. "The Marzannite Order ends here. Take your minions and get the hell out of here before I let Valentina have a go at you."

The sound of her name seems to rattle something loose in Dad and he rips his head to the side, connecting with the furious ghost of the shop owner behind me. His lips crash together and a burst of frigid air hits my back as Valentina approaches. She comes to a dead stop beside me, my body forming an invisible fence she cannot pass. Whether she physically can't move forward or is standing down out of respect for me, I do not know. A low growl emanates from her chest and her dead eyes pierce into my father, tearing his skin to shreds.

Dad takes in a breath and looks to me. "Don't be foolish, kid. You need me and you need us. We can help you, Nastya. Take them back to where they came from and come with us. We can figure it out together, the way we were meant to." He flips his palm and stretches it toward me. "Do what's right, Marzanna."

"I am doing what's right," I say.

Feet stomp on the shoreline, and I hear Mother's pitched voice in the distance. "Nastya! Move!"

I blink fast, heart leaping in my chest as I search for her. My body paralyzes when I notice Zasha barrel toward me with the rest of the Order snapping at her heels. In her hand, the silver sheen of a blade shimmers in the light. She pushes past my father, crashing an elbow into his shoulder to shove him out of her way, and lunges for me.

Everything moves in slow motion.

The tip of the knife flies at my throat and her heated breath brushes against my forehead as she snaps her teeth once before swinging the knife at me. I arch my back, gravity pulling me down. My shoulders hit the rock and I yelp as brutal pain rushes up and down my body. Zasha wings one leg over me, dropping to her knees to straddle my chest. Her weight pins me down and I kick my legs, but she is too strong. She raises her arm, readying to stab the knife into me.

"Nastya!" Daxon and Ally yell out in chorus and I hear their steps grow louder as they run to save me. My eyes roll to the back of my head. I breathe through the pain of Zasha's body crushing mine and glance past her to watch my father stumble away, not bothering to come to my rescue. My stomach lurches. Above me, Zasha growls and plunges the knife down. Before she can finish, her body is yanked to the side, and she is lifted off me. The sharp edge of the knife grazes my throat, nicking the rough skin of my exposed scar. I rise on my forearms, jaw gaping, and stare as Valentina wraps the fog of her being around Zasha and flings her into the air. My aunt screams and fights, but she cannot break loose.

Once death has its claws in you, it doesn't let go.

Valentina soars higher, dragging Zasha with her until they are but two dots in the sky. The shop owner flashes one last glance my way and the hair on my arms stands straight. Lightning strikes the sky, or so I think at first. What I believe to be lightning is in fact Valentina zooming down toward the water at an inhuman speed. Her figure blurs as she picks up momentum and flashes of gray fog trails behind her; the remnants of an airplane cutting the clouds. My tongue is too large for my mouth, and I press it into my teeth to free my mouth of its weight. A few feet from me, the river explodes as the shop owner cannonballs into the water with Zasha tight in her grip.

The cove grows silent.

When Valentina doesn't return, I face the remaining souls, trying to gauge their state of mind. It seems her act spurns a new emotion in them, and in seconds, they take to the shore. Panicked yells rise from the people standing there, and every member of the Order bolts into a hasty jog. Some are lucky enough to get away and disappear into the trees, leaving behind human shaped voids where they once stood. Others are not so fortunate. Their faces contort and they bat at the ghosts attacking them with little success. I stare, mortified, as more are snatched into the air and dragged to the river.

"Stop!" I shout. The souls don't listen.

Blood rushes to my face and I run from the water to the pit. My pulse thrums a steady beat in my chest, and I pump my arms and legs to get me closer to where my mother, Daxon ,and Ally stand banded together. A few gray shapes rush them and I slide in to block the ghosts from reaching my friends—my family.

The dead come to an abrupt stop a few inches from me. I look them over, my jaw set and my back ramrod straight. "Not them," I command. "Anyone but them."

The glow of my eyes lights up their blank faces and though the ghosts do not speak, I know they understand me. They swirl around and zero in on another unfortunate group, yanking a few people by their hair and arms to pull them away. Warm skin grazes my arm and I slowly turn to my mother, free of her bindings now and clutching me with long, frail fingers. Tears swell in her eyes, but she blinks them away. Despite all that's happened, mother stays exactly the same. She wraps an arm around my shoulder and drags me into her. Her body is rigid at my side and I wonder if she is as uncomfortable as me in this moment. We are not a hugging family.

"Can we leave, please?" Ally asks from somewhere behind us.

Another hand reaches for me, and I feel Daxon's fingers intertwine with mine. "She's right," he says. "There's nothing you can do for them now."

I want to argue. I want to tell him he's wrong and I can save everyone here, but I would be lying. My eyes stay focused on the water ahead and the turbulent waters in the distance as souls continue to drown members of the Order. Arms reach for the sky, fingers curled and pained, as more bodies disappear into the depths. Above us, the sky brightens as the sun returns and I stifle a cry and keep my attention on the waves crushing the shore. After a while, the water stills and the cove returns to its usual serenity.

I glance from Daxon to my mother. "Where's Dad? Did he..." I cannot finish the sentence.

"He ran off," Mother says, venom in her voice. "Once a coward, always a coward."

Though I do not say it, I am relieved. Dad's lack of a backbone saved his life today and while I can't ever forgive him for what he's done, I'm not positive how I'd react knowing he joined his sister in the end. I narrow my eyes with a singular focus, the river, and lean on Daxon's strong shoulder to keep from disappearing. I wait for the dead to return.

I'm not sure how long we stand there, Mother and Daxon at my side and Ally huffing and puffing at my back. Much too long, I think. We don't speak; not even when Mother nudges her head to the trees to signal us leaving and not when Daxon scoops out my legs from under me and pulls me into his chest to carry me away. As we part the trees, I stare over his shoulder, waiting. Always waiting.

The souls may be gone for now, but I know they will not stay gone forever. With me on the surface, all of me, there is nothing binding them to the palace. The keeper is free and so are they. For as long as I roam the Earth, I am bound to them and they to me. It's funny, really. All this time, serpents held the dead underwater and now, a different snake holds them hostage. I run a finger over the scar on my neck and sigh.

They are mine and I am theirs. Forever.

33

"Two sugars?" Daxon asks, hovering a spoonful of fluffy white grain over my cup.

I nod. "Yes, please."

He dumps the spoon into the coffee and whips it around, setting it on the table before sliding the cup closer to me. We are in the diner, sitting in a booth by the window with the sunlight steaming in. At the counter, Ally is arguing with the cook over an order and once in a while, she turns our way and winks, pleased with her ability to get a rise out of the man. I roll my eyes and smile, turning back to Daxon. "So," I say. "What's the plan for today?"

"You're looking at it," he answers. His lips curl and he reaches over the table to hold my hand; it's a strange feeling when I don't pull away from him. "Unless I'm not exciting enough company for you."

"You'll do," I tease.

He turns my palm over and rubs a circle with his thumb on my skin, reading off items on the menu for me. There is a fresh bruise on the inside of his arm, and I battle the urge to ask him about it. The last time I did, Daxon brushed me off, spinning lies about how it happened. Football practice, he said, but I knew better. It's never football practice.

I am yet to meet Damon's parents, and I often wonder how much of it is for my own good. Each time I bring it up, Daxon tells me they're busy or makes up an excuse against it. I don't press further, no matter how much I'd like to, and we never talk about the horror he lives with, like we don't discuss my being the Goddess of Death. One day we will, I tell myself. We have time.

There is no point pushing Daxon to speak of his dad, and if anyone understands his situation, it's me. Angry, hateful fathers are one thing we have in common. I squirm thinking of my dad while Daxon gives Ally our order. Somewhere out there, the bastard lurks and hides. The day at the cove replays in my mind, and I think about the sleepless nights I spent since looking out the window and waiting for him to show up. What a stupid habit to have developed. Children are supposed to be afraid of the nightmares in their closets, yet here I am, waiting for mine to return.

I'm not sure why I want to see my father, as unsure as I am as to why he refuses to come back. In the end, he got exactly what he wanted. His Marzanna. It's not my fault she wasn't what he was expecting. Then again, I don't think anyone was expecting the Goddess of Death to be a sixteen-year-old girl.

A chill steels my spine. I straighten in the seat to look out the window, blinking away rays of sunlight to peer through the dusty glass. Outside, the street is starting to fill up with people and they walk briskly to reach their destination, oblivious to the fact they are not alone. Cheek bones rising, I stare at the ghostly shape of a young boy floating behind a couple. The black holes of his eyes are cast downward, and he trails along with them, following as they turn the corner and vanish from my view. On another side of the street, a wide-set man carries out a menu board and plunks it on the sidewalk. He rubs his forehead with his sleeve to wipe the sweat collecting there and when he stretches his arms, one of them goes right through the ghost of a woman next to him. Her gray, foggy shape bristles and vanishes, reforming immediately a foot away from the man. Near to them, a crowd gathers and it doesn't take me long to spot the Warriors front and center with pamphlets in hand. They beckon people inward as they pass, and cram papers into their hands. I spot a picture of the cove on one of the pamphlets and shake my head, gaze landing on four gray figures behind the group. These souls are restless. Eager. They huddle together and follow the Warriors like leeches, buzzing around them as they continue to spread their message on the street. The ghosts don't acknowledge me, but they know I'm there. I am everywhere they are.

Death follows me now wherever I go. To Ally's house

when she asks me to spend the night and watch movies. While we apply face masks and laugh at whatever happened to Ally in school that day, they hover in the near distance. Silent and brooding.

They are with me when Daxon presses his lips to mine in the front seat of his truck as he drops me off from our dates. With me while I climb up the front steps to disappear into the funeral home.

They're even there when I shower, though I try not to think about that.

My life has become quite routine. Mother is still insistent I not to return to school, and while I wish it was different, I grudgingly agree with her. Simply because I changed doesn't mean the rest of the town has. They still whisper when I pass, and some of the kids still torment me as I make my path through town. The only difference now is more often than not, I am not alone. Either Daxon or Ally or Mother are usually nearby, and if they're not, someone less tangible is bound to linger near me. A protective circle of friends, alive and dead, keeps me together.

On the table, my phone vibrates and I tear myself away from the window to pick it up.

"Hey, Mom," I say, shaking my head at Daxon while grumbles a 'here we go again' under his breath. "Everything all right?"

"When are you coming home?" Mother asks on the other end.

"Um, soon. We're getting lunch."

She sighs loudly and I hear the sound of paper crumbling. "Make it a quick one," Mother says. "We got another one dropped off and I could use the help."

"I'll be there soon." I shrug at Daxon. "See you in a bit."

"Good. Bring some donuts."

THE WOMAN ON THE SLAB IS NOT SOMEONE I KNOW and as Mother finishes cleansing her body, I read over her file at the desk. Female. Thirty-seven. Blunt force trauma to the head. I glance back at the corpse and check the woman's head, seeing no evidence of a wound. Mother did a good job stitching her back together. Placing the file back in its folder, I wait for Mother to finish then help her slide the body into the cooling unit, locking the door shut. At the corner of my eye, I feel Mother's eyes on me as she removes her apron and tosses it on the metal rolling table beside her. She slicks back her hair, shiny strands escaping as her hand glides over them, then removes her glasses.

"I'm going to put on some coffee, then do you want to help me in the backyard?"

Since the day at the cove, Mother has taken to fixing up the house with a feverish drive. She started with the kitchen, making me help her tear down the linoleum floor to replace it with a beige tile I can't stand to look at. Next came the upstairs bathroom and I have to admit, she did a pretty good job with it. We now have a jet-stream tub to replace the old claw-foot one that had paint chipping off it around the edges. When the workers left after installing the giant thing, Mother spent almost two hours soaking in it and I had to check on her several times to make sure she didn't turn into a human-sized prune. Now, every time she passes by the bathroom, she smiles. Pride beaming off her like she won a lottery.

This week, Mother wants to tackle the backyard and I can already see her wheels spinning as she categorizes everything which needs changing in her head. When she first told me she's going to plant more rose bushes, I laughed. I had never seen my mother garden, but I'm pretty sure it's going to be hilarious to watch, which is one of the reasons I agreed to help her today.

That and seeing her overjoyed again.

It isn't that she's a different person now, she truly isn't, but she is closer to the woman I remember from long ago than she's ever been. Even the crow's feet near her eyes seem to have lessened, though not having to keep so many secrets from me probably has a lot to do with it.

The truth, no matter how dank and dark, tends to have that effect on people.

Mother's steps echo on the stairs as she leaves and I spin back to the morgue, not even remotely phased by the sight of the dead woman's soul before me. Deep fog surrounds her, and she reminds me a little of Valentina when I first encountered her ghost; the same scared expression on her face and the same vibrating gait as she floats toward me. I realize now all souls act the same this close to their death, and while they are afraid and confused, I am no longer terrified of them.

The woman's figure saunters closer and she is a few inches from me when she pries her lips open to scream. Her foggy arm loops around my neck and she drags me into her, so close I can smell the stench of decay rolling off her. My eyes water, but I keep them alert as I press my body into her and wait for the vision to arrive. Air pounds at my ears and my visions spots. I keep my feet sturdy on the floor as the morgue rearranges itself around me. Cabinets disappear, tables vanish. Everything goes away and becomes anew.

I am in a dark living room, the backs of my legs pressing against a flowery, soft fabric. I look down at the couch behind me, then stretch my neck to make out the room. A bay window to my right, a small bookcase to my left, two glasses of wine on the coffee table in front of me. Someone grips my shoulder and spins me around, pushing me into the couch. My mouth opens to scream, but I stop myself. This is not real. This is not me.

It's her.

In my periphery, a flash of movement catches my eye and I twist around to lay on my back on the couch. A dark shadow looms over my body and as my vision refocuses, I realize it is a man. Bright green eyes fill with hate, and he raises an arm, an object I don't recognize in his hand. The man swings down and a blinding pain rushes through me as whatever he was holding collapses on my forehead. My head sways and I fight to keep my eyes open, but they refuse to cooperate. I am still glued to the man's green eyes when my sight returns and I'm back in the morgue again.

This time, I am alone. The woman's ghost is gone and everything is as I left it.

I turn to the hutch where mother and I locked the body and press my palm to the icy metal. "I'll find him," I promise the woman. I do not know if she can hear me.

Pushing myself away, I walk to the table and grab my phone, typing out a message for Daxon to meet me, then head upstairs. The door closes behind me, and I make my way to the kitchen where mother stands at the counter, mixing creamer into a giant cup of coffee. She hears me coming and turns. Her face pales. "You saw her, didn't you?"

"Yes," I answer. "I have to leave for a bit. I'll be back later to help with the yard."

"You can let it go," she suggests. "Sit back and let the dust settle. You don't need to go running every time one of them dies and comes to you."

She means the people of the town and she is wrong. Who would I be if I didn't help the dead? If I did as Mother is suggesting, I would still see the woman's soul for as long as she is near me. I would still feel her pain and have her death follow me around like a festering wound. There was no peace in the way she died—the vision showed me that much—and if I can do something to bring her closure, I can't think of anything else more important. Deep down, I wonder if putting an end to the Marzannite Order helped Valentina somehow. I surely hope so, and maybe if I ever meet her again, I can ask.

I run my fingers through my loose hair and start for the door. "I'll be back soon," I say over my shoulder.

"Take a sweater," mother warns. Then adds, "And tell that boy to have you back before dinner."

She still refuses to call Daxon by name even though he comes by almost daily. Once in a while, I see them share a smile and my muscles relax in response. I don't know how long it will take mother to accept Daxon or his role in my life, but I will wait as long as it takes. She is wary and has every right to be; as far as she's concerned, every man ends up just like my father. I don't argue with her. In time, she'll learn Daxon is nothing like dad and until then, I settle for infrequent smiles and knowing glances. This is mother's way and only she can decide when it is time to rip the walls down.

"They still don't want you, you know," Mother says, her hand crushing the handle of the cup. There is no malice in her voice, only fact, and I know she means well. Even knowing who I am, she still tries to protect me. You can't shield death itself from the dead, I once told her. She only shook her head and walked away, as I am doing now. No matter what mother believes, I am of this town; of the river. And I belong to them whether they want me or not. Especially if they don't.

When death comes calling, they will need me, and I will be there. I will take their lifeless hands and I will listen to their stories. I will be the last thing they see because at least in death, they *will* finally see me and follow me as I carry them home.

It doesn't take Daxon long to get to the funeral home, and when he arrives, I meet him halfway down the driveway. He rolls down the passenger window. In the breeze, his hair tussles with every slick move he makes and his river-blue eyes penetrate my senses. I briefly recall the first time we met and my stomach lurches; he truly is exquisite.

Daxon asks, "What was it this time?"

"Nothing concrete," I answer. "I saw a living room and a man, the killer, I think. Green eyes. I remember green eyes."

His nose twitches and he leans over to open the door for me, waiting for me to climb inside. "Should we grab Ally?"

I nod, taking his hand as he slowly backs out of the driveway. We leave the funeral home behind, and I watch its reflection in the side mirror, tensing while the house shrinks in size. Above the porch, the rusty sign is tiny and unobtrusive; two snake eyes at my back.

"Think we'll find out what happened to her?" Daxon asks.

I don't answer. Instead, I watch the trees blur on either

side of the road like shadowy waves. Every so often, the wheels bump over the uneven road and I catch my reflection in the mirror. Gray eyes, wide and curious. A silver mane of loose hair. And an uneven scar cooling in the breeze of the wind. Exposed for all the world to see.

ACKNOWLEDGMENTS

The acknowledgement section is always a little tough for me. There are so many people that help me on my writing journey that it is hard to narrow it down. This book was no different.

First and foremost, I want to thank my husband. Writing can be a solitary existence and it's difficult not to get lost in your own world. Like a beacon, you are always there to reign me in when I forget reality and I cannot thank you enough for that.

To my parents who taught me at a young age to value my creativity. You are the reason I do what I do now and I cannot imagine living any other life.

Another big shout out to my beta readers and editors. We had quite a few rounds on this book and I am so grateful for your patience and support as I navigated the best way to tell this story. Your advice and hard work made this book what it is—pure magic!

To my fellow writers: thank you for listening when I got stuck on an idea or needed to vent. Our stories do not always go as planned and it can be a wild ride to get to the finish line. I am beyond thrilled to have you in my corner and offering tough love. You are all amazing.

Finally, to my readers. Humbled is not a good enough word to describe how I feel each time I receive an email or a message telling me you enjoyed one of my books. While I could never stop writing, it is for you that these stories exist. This book is no different. It is here because you took a chance on an author and I am forever thankful for each word you read.

In the words of Nastya, we are all of the river. Let the stream take you home.

ABOUT THE AUTHOR

A.N. Sage has spent most of her life waiting to meet a witch, vampire, or at least get haunted by a ghost. In between failed seances and many questionable outfit choices, she has developed a keen eye for the extra-ordinary.

Since chasing the supernatural does not pay the bills, she dabbled in creative entrepreneurship, marketing and retail management. A.N. spends her free time reading and binge-watching television shows in her pajamas.

Currently, she resides in Toronto, Canada with her husband who is not a creature of the night.

A.N. Sage is a Scorpio and a massive advocate of leggings for pants.

For more books and updates:

www.ansage.ca

Connect on social media:

Facebook Group:

facebook.com/groups/945090619339423/

Instagram:

instagram.com/a.n.sage/

Twitter:

twitter.com/ANsageWrites

Facebook:

facebook.com/ansagewrites

TikTok:

tiktok.com/@ansagewrites

Goodreads:

goodreads.com/author/show/18901100.Alexis_N_Sage

Amazon:

amazon.com/author/a.n.sage

CPSIA information can be obtained
at www.ICGtesting.com
Printed in the USA
LVHW050039080222
710481LV00018B/459/J

9 781989 868270